Jessica Huntley

My Dark Self

First published in 2021

This is a work of fiction. Unless otherwise indicated, all the names, characters, businesses, places, events and incidents in this book are either the product of the author's imagination or used in a fictitious manner. Any resemblance to actual persons, living or dead, or actual events is purely coincidental.

IBSN: 9798721361418

First edition

Website: www.jessicahuntleyauthor.com

Cover Design: Getcovers

Edited and proofread by: Jennifer Kay Davies

About Jessica Huntley

Jessica wrote her first book at age six. Between the ages of ten and eighteen, she had written ten full-length fiction novels as a hobby in her spare time between school and work.

At age eighteen, she left her hobby behind and joined the British Army as an Intelligence Analyst where she spent the next four and a half years as a soldier. She attempted to write more novels but was never able to finish them.

Jessica later left the Army and became a mature student at Southampton Solent University and studied Fitness and Personal Training, which later became her career. She still enjoys keeping fit and exercising daily.

She is now a wife and a stay-at-home mum to a crazy toddler and lives in Edinburgh. During the first national lockdown of 2020, she signed up on a whim to a novel writing course, and the rest is history. Her love of writing came flooding back, and she managed to write and finish her debut novel, *The Darkness Within Ourselves*, inspired by her love of horror and thriller novels, as well as complete the first in the series, *My Dark Self.* She has also recently completed a Level 3 Diploma in Editing and Proofreading and is working on further novels in the "My ... Self" series.

Other Books By Jessica

The Darkness Series

The Darkness Within Ourselves

My … Self Series

My Dark Self
My True Self

Acknowledgements

To my own identical twin sister Alice (who is not evil, but does have some similarities to the character of Alicia). Thank you for being my one-true friend growing up and for always having my back.

To my best friend Katie who I know loved this book and inspired me to make it into a trilogy.

To Lauren for reading it and suggesting the title.

To my husband Scott and our son Logan for always being there for me and supporting me.

To my dad who also knew I was destined to be a published author.

Connect With Jessica

Find and connect with Jessica online via the following platforms.

Sign up to email list via website to be notified of future books and her monthly author newsletter:
www.jessicahuntleyauthor.com

Follow her page on Facebook: Jessica Huntley - Author

Follow her on Instagram: @jessicah_reading_writing

Follow her on Twitter: @new_author_jess

Follow her on Goodreads: jessicahuntley88

Follow her on her Amazon Author Page - Jessica Huntley

Chapter One

My name is Josslyn and I'm a psychopath. Actually, that's not technically correct. I have psychopathic tendencies (don't we all a little bit?) and a personality disorder. Actually, no, that's not right either. It's really difficult to explain. Let me start over.

My name is Alicia and I am a psychopath.

It's me again. I sometimes get us mixed up. It's almost impossible to describe exactly what or who Alicia is because I don't know the answer myself.

I'm Josslyn Reynolds, a twenty-eight-year-old slightly crazy lady who lives alone and has no friends. Alicia is ... well, she's ... the psychopathic voice in my head. Wait, before you judge me as a lunatic, let me attempt to explain. She hasn't always been there (I'll get to that later), but she's been in my head a long time, so long in fact that I can't imagine her not being there. I know everyone has an inner monologue running through their minds, everyone has thoughts they keep inside that only they know about and that they would never say aloud, but Alicia isn't just my own thoughts and feelings: she's something else, something ... different.

If you met me on the street you'd never give me a second look. I'm average height, average build, have dull brown hair that's just below shoulder length, brown eyes and I'm a casual dresser. Boring, right? There's nothing interesting about me whatsoever (except for Alicia), but no one knows about her, so from the outside I'm perfectly normal, but on the inside ... oh boy, I'm fucked up. I've somehow managed to keep her a secret the entire time that she's been present within me. It feels like I have a secret superpower. It's what makes me special ... to me. I'm not special to anyone. I don't have anyone in my life that I care about (minus my parents and Oscar, which I'll explain soon). Most of the time I have to pretend to be normal and happy. I mean, I am happy (sort of). I'm not depressed, but I'm definitely not what you would call a sociable, happy person.

Let me get one thing clear: I don't like people. That's not Alicia talking, that's me. I guess you could say that I tend to push people away just by being me, which makes me feel very lonely. Yes, I know, I'm a walking contradiction. I don't like people, yet I feel lonely. Human beings need companionship or they end up going crazy, like me, although technically I'm not crazy, I just happen to have a voice in my head.

Loneliness is a funny thing, isn't it? Even the most popular, outgoing person can feel lonely, even if they are surrounded by friends and family. It's one of those things that you often hear about, but very rarely talk about. No one ever really stops and truly thinks about it because, the truth is, we're all lonely in our own way. We all have those moments where we realise that actually, sometimes, loneliness is our only true friend. It's always there, whether we want it to be or not. Some people like being alone and some people don't. As for me, I've spent my entire life feeling lonely, yet also knowing that there is always someone with me even though no one else can see her.

Alicia. What can I say about Alicia? She protects me, keeps me safe and sometimes even tells me what to say. She's always there, even on my bad days, and there are a lot of bad days. I'm not going to go into that right now. I'm sure you don't want to hear me complain about how dull my life is and all the problems that come with it, but what I will say is that she wasn't always around. In fact, Alicia never used to exist. You may not believe this, but I made her up. That's right. She was once merely a figment of my imagination, completely designed by my own subconscious mind. However, that's a story for another time because right now I'm late for work, which is quite an accomplishment considering I live directly above where I work.

Let me tell you a little bit more about me. Due to the fact that I don't like people I chose a career where I wouldn't have to deal with them too often: I'm a vet. Unfortunately for me this means I do have to deal with the owners of the animals I treat. I guess I didn't think about that part. The owners are so bloody whiney and always try and tell me what to do and how to deal with their precious pets. Despite this annoyance I do enjoy my job, mainly because I get to interact with animals on a daily basis. I may not like people, but I love animals. Animals are the best, aren't they? Who doesn't love animals? Idiots and crazy people, that's who. I always say that if a person hates animals then that person isn't worth knowing and can't be trusted. Animals never judge you, never shout at you or complain. They never call you a bitch or gossip behind your back. They are the best. Except cats – I hate cats. Actually, that's wrong: I like cats, but cats hate *me*. I've never met a cat that likes me, which makes treating them a bit of a pain in the ass. I constantly have scratches up my arms because every damn cat I meet takes one look at me and decides that I'm the devil and am clearly there to kill them, not cure them.

Dogs on the other hand are much easier to treat. I love them and they love me. I actually have a dog of my own called Oscar (I told you I'd get around to explaining about him). He's a six-year-old tan and white Jack Russell Terrier; a little pocket rocket who thinks he is the biggest and baddest dog in the world. That's why I love him, because he doesn't take any shit from anybody, but he does live for a belly scratch. I rescued him when he was a puppy. Some asshole brought him in to my vet practice saying that he was a menace and wouldn't stop yapping and he was going to throw him off a bridge if I didn't take him. So obviously I adopted him. I may have a psychopathic *something* inside me, but I'm not a completely heartless bitch. Not when it comes to animals, anyway. Even Alicia likes Oscar. She wasn't sure at first and told me that dogs were better off without humans to look after them, but when Oscar licked her (me) she melted a little bit.

That is a lie. I did not melt.

Okay, but you let him stay. That's the main thing.

As a vet animals have always been a big part of my life. I had a fair few pets as a child too, which is a lot more than most children can say. Despite not having a single human friend growing up I did have plenty of animal ones. My mum and dad bought a smallholding when I was just a baby and I grew up surrounded by the New Forest countryside. It was an idyllic place to grow up: fresh air, miles of wide-open spaces and lots of wildlife. I loved it. That was, until I started getting lonely and wished I had other children to play with. I was perfectly happy to play alone, but I didn't even speak to another child my own age until I was nearly ten. I was home-schooled. I'm not saying that all home-schooled children are freaks, but ... well, I mean, they're not *normal* are they? How can an only child be taught at home, not socialise with any other kids and expect to turn out normal? I didn't talk to a boy my own age until I was sixteen. I could go on more about this, but ...

Shit, is that the time? I really am late for work now.

I quickly finish my coffee and slam the empty mug down on the little table beside me. Oscar jumps in alarm off my lap and starts running around like a possessed demon. It's 6:55 a.m. I usually open up my vet practice at 6:30 a.m. Not that anyone will be waiting for me to open, but I do like to be on time for things. If I'm ever running late for anything, I get a tight, uncomfortable feeling in my chest, like I have right now.

I hurriedly wiggle my butt into my black work trousers. Black, boring, unflattering, like me. My keys are hanging on the single hook on the wall beside the door. I grab them and usher Oscar out the door. He comes with me to work every day. The little bugger barks all day otherwise. I don't think he likes being left alone. We're a team, him and me. It's actually nice having him as company. He's like my little shadow, except when I'm doing surgery; then he stays with Emma and Lucy, my two co-workers. They are ...

Bitches.

Alicia doesn't like them very much. She finds them annoying. They are okay. I guess I could call them my friends, but I find it very hard to connect with them properly. Emma and Lucy have a proper female friendship where they tell each other every little detail about their lives: who they have sex with, who they hate or love or whatever. I've never had that with anyone, not even my mum (not that I'd tell my mum who I have sex with. I mean, some things are just meant to be kept private, right?). I just listen from afar, always listening, never getting engaged in their conversations. I prefer it that way. So does Alicia.

She's not one for talking or expressing feelings or emotions, mainly because she doesn't have any. Sometimes I think she and I are very much alike. Maybe we rub off on each other a little bit.

I once researched what a psychopath was and the first thing that popped up on Google was:

Psychopathy is defined as an antisocial mental disorder in which a person shows a lack of ability to love or establish meaningful personal relationships, shows a lack of remorse or shame, is impulsive, a pathological liar and shows manipulative behaviour.

I mean ... that's Alicia down to a T! And I can actually tick off a few of those as well, especially the meaningful relationship one. The only meaningful relationship I have is with my dog.

The stairs down to the ground floor of the building are narrow. Oscar does his best to squeeze past my ankles, desperate to reach the bottom first, but I manage to block his way.

'Not today, buddy!' I jeer. On more than one occasion he's tripped me up and I've gone flying down the stairs, landing in a heap at the bottom while he stands over me barking like the asshole he is.

Oscar accepts his fate and waits until I reach the bottom of the stairs before barging past me. He knows that the first thing we do, after turning on all the lights and switching the computer on, is go and prepare the consultation room where I store the doggy treats. The little bugger won't leave me alone until I give him one. Dogs are creatures of habit. Actually, so am I.

I ritually do the same thing in the same order every morning and if something disrupts it then it throws my whole day off. I'm sure everyone has their normal morning routine. I always brush my teeth immediately after eating breakfast and drinking my coffee. Makes sense, right? However, before that, there's the ritual where the second my feet touch the floor after getting out of bed, I always pick them straight back up again and count to five. You know, normal stuff. I don't even remember when that weird obsession started.

Shit, I didn't brush my teeth! I was finishing my coffee and then realised I was late for work and rushed out the door. I was too busy telling you all about my life. Great, now my whole day is ruined.

Once I've switched on the computer and set up the consultation room (and given His Highness a treat) I go and sit in the reception area. This is my own vet business by the way. It's small, but it's mine. Yes, I'm up to my eyeballs in debt, yet I'm happy. At least, I'm as happy as I can be in my career. My personal life is a whole other story. My vet business is called Joss Pets. I don't know why it's called that. There's no special meaning behind it. I was in a rush the day I applied for my business loan and there was a blank spot where I had to write the name of my business and I made it up right there on the spot. It said I could change it later, but I never did. Just one of those things that has stuck.

Like I said, Joss Pets is a small practice. I don't keep any animals here overnight and I don't actually have a proper surgery area. I travel to a bigger vet practice in Bournemouth to conduct surgery. It's mainly a place where paranoid owners bring their pets when they have a sniffle or a blister or an infected eye. If there is anything major or life-threatening with them then they usually go further afield. I'm the only actual vet who works here. Emma is the receptionist and Lucy is a veterinary nurse who assists me and runs a lot of the consultations for me while I do the paperwork. That's always fun. It's about as much fun as making idle conversations with the pets' owners or stabbing myself in the eye.

Ring! Ring!

And so the day begins ...

That's the telephone on the reception desk. I stare at it blankly, praying to whatever Almighty God happens to be up there that it's nothing horrendously serious. I have neither the time nor the patience today. I let it ring a couple more times and then reluctantly pick up the receiver.

'Good morning. Joss Pets. Josslyn speaking. How can I help?' I say in the most happy, polite voice I can muster for this time of morning. I can almost *feel* Alicia rolling her eyes at me (if she had eyes, of course). 'Hello?' There's nothing but silence on the end of the phone. 'Hello?' I try again.

I listen really closely by putting my finger in my other ear (not that doing that ever works ... does that actually work for anyone?) but I still can't hear anything for another five seconds and then ...

Breathing. I can hear someone breathing heavily as if they are running or trying to catch their breath. It sounds a bit perverted.

'What the fuck?' I mutter to myself. 'Hello? Who is this?' More random breathing. I listen as intently as I can and then it goes quiet, like extremely quiet. Nothing. Not even a dial tone, which means whoever it is, is still on the line. Without realising it I'm holding my breath. I won't lie, I'm a little scared, but believe it or not this isn't the first time this has happened to me, but it is the first time it's happened at work and on a work's phone. A week ago I had a phone call on my mobile exactly the same: breathing and then silence. And the week before that. And the week before that, but I haven't been bothered about it. It's been more of an annoyance than anything and previously I've always slammed the phone down, but not this time. This time I'm going to sort this out and find out who this fucker is.

Let me take over.

No, Alicia, not now. The last thing I need is you taking me over at work. I can handle this on my own.

'Listen, whoever this is, please stop. If you do it again I'm calling the police.' And I hang up. There, that sorted it. Then why is my voice shaking and my heart rate going about as fast as it was when I attempted to sprint for the bus that one time and collapsed as I was about to climb on?

I stare at the receiver and then at Oscar who has joined me in the reception area. He's taken up his place in his little dog bed under the desk.

'I'm sure it's nothing,' I say out loud, not really sure if I'm talking to Oscar, Alicia, or myself. Jesus Christ, I'm messed up. The only people (they aren't even people!) in my life that I talk to and enjoy hanging out with are a dog and a ... I don't even know what Alicia is, but I know she isn't real.

I glance around the small reception area, focusing on random objects: a fake plant pot by the door that really needs a dusting, a picture of two dogs sniffing each other's butts on the wall above two blue plastic chairs and the small array of dog treats I sell. It's not exactly a well-equipped or inviting place to work, but it's all I can afford right now. When I first bought this building roughly five years ago it was in a dire state. Luckily my dad and I are pretty handy with a paintbrush and the odd DIY job, so we were able to spruce the place up and make it look semi-presentable and professional. My dad taught me all these life skills while we lived on the smallholding. To be perfectly honest I'd rather pay someone to do it, but beggars can't be choosers. Until I can afford it I'll be doing all my own jobs (or asking my dad). You never know, I could suddenly come into some money: win the lottery and become a millionaire overnight. Just have to buy a lottery ticket first. Or maybe mum and dad will die and leave me their house and all their money ... okay, that's a bit morbid for seven in the morning. Let's pretend I didn't just think that!

While I wait for my first appointment to arrive I may as well tell you a little more about myself. I'm sure you're dying to find out. What else would you like to know? Let me guess ... you want to know more about Alicia, don't you? Everyone always wants to know more about her. No one cares about Josslyn. Don't worry, I won't hold it against you. Out of the two of us she is the more interesting one anyway. So let me tell you about Alicia. Alicia is ... *interesting.* And her story is a long one, which I won't be able to tell you all at once, so I'll start with how she came into existence.

As you know by now, I was a lonely child and I grew up on a smallholding, so the only friends I had were animals. One day when I was five years old ... or was I six ... no, I was five ...

You were seven.

Okay, Miss Know-It-All!

I am just making sure you get your facts straight.

Well, thanks so much for that.

Anyway, where was I?

One day when I was *seven* I was out for a walk with a couple of my animal friends, a farm cat called Tornado and our pet dog called Milo. Tornado lived outside in all weather and was quite old (she was pushing fifteen I think). She walked with a limp and had a mean face. Milo was a scraggly crossbreed with grey fur who my dad adopted for me because he was the runt of a litter of puppies our neighbour's dog had and no one wanted him. Our neighbour had said he would probably die, but there he was, a year later and still alive. I had nursed him back to health and that was when I started to think that when I grew up I wanted to be a vet.

Milo, Tornado and I had stopped for a picnic at our local haunt (an extremely old, almost hollow oak tree in the woods). Seriously, this tree was gigantic and ancient. Dad had told me it was well over two hundred and fifty years old. It had even been struck by lightning once. One of the massive branches had cracked and fallen, but the tree still stood tall and proud, towering above the other trees in the woods. It was so old that the trunk was rotten and had been hollowed out by previous children over the years. It made the perfect den.

I had brought a few snacks and drinks for everyone. I sat down inside the tree (I called it My Place). Tornado then decided he didn't want to have a picnic and buggered off to hunt mice and Milo, the traitor, wandered off to sniff some bushes and pee on them. So I was left alone in My Place to drink my tea (it was make-believe tea because my mum wouldn't let me go wandering off with hot tea in my flask) and eat my snacks (chocolate digestive biscuits and cucumber sandwiches – how posh was I?) And at that precise moment I realised that I had no friends. I mean, obviously I knew I had no friends before that, but there was something about being abandoned by your pets (who are supposed to be loyal) that makes you realise that you really are lonely and also a complete loser.

So I made her up. Right there and then. She sort of materialised before my eyes. I quickly thought up a name (it was the first name that popped into my head) and started up a conversation.

'Hello Alicia, would you like some tea?'

'Hello Josslyn. Nice to meet you. I would love some tea.'

I poured the tea. 'I love your hair today.' Her hair (I decided) was the same as mine: dark brown and slightly wavy.

'Thank you,' she said. Alicia was the same age as me with the same dark eyes and she wore a simple top and green leggings. Oh, and she wore the coolest trainers ever: bright pink with silver laces and unicorns on the side ... because, you know, unicorns were cool back then.

She became my imaginary friend. She didn't talk much, but she was there and she listened to me prattle on about the weather and whatever else I felt like talking about. It felt so amazing to be able to talk to someone who actually spoke back to me. Tornado and Milo were great, but they weren't so good at holding conversations. Alicia sat with me and I offered her some of my biscuits and we shared the tea. For the first time in my short life I felt like I had a real friend, and I was happy.

At the end of our picnic I tidied the food and drink away and got up to leave. 'I better get back home. I told Mum I would only be an hour, otherwise she worries.'

'You will not tell anyone about me, will you?' Alicia asked, sounding quite serious and worried.

'No, of course not,' I said. 'You're my little secret.'

At that moment Milo and Tornado decided to make an appearance and the weirdest thing happened. Tornado took one look at me, arched her back, hissed and then ran off back home on her own. From that day on she never came on any other walks with me, Milo and Alicia, and she always hissed at me and ran away. Cats are weird.

So there you have it. That's how Alicia came to be. She started off as a figment of my imagination. She was so real I could almost reach out and touch her, but obviously as I grew up my imagination faded (as I guess do all children's) and then she was just stuck in my head. Of course, there's more to her story, but you know, I don't know you very well yet and I've got stuff to do and things to ...

'Arrggg!' I suddenly clutch my stomach and double over as a horrendous pain shoots through my abdomen. Oh my God, it hurts. It really hurts! I start gasping and moaning as I slowly slide off my chair and onto the floor where I immediately curl up into a foetal position. Oscar comes over and starts licking my face and wagging his tail, possibly thinking it's some sort of fun game. He then copies me by rolling onto his back and wiggling from side to side like an idiot. Dogs may be man's best friend, but I do wonder about their sanity from time to time.

'Fuck off, Oscar,' I mutter as I reach up past him for my mobile phone which I've left on the reception desk. I manage to brush it with my fingers and knock it off the desk, all the while trying not to pass out from the continuing pain. I fumble around with the phone, trying to unlock the screen, but my hands are shaking so bad and I'm sweating, like literally sweating. Even my fingertips are sweaty so I can't unlock it. They just slide around and do absolutely nothing. Fuck.

Then the pain vanishes. It's gone. Just like that. I continue to lay on the floor, too scared to move in case it strikes again, but it seems to have completely vanished. Maybe it was wind. Yeah, right. Period pain? No, not quite time for that yet. I don't know what the hell it was, but it wasn’t pleasant by any stretch of the imagination. It has also never happened to me before. I’ve had stomach aches and indigestion before, but nothing as bad as that.

Oscar is still squirming about on the floor, so I ignore him, grab my phone and pull myself up into a sitting position with my back leaning against the leg of the desk. I take a deep breath and compose myself, finally able to unlock my phone with my fingerprint, but it seems irrelevant now because I had been trying to unlock it so I could dial 999 (honestly, the pain had been so bad that I thought I was going to die). Out of sheer habit I check my usual apps: Facebook, Instagram, WhatsApp, and my e-mails. There is one WhatsApp message from my mum, so I open it:

Hello darling. How are you? I'm just checking in and wondering if you are able to pop over tonight to help with clearing out the attic. I've been meaning to do it, but I find it difficult getting up and down the ladder and your father has hurt his back again. I'll make dinner for you, your favourite. Let me know. Bye darling. Love from Mum xx

And yes, she really does text in full sentences. None of this short-hand nonsense, as she calls it. I mean, it's 2019, you would think she would have caught up with the technology by now, but no. She would live in the 1930s if she could. I quickly type a reply, knowing full well that she will struggle to read my message:

Sure Mum. C u l8r abt 6. Luv u x

Well it's better than spending another night alone in my flat while eating another takeaway from down the road (Donald's Delights). My parents live about thirty minutes away. I finish at half past five tonight. I'll spend a few hours clearing out their attic, have a decent meal for once and then get back home for about eleven o'clock. Sorted.

Oscar finally stops rolling around on the floor and returns to his bed. I peel myself off the floor and brush myself down just in time to see my first patient arrive outside the front door with its owner. It's a cat.

Fucking perfect.

Chapter Two

It's 7 a.m. and a strange looking old lady is attempting to open the front door to my practice. She has a cat-sized pet carrier wedged under one arm and an over-sized blue handbag in the other, all whilst wrestling with the door handle. It's fascinating to watch and fairly amusing. Maybe I should go and help her.

Leave her.

That's not nice, Alicia. It is funny to watch though ... oh shit, she's seen me watching her. I have to go and help her now.

I get up and go to open the door. It's locked. I had forgotten to unlock it earlier. Wow, my day really is starting off badly all thanks to me forgetting to brush my teeth. I make a mental note to rush back upstairs in-between patients and brush them. No point in having bad breath all day.

'Sorry!' I yell through the door as I fish around in my pockets for the keys. I finally get the door open and the old woman huffs at me and stumbles over the threshold.

'It's freezing outside!' she exclaims. 'Poor Mrs Mittens.'

Now (and I'm taking a wild guess here) I assume that Mrs Mittens is the cat and this old lady isn't referring to herself in the first person. She's a new customer to the practice so I've never met her before. Emma booked her in yesterday at the last minute. Apparently it was an emergency, but not so bad as to warrant driving to the out of hours vet practice.

'I'm so sorry, Mrs ...' Shit, I don't actually know her name. I didn't even have time to check the details this morning when I switched on the computer – what with the weird phone call and the horrific pain it had completely slipped my mind.

The old lady stares at me and huffs again. 'Mrs Smith.'

'Right, of course, Mrs Smith. Good morning. Please, this way.'

I usher her further into the reception area and close the door against the cold and the wind. It's blowing a gale out there. A load of brown, crispy leaves float in from outside and find their way into the corners of the room. I hate winter. I hate the cold: the wet, the wind, the darkness. I also hate summer: the heat, the long days, the light. My favourite season is autumn, but early autumn, like in September when it's warm, but not too warm, cold, but not too cold and all the leaves are starting to turn. It's the beginning of November now (the 7th to be precise), the time of year when things turn properly wet, cold and miserable.

I can hear the cat making pathetic meows from inside the carrier as Mrs Smith thumps it down on the consultation table in the little room at the back. I wash my hands in the small sink and then cautiously approach the table, aware that a pair of eyes are watching my every move.

'So ... tell me about Mrs Mittens.' I reach to open the carrier door and suddenly the cat hisses and snarls. 'It's okay, happens all the time,' I say with a forced smile.

'Mrs Mittens usually eats dinner with me at five in the evening, but yesterday she wouldn't touch her food. She went and slept in her bed by the fire instead.'

I wait for the rest of the story, but it appears that was it. The end. 'Okay,' I say slowly. 'And she appears normal otherwise? Did she eat breakfast this morning?'

'Yes, she did. She is perfectly herself otherwise. It just worried me. Usually she enjoys her food and eating dinner with me. I always tell her about my day. Like, yesterday, I wanted to tell her about the shopping trip I had with Edith from down the road. You know, she is getting very slow these days, is poor Edith. Her knees aren't as strong as they used to be, so our shopping trip took much longer than usual. I even—'

'Can you get Mrs Mittens out for me?' I interrupt. I really didn't need to hear any more about Edith and her weak knees.

Mrs Smith opens the carrier door and pulls the cat out. I must admit that Mrs Mittens is a beautiful cat: a long-haired silver-grey with blue eyes. Mrs Mittens immediately hisses, arches her back and then hisses again. I'm pretty sure if I try and give her a physical she will take one of my eyes out. I should probably at least try and check her over, after all Mrs Smith will be paying forty quid for this visit whether there's anything wrong with her cat or not.

Mrs Smith gently strokes her cat while I do my best to check it over, all the while getting hissed at. I finish my checks and take a step back, relieved that I no longer have to touch the writhing beast.

'Mrs Mittens looks healthy to me. I can't see or find anything wrong with her. My advice is to keep an eye on her and offer her plenty of water. If she refuses her dinner again maybe offer it to her again a bit later ...' I stop myself before I add *and stop telling her such boring stories. Maybe your cat is sick of you and wants to be left the hell alone.*

Mrs Smith nods in agreement. 'Okay, well that's a relief. You know, Mrs Mittens usually likes new people. She liked the last vet we saw. Cats have a sixth sense you know. They can tell when something is off about a person. They can tell when someone has an evil streak.'

I smile politely. 'Good to know. Thank you, Mrs Smith.'

'I wasn't saying you are evil dear, but ... you know, cats are never wrong.' Mrs Smith leans in towards me, getting her face as close to mine as she can without moving from the spot. She stares straight into my eyes, which, I won't lie, unnerves me slightly. 'Hmmm,' she says. 'Interesting.'

'W-what's interesting?' I ask with a nervous smile.

'Your eyes. They are ... interesting.'

What the fuck does that even mean?

After Mrs Smith and Mrs Mittens leave the building I disinfect the examination table and type my notes on the computer, leaving a note on the bottom mentioning that Mrs Smith is a strange old cow (no, I don't really put that, but I want to). I merely mention that she should be handled with care.

At 8 a.m. Lucy and Emma arrive together to start work. I'm not sure if they live together or carpool or what, but they always seem to arrive at the same time. I've never asked. We aren't that close. Plus, I don't actually care.

They both beam at me and give Oscar a tickle. 'Morning, Josslyn!' they say together.

'Hi. Morning,' I say back as enthusiastically as I can.

'How was Mrs Smith this morning?' asks Emma. 'She sounded like a bit of a weirdo on the phone last night. What was wrong with her cat?'

'Nothing, it appears,' I say with a sigh. 'Other than the fact the cat doesn't like me.'

'Why is it that cats don't like you?' asks Lucy, as she starts changing into her work scrubs.

'Who the hell knows,' I say with a laugh. Urrgg, all this small talk is infuriating.

Lucy laughs. 'I've never known any cat that comes here to like you. How strange!'

The girls share a laugh together, probably at my expense, but I choose to ignore it. I'm almost certain they talk about me behind my back, but then again so do I ... well, I talk to Alicia and Oscar about them. I'm pretty sure that doesn't count though. Oscar never says anything back and Alicia despises pretty much every human on the planet, although I have noticed she does have a fondness for my dad.

Emma takes up her position at the reception desk and starts typing and checking emails or whatever it is she actually does. When I hired her I merely asked her to do the inventory, send emails and order whatever medical supplies I needed, but she does so much more than that now that I can't keep up. She just randomly hands me a form and says, 'sign this!' so I do, without looking at what I'm actually signing, but it works. Everything runs smoothly. I'm not losing money and the customers are happy.

Emma has short, black hair and lots of make-up on, along with big hoop earrings. It looks as if she's ready for a night out. Who the hell has that much energy or time in the morning to apply that much make-up? I guess I would have the time if I went to bed at a more reasonable hour and got up at a more ungodly hour, but I happen to like staying up till gone midnight, alone in my flat with no one but the dog and my made-up, psychological disorder for company. I also like passing out on my small two-seater sofa and waking up with a sore neck and drool dangling from my mouth.

Lucy flicks on the small kettle we have in the tiny room at the back of reception and starts making coffee for all of us. Despite what Alicia says, these girls aren't that bad. I mean, I never have to make my own coffee when I'm at work so that's a bonus. Plus, they often bring me biscuits, which they don't actually eat (because 'carbs and sugar, ewww!') so it's all for me.

Lucy has long, straight, blonde hair tied back in a ponytail and a bit less make-up on than Emma, but she still looks fresh and done-up. As I mentioned before she is a veterinary nurse and, although she doesn't know as much as I do regarding pet illnesses, she does know a lot, but I do feel special when she asks for my opinion on a case. Only on very rare occasions do I disagree with her and offer a different medication or treatment, but she always accepts my help with a smile on her face.

Compared to Lucy and Emma I look like a disgrace. Here I am with a bare face, dark bags under my eyes and dull brown hair scraped back in what I can only describe as a messy bun. I don't wear make-up. Actually, that's a lie. I do wear it, but only when Alicia is in charge. If Alicia had her way she would probably look as good as these girls do all the time. Even I'll admit that we look quite attractive when we have make-up on, but it's very rare that she takes charge nowadays. She's just there in the background, like an internal monologue, constantly criticising and trying to tell me what to do. Alicia is always getting on at me to look after myself, get a haircut, go to the gym, stop eating crap, stop drinking wine, but I never listen (yet I still complain when I put on another pound or two). It's a never-ending vicious circle of life.

'So,' says Lucy, coming to join Emma and I in reception. 'What did you get up to last night?' she asks me.

Honestly, this infernal small talk.

Just let me take over and they will never talk to us again.

Thanks Alicia, but I got this.

'I watched that programme you girls always go on about.'

'Love Island!' they squeal together.

Just let me kill them both right now and put us all out of this misery.

'Um ... no,' I say with a stutter. 'That Bake Off programme ... thing.'

'But that's not on at the moment,' says Lucy with a frown. 'And it's usually on Tuesday nights.' Today is Thursday.

'It was a repeat,' I add hastily. Let me just clarify that I wasn't actually watching Bake Off, but I didn't want to tell them the truth which was that I watched a programme about serial killers and actually found it very informative and educational and could totally see where most of them were coming from.

'Did you enjoy it?' asks Lucy.

'Uh ... yeah, it was ... good.' Note to self: I really need to work on my small talk or at least come up with some new words for *good*.

Lucy just smiles at me.

Look at that condescending bitch smiling at us. I could easily wipe that smirk off her pretty, overly made-up face.

'Hey Josslyn, you want to come out with us tomorrow night? It's Friday, after all. We're gonna hit a few bars, maybe go dancing. Wanna come for a girls' night?' Emma says in her usual high-pitched voice. Both of them start doing some weird dance together.

I blink a few times, bringing myself out of my dark thoughts, which was that I'd rather slit my own wrists than go dancing in a nightclub. Seriously. I'm twenty-eight for fuck's sake, far too old and boring to be setting foot in a nightclub. Who even likes nightclubs these days? They are a breeding ground for germs, the floors are always sticky, there's always a drunk girl in the corner being felt up by some sweaty bloke and every man in there seems to think it's his god-damn right to squeeze every girl's butt and laugh. How do they expect us to react exactly – turn around, swoon and say, 'oh my God, take me now!' I don't think so! The last time a drunk guy did that to me in a nightclub Alicia made me punch him in the face. Actually, that's a lie. I punched him in the face, but Alicia told me to, although I didn't need much convincing. Anyway, I digress …

My immediate reaction is to say no to Emma's offer. I always say no when they ask me to go out with them, which annoyingly they do quite often. I'm not sure why they continue to ask me to be perfectly honest. You'd think after turning them down a dozen times they would get the hint. Maybe they're just being polite.

Say no.

'I … um …' I start. But then I get one of those brain waves (which is never a good thing in my opinion) and I think why the hell should I always do what Alicia says? She's not the boss of me. I'm the boss of me. Maybe it's time I turn things around and try something different rather than watching serial killer documentaries and taking notes while drinking myself to an early grave on cheap wine every night. Okay, maybe not every night.

Say no!

'Err ... sure!' I suddenly say with a higher voice than I originally anticipated.

Both girls stare at me, probably just as shocked as I am that I actually said yes.

You bitch.

'Oh ...' says Emma with a half-laugh. 'That's great. You never come out with us. We'll pick you up at ten.'

'P.M?' I ask in horror.

'Well yeah!' laughs Lucy. 'Any earlier and it's dead in town.'

'Right, of course,' I say with a sigh. Dear God, what have I done?

Funny she should mention the word dead ... because that is exactly what she is ... dead.

It seems I've made Alicia angry.

The rest of the day passes by fairly uneventfully. We have a walk-in patient (a dog who had somehow got his head stuck in a traffic cone), a few regular patients for their jabs and check-ups and one rabbit who had a weepy eye. Since it was a quiet day I spend most of it hiding away doing paperwork while Lucy and Emma man the desk and the consultation room. I take Oscar for his routine lunchtime walk up to the local dog park and throw his tennis ball a few hundred times. Honestly, don't dogs ever get tired of chasing the same old ball over and over? Clearly Oscar doesn't, because he has the same amount of enthusiasm the last time I throw it as he does the first time. That's what I love about dogs: they always have such amazing enthusiasm and passion for life, as long as they have a ball and you. Dogs are one of those wonderful things that make the world a better place.

It seems that Alicia is no longer speaking to me as she remains quiet for the rest of the day until, that is, I start doing the close-down procedures at half past five. Lucy and Emma have already left for the day, leaving me to finish up. I actually prefer it that way. Last one in, last one out. It is my practice, after all. They sometimes offer to help, but I always say no. Just because I have no life it doesn't mean I want to keep them from theirs.

I'm just finishing off the last email when my mobile starts buzzing in my pocket. Without even looking at the screen to see who it is I answer it.

'Hello?' No answer. 'Hello?' Nothing. Then ... breathing. Shit, it's him (of course, I'm jumping to an extremely sexist conclusion here and assuming it's a man). That's when I sense Alicia stirring. I look at the number on the screen, but it's a private call.

Allow me ...

What are you going to say?

You shall see ...

Thanks, but I'll deal with it.

'Listen up, whoever you are.' My voice is shaking, I can feel it, but I do my best tough girl impression. 'I told you I'd call the police if you did this again, so that's what I'm doing right now ... as soon as I hang up the phone. I'm going to call the police and—' The phone goes dead.

Smooth.

Shut up.

I try and put the creepy phone calls out of my mind as I bundle Oscar into my beat-up old red Corsa and point it in the direction of my parents' house. He always sits in the front passenger seat, despite my frequent half-hearted attempts to put him in the back. He prefers riding shotgun and being able to see out the windscreen, but after about five minutes he usually curls up into a ball and goes to sleep, which, predictably, he does. I'm left to listen to my own thoughts and his gentle snores. I'm actually really looking forward to my mum's awesome cooking. She's making my favourite meal: lasagne with garlic bread. My mouth starts watering at the thought.

It's dark already. Damn these short winter days. The lights on my car are looking a little dim, probably because they're caked in dirt and grime due to the fact that I haven't washed it in months, possibly a year. I squint ahead at the road, making a mental note to get my car washed this weekend. Yet another one of those annoying adult jobs that constantly need doing, like paying bills and doing the washing. I can't help but notice the bright lights in my rear-view mirror. Jesus, turns your high-beams off, jack-ass! Then the lights disappear.

While I have some time, I think I'll tell you a little bit more about Alicia. As you may have noticed she isn't tactful or even very nice, but she is always there for me, so I admire and love her for that. Yes, I love her. She's my friend, the only friend I have and she understands me. I don't always understand her, but I'm learning to. Sometimes we have our disagreements, but overall we have similar thoughts and feelings. I'm just better at hiding them. If Alicia had her way all the time I'd probably be locked up in a mental institution with wires hooked to my brain and on a considerable amount of medication.

Alicia started off being relatively nice and normal and we would talk for hours about what we wanted to be when we grew up (I always wanted to be a vet and she wanted to be some sort of business owner who lived in a foreign country. She said she hadn't worked out the details yet). However, when I was eight, she started to change. She started to make me do things: bad things. They were things I didn't always agree with or want to do, but she said it was for the best, so I believed her because she was my friend.

One day I was walking through a field near the farmhouse. The grass was really over-grown and almost up to my waist in certain places. I was struggling to make a path, constantly having to untangle my legs from the long grass. Alicia was walking in front of me, but because she was invisible (and therefore not real) she didn't make any impression in the grass, nor was she able to help me clear the way. She just glided through it, like a ghost. It was fascinating to watch.

'What's it like to be invisible?' I asked her.

She shrugged her shoulders. 'I am not sure. You get ignored a lot I guess because people do not know you are there.'

'I don't ignore you.'

She turned her head and looked over her shoulder at me, grinning. 'No, you do not.'

'Do you think you'll ever be able to be seen by anyone else?'

'One day.' I remember her sounding so sure, so unbelievably certain about that fact. Her whole face became focused and she seemed to light up. I would have loved for her to be real because then I'd have a real friend and not just a figment of my imagination.

'But when other people can see you will that mean that you leave me and talk to them instead?' I asked.

'I will never leave you.' Again, a certain statement.

'Good, cos I'd be so lonely without you, Alicia. I'd do anything for you.'

'Anything?'

'Of course. You're my best friend.'

We arrived at My Place, the big tree in the woods. We always went there, just Alicia and me. It was in the middle of nowhere, away from prying eyes and ears. It was where we talked about stuff; personal stuff. The kind of stuff you talked to your best friend about. Of course, we were only eight years old, so there was no talk of sex or anything like that, but we did talk about very serious topics, like ...

'I wonder what it is like to be dead,' said Alicia out of the blue.

Yeah, that sort of stuff.

'Lonely I guess. If you're dead then people can't see or hear you.'

'So does that mean that I am dead now?' I remember not being sure how to answer her because for all intent and purposes Alicia *was* dead. I stayed quiet for a moment. 'Go on. You can tell me.'

'Well, technically Alicia, you've never lived because you aren't a real person, so therefore you can't die.'

'But I am part of you and you are a living person.'

'True.' This had all been a bit too much for my young brain to handle. There I was discussing life and death with my invisible friend.

'Have you ever wanted to be dead?' she asked me quietly.

'Sometimes,' I answered truthfully. 'Before I met you I wished I was dead. I used to think I would be better off dead because no one would miss me because I had no friends, but then I remembered mummy and daddy. They would miss me.' It was true. I may have only been young, but I considered myself a troubled child. I hadn't been mistreated. My parents loved me, but I knew I was different somehow. I kept so many secrets from my parents; Alicia being one of them. I still hadn't told them about her, but I knew I couldn't keep her a secret forever, even though she wanted me to. The truth was bound to come out one day. The amount of times they had caught me talking to myself was starting to creep up. They must have suspected that something wasn't quite right with me by now, unless they chose to ignore it.

'Will you do something for me, Josslyn?' asked Alicia, changing the subject.

'Of course.'

'You know I rarely ask for anything, but this is important. It is about Tornado.'

'What about her?'

'I need you to kill her.'

'What!' I gasped. I remember thinking how calmly she had spoken those words, like she had merely asked me to pop to the shop to buy a carton of milk. It was weird ... and creepy and for the very first time I felt a little bit afraid of my best friend.

'Poor Tornado is getting old now. She is suffering. You have seen her limping around and she cannot catch mice like she used to. I think it is best we put her out of her misery. It is what you would have to do in the future when you become a vet. You would have to kill animals that are suffering for their own good.'

'Yeah, but ...' Again, she made a good point, but it was the way she had said it that put me on edge. Cold, callous, unemotional.

'I will help you.'

'How?'

'Let me take over.'

'What do you mean?'

'Let me take over your body.'

I stared at her with my mouth open. 'You can do that? How?'

'I can try, but you have to let me in first. You have to want me to take over.'

'I'm not sure I do.' It was at that moment that Alicia got up from sitting on the ground and moved right up close to me, her face only inches away from mine. I started to shake with nerves, but she remained calm and had a strange look in her eyes. Her stare seemed to go right through me. It made my heart beat twice as fast as normal and a lump formed in my throat.

'Y-you're scaring me, Alicia,' I stuttered.

'It is good to be scared sometimes,' she replied. 'It makes you feel like you are really alive.' She smiled at me and stroked my hair. 'Let me take over and I promise that you nor Tornado will feel a thing. I will make it quick.'

I blinked, a few tears escaping from my eyes and then slowly I nodded, finally succumbing to her wish.

And that was the last thing I remembered until a few hours later. I was standing in our barn, looking down at the ground which was covered in yellow straw and spots of deep red blood. I was holding one of my mum's kitchen knives in my right hand and Tornado the cat's head in the other.

I screamed louder than I had ever done in my life and ever have since.

Chapter Three

So yeah ... that happened.

After that horrendous day I didn't hear from Alicia again for nearly two years, which to be perfectly honest, I was relieved about. I'm not sure why she stayed away for so long. Maybe she thought I needed time to get over the incident or maybe she had quenched her thirst for evil deeds. Whatever the reason, she left me alone to deal with the aftermath and I've never totally forgiven her for that.

By the time my parents turned up I had hidden the body and the knife under some straw and I told them I'd seen a rat. They decided to ignore the fact that Tornado mysteriously disappeared after that. No one seemed to really care about the cat anyway. She was old, my parents had said, but I cared. Despite the fact that Tornado had taken a disliking to me ever since Alicia had been on the scene, that old cat had still been my friend. And then she was dead and Alicia was gone and ...

What the fuck! Those damn headlights are on full beam again. I assumed the asshole had turned off the road ages ago. Are they following me? I can't work out if it's the same car, but my gut instinct is telling me that it is. I try and focus on the road ahead, but my frustration with constantly being blinded is starting to show. I grip the wheel harder, grit my teeth and speed up to try and get some distance, but the car is still there. It's keeping up with me. Maybe it's *him* – my weird stalker. The thought pops into my head suddenly, but before I can properly react to the idea the lights disappear. I breathe a sigh of relief and continue to my parents' house, determined not to let it shake me up again.

My parents, Ronald and Amanda Reynolds, live in a quaint little area on the outskirts of Brockenhurst in the New Forest. They moved there about ten years ago when I was eighteen, finally fed up with living on the farm. They didn't move far though, only about fifteen miles, but the farm had been very rural. The upkeep of the animals and the grounds had been too much work, especially with my dad's declining health. He had developed a bad back (from years of hard labour) and arthritis in his hands, so he and my mum decided to sell and move to a location which was a little more bearable. I was annoyed at them for not moving sooner. Maybe then I could have had some form of a social life. I went from being an isolated, home-schooled eighteen-year-old who had barely spoken to another human being my own age in her entire life, to a terrified university student who had no idea how to interact with other people, let alone hold a decent conversation. I decided to stay close to home and went to the University of Bournemouth so that I could still live with my parents. It was a bit of a trek each day to get to the university, but it meant I could escape the terrifying city and return to my home comforts.

I love this house. It is one of those old-fashioned, thatched houses (a cottage, if you will) and has its own name plaque by the front gates, which are wrought iron and sturdy. The name of the cottage is The Old Mill. I'm not sure if it was an actual mill years ago or if it's just one of those quaint names people give quaint cottages, but in any case I think of this as my home because wherever my family lives is where I feel most at ease. My flat in Ringwood is just a place I live and sleep and work in. This is my home.

I left home five years ago in 2014 when I finally cut the cord and decided I wanted to face the world alone. I moved a mere thirty minutes away to a beat-up flat above a decrepit old shop where I eventually started my own vet business (as you already know). My parents loaned me some money to start with, just to get me up and running, which I'm slowly paying back (very, very slowly), but luckily they aren't as judgemental as the bank or the loan company, who make it their mission to put me in a bad mood every month when they call and remind me that my bills are overdue. As if I had magically forgotten that I had an outstanding amount of debt to repay.

I push the fancy automatic fob on my key ring and the iron gates magically open, as well as turn on an alarm in the house, which alerts my parents to my arrival. I pull up into the massive expanse of a driveway and park behind their BMW. Yes, my parents are fairly wealthy. My dad worked his butt off on the farm and they managed to sell the place for a handsome profit, as well as invested heavily in some high-yield stocks (don't ask me which ones), which paid out five years ago (another reason why they sold and bought this place and could lend me some money).

The outside light above the front porch is on, a clear sign that they are expecting me. Whenever I would come home late from studying at university they'd always leave the light on for me, like a shining beacon to find my way home. I smile at this thought. They may have their issues as parents (whose parents don't have issues?), but they do love and care about me. I can't deny it.

Oscar forces his way out of the car the moment I open the driver's door and runs at full speed to the front door where he immediately starts to bark, making a quick pit stop to pee on the near-by potted plant. That poor plant. I'm not sure how it's survived all these years with the amount of dog urine it's absorbed. There's no creeping up by surprise on my parents with Oscar in tow.

By the time I reach the front door my mum is standing there with a huge smile on her face, whilst holding a saucepan and stirring the contents with a wooden spoon. Dear God, it's like something out of a olden-day story.

What can I say about my mum? She's old-fashioned, annoying, bossy and over-protective, but that's what I love about her. Some mums are cool (mine is most certainly not) and some mums are classy, but mine is the best of them all. She has beautiful auburn hair which is starting to turn grey in places, but she doesn't seem to mind that (you'll never see me with poisonous dye in my hair, she always says). Her clothes are actually quite sophisticated and up to date, but she still doesn't know how to work her mobile phone properly and has no idea what Netflix is.

'Hi darling!'

'Hi Mum.' I give her a quick peck on her cheek and take a good sniff of the saucepan. Chocolate sauce. For good measure I stick my finger in the chocolate and give it a taste. 'Just as yummy as ever.'

'I'm glad you think so. Your father is in the attic.'

'I thought you said he couldn't get up there very easily.'

'I did, but that doesn't stop him. You know how stubborn that man is.'

'I'll go and get him.'

'Dinner will be ready in twenty minutes.'

'Thanks Mum.'

I step inside and am immediately hit by an almighty gush of warmth and loveliness. I can smell the strong scent of garlic coming from the kitchen, as well as the chocolate sauce which fills my nostrils with its dark and gooey aroma. The interior looks immaculate and like something straight out of a home magazine. Everything has its own place and job. There are no random corners of junk (unlike my flat, which my mum doesn't visit very often, thank fuck).

Oscar follows my mum into the kitchen to no doubt scavenge for scraps while I head upstairs to the main landing where I find the attic trap-door open and a load of boxes packed randomly in the hall. They look completely out of place in the otherwise neat and tidy hallway. I can hear a man swearing from somewhere above me.

'Dad?' I call out.

'Jossy? Stay there, I'll be right down.'

While I wait for my dad to make his appearance I start rifling through a near-by box, which is very damp and smells musty. I'm guessing the attic is still in need of an upgrade, as it was ten years ago when they moved in. Jesus, some of this stuff is ancient. Who even owns videos anymore? My parents, that's who. Oh yes, and there's the video player covered in dust. I pick up an old video cassette case: The Lion King. I must have watched this film a thousand times as a child. It was my favourite. I think the video got worn out because eventually it stopped working and that was when my parents bought me the DVD, but then I refused to watch it because I liked to rewind the tape back to the beginning. There was always something about that whirring sound I liked, erasing all the things that had happened, then pressing play and it starting all over again, like it never happened. With a DVD you don't get that. It just gets to the end and that's it – no whirring sound. It always seems a bit of a let-down. Of course, I did watch The Lion King again eventually, many, many times, but never again on this video cassette.

My dad finally touches down on the floor next to me and gives me a kiss on my cheek and a quick squeeze. My dad is awesome, like seriously awesome. I can always tell him anything (except about anything to do with Alicia, because, you know, that's a whole other level of freaky) and he is the best at cheering me up. His hair is jet black, not even a fleck of grey despite the fact he is five years older than my mum, but at fifty-five he still looks pretty damn good. He always says that he looks young, but feels old. His body is finally starting to give up on him, but he still does jobs around the house and mends anything that needs fixing, even though it's bound to cause him serious pain the next day.

'Dad, you shouldn't be up there,' I scald.

'I know, but I wanted to find this before you got here.' He hands me an old photo frame. It's practically falling apart in my hand, covered in dust and cobwebs, but I recognise it instantly. It's a picture of me, Milo and Tornado back before Alicia made her first appearance, when Tornado was my friend ... and still alive. A solid lump forms in my throat and I have a hard time holding back a tear, but I quickly cover it up by smiling at my dad.

'Thanks Dad.'

'You can take that too if you want it.' He points at the videotape in my hand. 'It was always your favourite.'

'I don't have a video player anymore.'

'No, but it's always worth holding on to these things – makes us remember the good times.' I think that's my dad's one good excuse for keeping a load of junk rather than throwing it away or donating it to a charity shop.

Rather than arguing with him I just say, 'Okay, I'll keep it.'

'Who knows what else you will find up there later!' he jokes.

'Yeah ... who knows.'

Is there anything better than your mum's home cooking? If there is then I don't want to know about it. Right now, all I'm focusing on is the most amazing lasagne I have ever tasted in my life. My mum has outdone herself tonight. The garlic bread (home-made) is hot and buttery and garlicky just like it should be. Plus a glass of crisp white wine straight from the fridge, which will be out of my system by the time I've finished clearing the attic, so I sit back and enjoy it. My mum has always been a good cook, but I never showed any interest in learning from her. The only meal I do know how to cook is a roast dinner (but only if my life happened to depend on making it). She forced me to learn that particular meal. Apparently it's an important meal to be able to make, especially for my future husband.

'If you don't know how to cook how do you expect to land a husband?' she asks me. Ah, the mum interrogation has begun early tonight. She still lives in the dark ages where women are expected to cook for their husbands.

I look at her with a mouth full of food and answer. 'My charming good looks?'

My dad stifles a laugh and takes a drink of red wine. 'This isn't the forties, Amanda. Jossy doesn't need to land a husband. She is perfectly fine on her own. Aren't you love?'

I mumble some sort of response and continue to scoff my dinner.

'Have you met anyone you like yet?' continues my mum. 'The last man you dated was so lovely. Daniel, wasn't it?'

My mum knows full well that his name was Daniel, but she still feels the need to ask me if she remembers his name correctly. One of those annoying mum things. I mumble another reply.

Daniel. *Fucking Daniel.* Jesus, if there's one thing I regret in life it's going out with that loser. I'm sure you've had those sorts of regrets too, unless you happen to have found the perfect man or woman straight away and haven't had to suffer through the unbearable realisation that you are dating a fuck-tard. My mum only saw the polite and kind side of him and so did I, at first, but then he started to change, as they all inevitably do, and I saw the real monster within ... and he saw mine.

Daniel and Alicia never got on (not that he actually knew about her, of course). The whole time I was dating him I had to try and convince her not to strangle him in his sleep. One night I actually woke up straddling him with my hands wrapped around his neck. It was pretty scary. I got beaten up pretty bad that night, not strong enough to fight him off and I refused to let Alicia take over again. Anyway, to cut a long story short, he apologised, I apologised, we moved on from that incident and then he started getting clingy, weird and annoying so I dumped his ass. The end.

'Darling, I know you find it hard to meet men and make friends, but ... you need to try.'

'I do Mum. In fact, I'm going out with the girls from work tomorrow night.' I feel somewhat proud of myself that I can tell her this fact. Her face lights up like a glow-stick.

'That's wonderful, darling!'

I can tell you in absolute certainty that it most positively will not be wonderful.

'Have you made any other friends?'

'No Mum, I haven't.'

'Aren't you lonely? It's not good for a young woman to spend so much time by herself. It does things to people.'

You are telling me.

'I have Oscar.' Oscar responds by yapping and licking my fingers which I offer to him covered in sauce.

'You always did like animals more than people,' says my mum with a huff to her voice.

'They don't annoy me like people do.'

'They also don't speak to you like people do,' corrects my mum.

'Thank God for that.'

My mum appears to get bored with trying to convince her hopeless daughter to get a boyfriend and make friends so she moves on to discussing my work. This is the price I have to pay to eat a decent meal these days.

'How is work going?' she asks.

'Fine.' I'm not exactly one for opening up to people; even my parents get the shortened version of events most of the time.

'Have you had any interesting cases?'

'Errr ...' I think back to Mrs Smith earlier this morning. 'Cats still don't like me.'

'Why is that do you suppose?'

Maybe it's because I beheaded one of their own kind when I was a child and they can sense I'm a murderer. Although technically cats hated me before that happened, ever since I made up Alicia. It's Alicia they don't like, not me, but of course my parents don't know about her, not really anyway. They are vaguely aware that I had an imaginary friend when I was a child, but I never told them any more than that.

'Cats are evil,' answers my dad with his mouth full. 'I never liked them. I don't trust them. Dogs on the other hand ...' Without finishing his sentence he leans off his chair and ruffles Oscar's fur and starts playing with him. Both man and beast start playing tug of war with the tea towel that has fallen to the floor from the edge of the table during dinner.

'That's one of my best tea towels,' warns my mum, but she doesn't stop them. No doubt she has a dozen other tea towels tucked away somewhere. She continues to eat her dinner with a bemused smile on her face. Watching my dad and Oscar play seems to distract her and she doesn't ask me any more questions.

After dinner she brings out the biggest chocolate cake I've ever seen. Seriously, it's huge and with mountains of chocolate frosting and whipped cream on top. It's not even my birthday. She cuts me a massive wedge and sticks a fork into the top of the cream, which can't support the weight and immediately the fork plummets to the plate with a clang. I'm pretty sure she is trying to fatten me up.

Isn't that what all mums do? Not that I need fattening up. I could actually stand to lose a few pounds. Even though I'm stuffed from dinner I still manage to eat the whole slice of cake without barely pausing to breathe.

'Right, tell me what needs doing up in the attic,' I say with a sigh. I'm so full that all I want to do is slouch in front of the television with my dad. I don't even care what's on, but I'm here for a reason. I said I'd help my parents so that's what I'm going to do.

'Most of it is for keeping such as the Christmas decorations and the stuff on the right-hand side as you go up, but the boxes right at the back in the corner need to come down and be sorted. Anything that's rubbish can go in black bin bags out the back. You can keep anything you want.'

'Okay, I'll see what I can do.'

'You don't have to get it all done tonight, darling. You can always come back another time.'

'I'll get as much done as I can.' It's probably going to be a long night.

Attics are creepy, aren't they? I don't think I've been in an attic that didn't give me the creeps. Watch any horror movie and the attic is always the place where the scary things are hiding. Monsters always jump out or hide in the shadows or behind boxes, but luckily so far I haven't come across any dead bodies, scary-looking objects or ghosts. The single light bulb dangling above does a good job of lighting up the entire space. Dad kitted out the attic years ago, laying a load of decent floorboards so he didn't have to balance on the wooden beams. It smells damp up here. The last month or so has not been kind. We've had rain almost every day. There are a load of cardboard boxes stacked fairly neatly on the right-hand side of the attic (the ones Mum wants to keep). I immediately spot the old boxes at the back in the shadows. There are six of them, all different sizes. I've carted up a few black bags with me.

I get to work by opening the first box: old cutlery and kitchenware from the 60s it looks like, most of it broken. I can tell it's from that decade because of the ridiculous patterns and designs. In the bin it goes. In fact, screw it, the whole box can go. I pick it up and take it to the trapdoor, then gingerly walk down the steps to the landing below. I take it straight outside and put it by the bins. I'm ruthless when it comes to getting rid of crap, yet my flat still looks like a tip. Next one.

I find dozens and dozens of old magazines and newspapers from about thirty years ago. I pick up a random newspaper, which is from 1988 and flick through it. Apparently that was the year that O-Levels ceased to exist and the first group of sixteen year olds sat their GCSE's. I guess it's true what they say ... you do learn something new every day. Good to store as general knowledge in case I ever need that information. Well I can't see why my parents would need these so I cart them down to the bins as well and put them in the recycling bin. Next.

All this walking back and forth and up and down the stairs is hard work. I take a quick rest at the top of the stairs before starting on the next box. This one is really old and dusty and sealed shut with sellotape and has a message across the top in big red letters saying "Baby Stuff". Ooh, this must be mine. I just have to have a peek. Mum never showed me any of my baby things, so I'm intrigued as to what I will find as I rip off the tape.

The first thing I notice is a teddy bear. I pick it up. It's one of those really old-fashioned bears that are designed to look freaky and weathered. I don't recognise it at all. Maybe I had it when I was a tiny baby. I put it aside and dig further into the box, pulling out a blanket. Now this I remember. Mum said she made it for me while she was pregnant. It's a blue and pink crochet blanket (I guess she didn't know whether I was a boy or a girl at the time). I remember sleeping with it night after night until I was about ten and then I decided one day I didn't need it anymore. Isn't that sad? The way children just grow out of needing things one day. I decide I want to keep it and set it aside and then dig a little deeper. I bring out a sealed wooden box. It's about six inches square in diameter and has no decoration on it at all. It's locked shut with a tiny padlock. The key is nowhere to be found. My curiosity gets the better of me and I whack the padlock with a nearby wooden coat hanger. It breaks easily.

I slowly open the lid and my curiosity is quickly diminished when I see absolutely nothing inside. I'm about to toss it back into the box when I realise that actually there is something in there. It's a piece of paper or, more appropriately, a photo. It's very old and torn and not very clear at all, but I can just make out what it is. Oh wow, it's an ultrasound photo! This must be me! I've never seen it before. Mum never showed me or spoke to me about her pregnancy. I stare at the blurry image, trying my best to make out the blob, but it's not exactly clear. In fact, it almost looks like there are ... no, that can't be right. I'm no expert at reading baby sonograms, but I could swear there are two ... I turn the photo over and there, in tiny scribbled writing, are the names:

Josslyn and Alicia.

Wait ... what?!

Chapter Four

My immediate thought is that I've read it wrong or that I'm imagining the whole thing, but my heart is beating so fast and hard that I can feel my blood pulsing around my entire body. My heartbeat is deafening and it feels as if it's trying to leap out of my chest. It can't just be my imagination.

I clutch the photo in my hand, slowly sinking to the floor, desperate for the support before my legs give out on me, each of them about as strong as cooked spaghetti at the moment.

I'm a twin. Her name is Alicia.

That's what is going round and round in my head, but it doesn't make any sense. How can it? It's utterly ridiculous and completely impossible. Well, technically I guess it isn't impossible, but surely my parents would have told me. I mean, in my entire life they had never mentioned, not even once, that I was a twin. Why is that? Why would they lie to me?

Technically they have never lied to you. They have merely omitted the truth.

Oh my God. Alicia! What the hell? Did you know about this? What's going on? Tell me! I don't understand what's happening.

There are so many questions buzzing around my brain dying to get out, but my mouth doesn't work fast enough so it all comes out in a jumbled mess. I take a deep breath and slow down my breathing.

Alicia. Tell me what you know ... Alicia!

After what seems like an eternity she finally speaks.

Ask your parents.

I feel as if I'm literally sprinting at full speed around a 400-metre track. I'm so out of breath and panic is rising rapidly from within. The attic walls are closing in. I need to get out of here before I suffocate.

Still clutching the photo as if my life is depending on it I hastily scramble to my feet, willing them to work long enough to get me downstairs. It takes a few seconds for them to respond as I try and grab something to pull me up to standing. I've never felt like this before. Never. It is a whole new experience for me and I don't like it. I don't like being lied to and being kept in the dark. I launch myself in the direction of the stairs and almost collapse down them. My legs still aren't working properly and I feel physically sick. I try and call out for my parents but no words are forming. I don't know what else to do to get their attention so I start banging on the floor with my fists like a toddler throwing a tantrum. Tears are streaming down my face. I need answers. I need them now.

Mum comes running up the stairs towards me in a blind panic, still with a tea towel and a wet plate in her hand.

'Josslyn, darling, what on earth? What's wrong?'

I stare at her dead in the eyes as I shove the photo in her face, my hand trembling so much it takes a few seconds for her to focus on what it is. I watch as the colour drains from her face and her eyes fill with fear and pure horror. She drops the plate which smashes and clutches her chest as she reaches for the nearby banister for support.

'R-Ronald! Come here now!' she screams. She starts crying hysterically, covering her face with her hands, shaking her head over and over. She's ashamed to even look at me. I know she is. She won't look me in the eyes.

Dad comes thundering up the stairs. 'What the hell? What's wrong?'

'She knows,' sobs my mum.

'What? What does she know?' My dad looks completely confused and his eyes dart around frantically trying to make sense of the situation. I see the immediate understanding on his face as he sees what I'm holding in my hand. I can't let go of it, but he can see it. My mum nods at him as she continues to sob quietly. My dad appears to be handling the situation a lot better than either me or mum because he crouches down next to me and gently lays a hand on my shoulder. I wince away from him, not wanting anyone to touch me.

'Jossy, we can explain.'

'Explain!' I shriek.

Then it all comes pouring out at once. My words sound so angry and all seem to mix into each other because I'm speaking so fast, but I have to get them out. The questions and the confusion inside me need to be released or I fear I may explode.

'What is there to explain, that I'm a twin, that I have a twin, a long-lost twin that you never told me about?

Is she chained up in the basement, is she dead, is she alive, where is she, why didn't you tell me, why wouldn't you tell me? I have a twin called Alicia. Why? Why is she not here? Tell me now or I swear to God I'm leaving this house and will never speak to either of you again, the truth, I want the truth!' That speech has drawn out every ounce of breath and energy I have left. I'm left panting on the floor, my body physically trembling all over. I may be over-reacting and if I am I don't care. My parents may have had the answer to who Alicia is all this time and never told me. That is unforgiveable in my eyes.

My dad takes a deep breath and glances at my mum. 'It's time,' he says slowly. 'I think it's time. Why don't we go downstairs, have a cup of tea and a chat?'

The first question that pops into my head is why the hell is he being so calm? It actually fills me with more rage. The fact that he can stand there and speak so calmly and act so relaxed makes me mad. At least my mum has the decency to be having a mental breakdown on the floor. Despite the fact that I'm seething inside I nod slowly in agreement and my dad helps me to my feet. We leave my mum on the floor and make our way slowly down the stairs. He leads me into the lounge where I gently sit on the edge of the sofa. Oscar is next to me on his back with his feet in the air, his mouth open, his bits on show and is snoring his head off. Clearly he is blissfully unaffected by the commotion that had happened upstairs just now. Oh, to be as care-free as a dog.

My dad leaves me on the sofa and goes into the kitchen to make the tea. I can hear him taking the cups out of the cupboard and filling the kettle with water. I could actually do with something a lot stronger than tea, but maybe alcohol isn't the answer right now.

The photo is still in my hand, but now I can't bear to look at it, yet I cannot let it go. I still have so many questions, but I don't know which one to focus on and ask first. I do know that I have to be careful with how I phrase my questions. They may not know about Alicia being inside my head. If they don't then I can't tell them. What would they think if I told them that Alicia is in my head and is a complete psychopath? I have to protect her and myself. It wouldn't shock me if they sent me to a mental hospital if I told them the truth. I must be cautious.

Thank you. I appreciate you not telling them about me.

You know, I think that's the first time she has ever said those words to me, but now I don't know what to think. Is she even real? Why is she in my head? I won't lie: I'm absolutely terrified about this situation and finding out the truth, whatever it might be, but I need to know. I'm not even sure if Alicia knows what she is as she's being extremely cryptic at the moment.

At that moment my mum makes an appearance in the lounge doorway. She looks terrible. Her face is as white as a sheet and her eyes are red and puffy from crying. She is physically shaking as she sits down on the stuffed armchair opposite me. I don't move a muscle or make a sound. I just stare at her, unsure if I hate her or not. My parents have a hell of a lot of explaining to do, that's for sure. I can tell she wants to say something because she keeps opening her mouth as if to speak and then clearly thinks better of it and closes it again.

My dad finally comes in and puts a cup of tea down on the coffee table in front of me, but I don't want tea; I want answers. Right now.

'So ...' I say abruptly, which makes my mum jump. 'Who is this?' I point to the scan photo without actually looking at it. 'Who is Alicia?'

My mum lets out a whimper, but it's my dad who speaks first. 'Alicia is your twin sister.'

For a few seconds I'm startled by that tiny, seemingly insignificant word. *Is.* 'Does that mean that she's still alive?'

My dad nods. 'Yes, she's alive. At least, I assume she is.'

I frown. 'What do you mean by *assume?* What happened to her? Tell me the whole story, dad. If she's alive and she's my twin then why isn't she here? Why am I an only child?'

My dad doesn't reply. He looks over at my mum, who shakes her head, sobbing. 'We can't tell her, Ronald. Please, don't tell her.'

'Tell me what? Tell me what!'

The air is fraught with tension. I'm not entirely sure what I'm expecting them to say, but never in a million years did I expect my dad to say what he says next.

'You're adopted.'

All of a sudden my view of the room is distorted and my vision goes blurry. I think I'm about to pass out. This is all just too much information to process in the space of a few minutes. In the past five minutes I have gone from being a happy only child of loving parents to finding out I have a long-lost twin and that my parents are not actually my real parents. Who the fuck am I? I shake my head to try and stop myself from fainting.

'Ronald, get her a whisky or something,' says my mum (if I can even call her that now).

'I don't want whisky!' I shout. 'I want gin!'

Honestly, does she even know me at all!

I watch as my dad (or not my dad) scrambles to fill a glass with a shot of gin. Both of them are in full panic mode, clearly unsure how I'm going to react so they are just giving me whatever I want. He shoves it in my face. I take the glass, knock the clear liquid back and hand it back to him for a refill. It looks like I won't be driving anywhere tonight after all. He refills the glass and returns it to me. I take another shot.

'Better?' he asks. He then pours himself one and knocks it back. Honestly, we aren't alcoholics. It's just in times like this tea just won't cut it.

'Are you ready to hear the rest?' he asks with a hint of apprehension in his voice.

'There's more!' I gasp. Dear God, I don't think I can take any more life altering news tonight. My brain can't comprehend it.

'No,' he quickly replies. 'That's pretty much it, but there's a lot of detail to fill in.'

I take a deep, cleansing breath, the way I was taught when I went to that yoga class one time. I never went back because it was stupid and the whole time I was supposed to be clearing my mind of any thoughts, Alicia was talking, so my inner peace was non-existent. I had ended up shouting 'Shut the fuck up!' in the middle of class. I wasn't invited back.

'Fine,' I say. 'Go on then ... tell me.'

My dad hands me another gin. I take it but don't knock it back straight away. I just keep hold of the glass in case he throws another ridiculously shocking piece of news at me.

'Your mother and I found out quite early on that we couldn't have children. We tried for many years, but eventually we realised that adoption was the only way we would have a child. We went through the proper agencies and did all the paperwork and a woman was found for us who was pregnant. She made it perfectly clear that she did not want to keep you. It was arranged that we would adopt her baby – you – as soon as you were born. Then she had a scan and she found out she was having twin girls. The adoption agency asked if we wanted to adopt you both, but we weren't ready for twins and we decided to not adopt the other one. It was a very hard decision, but we feel it was the right one. We named you Josslyn and your biological mother named the other girl Alicia. We never saw Alicia, but we first saw you when you were two hours old. You were ours and we were so happy.' My dad finishes his story.

I stare at him without blinking, but then my eyes start watering and I have to blink. There's something about that story that doesn't feel quite right, but I can't put my finger on it.

He is lying.

I agree with Alicia. Oh my God, what am I saying? This voice in my head can't be Alicia. It's me. I really am crazy. I'm a psychopath. I have two personalities ... oh shit, what's that condition called where—

Multiple Personality Disorder, or more recently it is known as Dissociative Identity Disorder.

Fine. Thank you Miss Know-It-All.

My dad is frowning at me. Little does he know what is going on inside my head right now. My parents clearly don't know about the voice in my head, which makes things even more confusing. What the hell is Alicia? She can't be my twin sister if the real Alicia is alive ... can she? It's like something out of the Twilight Zone.

'Why me?' I finally ask. 'Why choose me and not Alicia? What did you do, flip a coin to decide which one of us you chose?'

My parents glance at each other. 'We chose the bigger and healthier of the two. We were told you were the oldest, but you were born by caesarean.'

Bullshit.

'How could you do that? How could you just decide to adopt one of us but not the other? Don't you have a heart? We're twins for fuck's sake. Twins have a special connection. Were we identical?'

'N-no, I don't think so. You were fraternal.'

I'm not sure why, but a part of me suddenly feels disappointed that there isn't another person out there who looks like me. It would have been kind of cool having an identical twin growing up.

'Why couldn't you have just adopted Alicia as well?'

'We ... we couldn't ...' my mum begins, but then she stops. I'm no detective but even I know when someone is hiding something.

'Okay, so answer me this: didn't you find it weird that I once had an imaginary friend called Alicia?' Ha! Let's see them answer that one.

My mum's jaw drops open and my dad chugs another gin. Between us we are getting through the bottle, which was supposed to be saved for Christmas.

'Y-You did?' stutters my mum.

I roll my eyes at her, something I haven't done since I was a rebel teenager. 'Don't give me that, Mum, or whoever you are, you remember full well about my imaginary friend.'

'I-I am your mother,' she says, not very convincingly. 'I may not have given birth to you, but your father and I raised you. You are our daughter.'

'Yes, lucky me that I happen to be the bigger of the two. I really am the chosen one.' I gulp back my third gin. Okay, maybe I should slow down. My head is beginning to feel fuzzy. I decide to change tactic. 'What happened to Alicia? Where is she now?'

'We don't know. She was adopted by another family, that's all we know.' My dad has stepped back into the conversation because my mum looks to be on the verge of another breakdown.

'You never thought to find out what happened to her? Were you ever planning on telling me that I have a twin sister?'

Silence.

That would be a no.

'Don't you think I have a right to know?'

Silence.

'We ... we thought we were protecting you.'

'Protecting me from what exactly?'

Silence.

Jesus Christ, I may as well be talking to a brick wall. What is it they aren't telling me? I can feel the anger starting to build again from somewhere deep down inside. I want to scream, shout, kick, hit something. I need some sort of release. I need to know more and my parents are clearly not going to tell me.

'I'm going to find her.'

'What?' stutters my mum.

'You can't,' says my dad.

'Why not? I want to meet my sister. I want to know the truth and you aren't going to tell me so ...'

'Please Alic ... I mean Josslyn ... don't.'

Did my mum almost call me Alicia? What the fuck is going on?

I stand up to storm off, but my gin buzz has suddenly hit and I stumble back onto the sofa. Maybe I shouldn't have had three large shots in such quick succession. Now my body feels numb and my head is spinning.

Then suddenly it hits me: the pain. The same pain as I had this morning, but this time it feels worse, so much worse – like something is trying to burst its way out of my body. It's not just in my abdomen either, but all over, especially in my head. I scream and grab my head as I throw myself on the floor in agony. I can feel my mum's hands on me, trying to help. I can hear her panicked voice, but she is so far away. All I can focus on is the pain. Nothing else matters.

Dear God, make it stop! Or let me die. Either one. I don't even care what happens right now. All I want is for this to be over. Then, as quickly as it started, it stops. I continue to lay on the floor, gasping for breath. Everything slowly comes back into focus and I can see my mum hovering over me, a look of sheer terror on her face. My dad has another gin in his hand ready to give to me, like gin is the answer to everything. I push the glass away and manage to sit myself up. It's at this moment that Oscar decides to wake up and he comes up to me, wagging his tail in excitement. He licks my face.

'Josslyn, what on earth? What happened? Are you okay?' My mum sounds genuinely concerned.

'It's nothing. I've just been getting a sharp pain for a few seconds at a time.' Although it feels as if it lasts a lifetime.

'Since when?' she gasps.

'This morning.'

'You should see a doctor.'

'I don't need a doctor,' I snap. 'What I need is to get out of this house right now.' I struggle to my feet, staggering slightly. Whether that's down to the gin buzz or the shock of the intense pain, I'm not sure. Maybe it's both. I grab my stuff (bag, photo, video) and head for the door.

'Oscar, come!' I order.

'You can't drive home! You've had too much to drink!' warns my mum. By the way, I am only calling them Mum and Dad for the sake of not making things any more confusing than they already are. To be honest I don't know what to call them, although *liars* seems appropriate.

'You can't tell me what to do! You're not my mum!' Okay, maybe that's a little harsh, but right now I don't care.

'You're drunk,' states my dad.

'Please! I've only had three gins ...'

'They were big glasses.'

'I can handle my d-drink. Remember that time I came home at New Years for dinner? I was so drunk and you didn't even notice.'

'Of course we noticed. You started talking to the lobster we were having for dinner and kept asking if the water was too hot as it was cooking.'

I attempt to open my mouth, but then shut it. I honestly don't remember that happening.

'I'll drive you home,' says my dad slowly.

'You've had a few too many yourself,' answers my mum. Right, so the bottom line is we are all too hammered to drive a car, apart from my mum who can't drive anyway. I told you she was old-fashioned. 'I'll call a taxi,' she says.

I finally admit defeat and nod my head, but there's no way I'm going back inside the house so I take up residence on the doorstep and wait for my taxi. Oscar busies himself with sniffing the garden plants and peeing wherever he fancies.

'Jossy,' says my dad quietly. He's standing behind me inside the house. 'I'm sorry for everything. I'm sorry we didn't tell you and I'm even more sorry that you found out this way. We love you.'

I ignore him and continue to stare into the darkness of the night. I wait until he closes the door. Then I start crying.

Chapter Five

I get home and collapse into bed fully clothed. I won't lie: the gin has hit me hard and I need to sleep it off. I have work in the morning, but this is definitely one of those days where I wish I didn't have to work. I'm sure we all have those days, weeks, months, years, whatever. My head is also fuzzy because of the sheer amount of shocking information that I have received. I can't think straight and Alicia isn't talking to me for some reason. So I fall asleep (or pass out is probably more accurate) in silence and have a dreamless sleep until my alarm buzzes at 5:30 a.m. the next morning.

Dear God, just kill me now. Gin hangovers are the worst. Actually no, vodka hangovers are the worst, but I don't get them anymore because I no longer drink the death juice (ever since a very horrendous throwing up incident at university and the worst hangover known to man). This hangover is still pretty bad. My head is pounding, my throat is dry and sore, my head is still spinning, I feel sick. Ah alcohol, you sneaky son of a bitch. It promises you a good time and a happy high and then it punches you clear in the face and runs away laughing saying 'sucker!'

I smack my alarm clock to the floor just as Oscar jumps on me and starts licking my face. He doesn't care that I feel like death warmed up. He just wants his breakfast. I swing my legs over the side of the bed, touch the floor, pull them back and count to five. Then I'm reluctantly ready to start the day. As I struggle to my feet it all suddenly comes flooding back – I have a twin sister and I'm adopted. Well I guess that's it, but it's enough! Shit. What am I going to do? I need to find her. I need to know ...

You do not need to know anything.

Oh, I see you're finally talking to me. Where the hell have you been?

Thanks to you I also have a hangover, so I have been sleeping it off.

Are you going to answer my questions now?

I do not know anything.

Bullshit. Who are you? Why are you in my head?

I am Alicia.

You can't be. Alicia is a real person, not a voice in my head.

I am real.

'No you're not!' I scream out loud. I cover my ears, as if to block out her voice, but it's still there ringing in my ears.

I finish all my morning routines and sit in my usual spot in my armchair sipping a very strong coffee. I can't stomach food right now, but coffee is my friend, my only friend. Alicia is fucking ignoring me again, but I can still hear her voice echoing in my head: *I am real.* Those words are repeating over and over until eventually they stop making sense. They just become meaningless sounds. What does *real* even mean?

Oscar eventually reminds me that time is ticking by, so I begin the day. I open up downstairs, do all the usual procedures, give Oscar his snack, unlock the front door and check if there are any new messages since last night. There are none on my work phone, but I do have one from my mum on my mobile, which I haven't listened to yet. I don't want to listen. There is nothing she can say that will make me feel any better so that message can sit there a bit longer for all I care.

The day drags by one excruciating second at a time, but I can't focus on anything, not the cute puppy that comes in for her set of jabs, not the fluffy bunny who needs a health check-up, nothing. Even Lucy and Emma's annoying girly voices don't really register in my head, until somewhere in the background I hear ...

'What are you gonna wear tonight, Josslyn?' It's Emma who speaks.

'Huh?'

'You gonna wear a dress and heels? I don't think I've ever seen you in a dress and heels. I'm wearing pink.'

'Okaaayyy.' I elongate the word because, to be honest, I have no idea what she is talking about, but then it hits me. Shit. Tonight. I agreed to go out with them ... fuck, mother fuck—

'Errrrrr.' It's like I've lost the ability to speak.

Lucy and Emma are staring at me waiting for an answer, as if the answer of what I'll be wearing is all that matters to them in the world at this precise moment. There's no way of getting out of this. Maybe I can make the most of this situation. I can get blind drunk and dance my troubles away. Sounds like a good idea to me.

That is the worst idea you have ever had and you have had a lot of bad ideas.

This time it's me who ignores Alicia. She doesn't know what she's talking about. Getting drunk is always a good idea. Yes, I got drunk last night (okay, tipsy), but tonight I'm going all out. It's the weekend, after all. I don't open my practice at weekends, unless there's an emergency.

'I'm wearing black,' I finally say. Black like my heart.

'Oooh, I love a little black dress,' says Lucy excitedly.

I don't remember saying I was wearing a little black dress, but I'll roll with it for now.

'Uh huh,' I manage to say.

Luckily these girls won't be half as annoying when I'm hammered. Who knows, maybe we will even become girlfriends and go to the toilet together or hold each other's hair back while one of us vomits. That's what friends do, right?

It's after work, my hangover luckily subsided hours ago (and I was able to grab a taxi back to my parents' house and drive my car back home without them noticing me because I still don't want to see them) and I finally summon up the courage to listen to my mum's voicemail. I've also chucked a frozen pizza in the oven to eat because I'm absolutely starving. I eat with my mouth open while I hold the phone up to my ear.

'Hi darling. It's your mother. I hope you got home okay and you don't feel too unwell after all that gin. I'm so sorry, darling. Please believe me, your father and I never meant to hurt you. We thought it was better that you didn't know about Alicia. We love you. Please call me back.'

Sorry Mum, but not tonight. I'm not ready to talk to you yet. I'm not even sure if I'll ever be ready to talk to my parents. I feel so betrayed and hurt. I just can't believe they have let me carry on for twenty-eight years thinking they were my biological parents and that I was an only child. It's only by pure chance that I found out. I'm sure that if it had been up to them they never would have told me the truth.

My parents are liars and it's going to take a long time to get over that fact.

I eat my pizza while I'm raiding my untidy wardrobe for something to wear. I'm convinced there's a random black dress hidden away somewhere, remnants of my university days (not that I socialised much, but I quickly learned that to fit in you had to wear a mega short dress and get drunk at least five times a week). So I bought a cheap black dress from Boohoo and, to be fair, it paid for itself in free drinks alone pretty quickly, so I decided to keep it. It has been stored away at the back of my wardrobe, never to be seen again for years ... until tonight.

There it is. Urrgg, it could do with an iron, but I've never ironed anything in my life and I'm not about to start now (I don't even own an iron anyway). I hang the skimpy black halter-neck dress on a hanger. I'll let gravity do its work for a few hours.

My pizza has now gone cold and I'm laying on my bed on my back staring up at the ceiling. I have a plan. Tonight I'm going to get wasted and tomorrow I'm going to start the search for my long-lost twin sister. A quick Google search should be of some use. If not then I'll try and get Mum or Dad to tell me which adoption agency they went through to get me. Maybe the same agency was used to adopt Alicia. I don't even have a last name for her though. Maybe my parents know my biological mother's name ...

I still do not understand why you need to find Alicia when you have me.

Because you're not my twin sister. You're a figment of my imagination and a severe psychological problem that I need to get resolved.

If you wanted to get rid of me you would have told your parents about me years ago and would probably have gone through years of therapy, or been locked up in a mental institution.

She has a point. It's not like I want to get rid of Alicia (or whoever she is). I've kept her a secret for over two decades because I'm afraid to be without her. Without Alicia I'm alone, like properly alone. I'd have no one. She's my friend (albeit a slightly terrifying, crazy friend) but she's still my friend and friends always stick together.

Friends also tell you when you look like shit and need to put some make-up on before going out tonight.

I don't look that bad.

Have you looked in a mirror lately? Have you seen the state of your hair? Go and take a shower and wash your hair, then put some make-up on so you do not look like a mummified homeless person.

Hey, go easy on me, I'm very delicate right now.

The truth hurts, Josslyn. Deal with it.

I get up with a sigh and do as I'm told.

Finally 9:45 p.m. rolls around and I'm ready. Alicia talked me though how to apply my make-up properly. She kept wanting to take over, but I refused so she settled for bossing me around until I'd got it right. Now I'm standing in front of my full-length mirror in a tight black mini dress, complete with a halter-neck design, black stripper heels and a black clutch bag. My hair is poofed up into a beehive style and tied back into a stylish ponytail. My eyes look quite striking with dark, smoky eye shadow and thick eyelashes. I'll give it to Alicia – the girl knows how to dress! I haven't looked this good in years, not since my student days. Maybe I should make an effort more often, but then it really has taken an enormous effort to look like this. How do some women do it every day? It took me five attempts to put false eyelashes on (I'd found them in the back of my drawer stuck to a hairbrush). My skin is still as pale as paper, but I don't mind. It sets off my tattoos nicely. Oh yeah, I guess I forgot to mention my tattoos. I often forget I have them because it's extremely rare that I have this much bare skin on show. I'm not sure Emma and Lucy have even seen them.

Let me tell you about my tattoos quickly because they have their own story to tell. I think there are two types of people in this world: those that love tattoos and those that don't. I happen to love them. I got my first one when I was eighteen; a small Gemini symbol (because I'm a Gemini ... duh), which is actually quite interesting because Gemini is the symbol of twins. Anyway, after I got my first tattoo and my mum stated that she hated it I obviously had to get more just to piss her off because that's what teenage girls are supposed to do. I added to my tattoo collection over the years: a few animals, phrases, fairies and skulls. All in black and white, no colour and all of them are fairly small. The biggest one I have is on my side. I have a little dog and cat paw each for Milo and Tornado ... and later I got one for Oscar. I have one of some lips on my ass (which is a representation of my ex-boyfriend when I told him to get lost and kiss my ass).

Anyway, I'm sure you get the picture of how I look, which is to say I look awesome if I do say so myself. I'm also slightly tipsy already because I started pre-drinking by myself hours ago.

At 10 p.m. the girls text me to say they are outside in a taxi. We are off to Bournemouth. Time to get this party started!

Being drunk is awesome! Fact. I've lost count of how many gin and tonics I've had. Emma bought a round of three shots each, which we did at the start of the night as soon as we entered the club. Each shot was a different colour. I'm not sure what they were, but one was definitely vodka because it immediately made me gag, but I womaned up and got it down my throat. It burned! Emma and Lucy found us a booth to sit in. They both look glamorous as usual, but for the first time ever I actually feel like one of the girls. It is ... surprisingly nice. They gasped in pure shock when they saw me and couldn't give me enough compliments about my dress and tattoos.

A few hours later (I have no idea what the actual time is) I leave the girls to go and get another drink. They had started to talk about sex and how often they did it while they were single versus how often they did it when they had boyfriends. I didn't want to admit that my record while I was single was twice in one year. They said to hurry back. As much as I have been enjoying their company I decide it's time for me to spend some time alone. I'm sure they won't mind or miss me.

My feet are killing me because of the amount of dancing we'd done at the start of the night. I'm sipping on my straw even though I've finished my drink. The club is heaving. I really hate clubs (who over twenty-five doesn't?), but it's doing a wonderful job of distracting me from my internal monologue. The music is so loud I can barely bear Alicia's voice in my head. I'm pretty sure I keep hearing her telling me to leave or stop drinking, but I'm ignoring her like she often ignores me.

Then I see him. The guy who beat me, called me names, made my life a living hell and then turned around to my parents and told them he wanted to marry me one day. Daniel. Fucking *Daniel.* Shit! Annoyingly he actually looks pretty good, although that could be because of the copious amount of gin I've ingested. His hair is long, falling in some wavy curls around his ears. His smile is the same though; still fake and dazzling. He's using that same smile on an innocent drunk girl who seems to be hanging on his every word, touching his arms and stroking his chest as she throws her head back and laughs, probably at some dumb chat up line or joke he's just used.

I suddenly realise that I've been staring at him way too long. I should look away, but for some reason I can't. I just keep staring. Now who's the creepy weirdo. Shit. I should have looked away. He's finally noticed me. His eyes lock with mine, but instead of quickly looking away and pretending like I hadn't seen him I continue to stare at him. There's something wrong with me. I feel pure anger welling up inside. I'm staring him down like a predator hunting its prey. My eyes burn into him, hating him, wishing I could blow up his head with my mind.

That prick needs to die.

Okay, now I know Alicia and Daniel never got on and she did try to kill him once, but I can't help but slightly agree with her. He's walking towards me, making his way through the sweaty crowds with a smug smile across his face. I'm actually relieved that I look drop-dead amazing. There's nothing worse than seeing an ex-boyfriend and looking like shit.

Daniel stops directly in front of me and moves forwards to hug me. I shrink away slightly at his touch. I try to hold my nerve as I get flashbacks of him pinning me against the wall, a knife pressed into my ribs.

'Hey babe, looking good.' I can smell the beer on his breath and the stale smoke. It makes my stomach churn.

'Errr, hi, thanks.' I clear my throat nervously.

Jesus Christ Josslyn, come up with some better replies. Do not be weak.

She's right. I mustn't be weak.

'Can I buy you a drink?' he asks, stroking my arm with his sweaty hand.

'I'm not thirsty.'

'Wanna dance?'

'Not with you.'

'How've you been?'

This guy does not give up, does he?

'Daniel ...' I turn square on to him. We are almost the same height because of my super hooker heels. He grins at me. 'Fuck off.' The grin still stays. 'Now.' The grin falters slightly.

'Are you still mad at me?'

'What do you think?'

'Babe, come on. You tried to strangle me in my sleep. I was defending myself.'

'That happened one time. What about all the other times?'

'What other times?'

'W-what the hell? Are you serious?'

Daniel grins at me some more. 'You'll never do better than me.'

Punch that motherfucker in the face. Now.

'Then I guess I'll stay single for the rest of my life. Now kindly fuck off.'

I push past him and attempt to storm off, but the crowd of sweaty dancers hinders my progress. So much for the huffy exit. I can feel his eyes burning into the back of my head as I walk away. He still gives me the creeps and I want nothing more than to get as far away from him as possible.

I head to the bar, buy a shot and another gin and tonic and chug them both within seconds. Then my head explodes with pain and I pass out.

My body doesn't feel like my own. It feels ... different. *I feel different*. I also feel sick and my head is pounding with what I can only imagine is a catastrophic gin (and God only knows what else) hangover, but there's something more I can't quite explain. My hands feel weird, sticky even. I can smell ... *something*. There's definitely a whiff of alcohol in the air, but also something more, like a metallic smell. I still have my eyes closed because not only am I scared to open them, but my eyelids also feel fused together, probably due to the layers of mascara Alicia made me apply last night and the ridiculously long false eyelashes.

Alicia ... are you there? What happened last night? The last thing I remember is downing those drinks at the bar after walking away from Daniel and then ... darkness. How did I get home? Where's Oscar? Alicia ... answer me.

Silence.

Fine. Fuck you.

It's at that moment I peel my eyes open and am met with more darkness. Damn these dark winter mornings. I resist the urge to gag as I roll over and switch on my bedside lamp. It's then that the room around me comes into focus. It's utter chaos. Clothes are strewn everywhere, a chair is knocked over, left-over pizza is scattered over the floor (which is weird because surely Oscar would have finished that off by now).

I clutch my head in agony and that's when I feel the wet sticky stuff on my hands. I pull my hand away and stare at the red blood that's staining it. It's not like when you accidentally cut yourself and a trickle of blood oozes out. My whole hand looks like it's been dipped in a pot of blood as if it were paint. And that's when I see more blood. It's covering my hands, my dress, my bedding, parts of the floor, the walls and even areas of the ceiling.

I begin shaking uncontrollably and then quickly scurry to the bathroom to be sick, leaving footprints of blood behind me. I clutch the bowl of the toilet for support, still trembling.

'Oscar!' I yell. My first thought is where the hell is my dog and why isn't he jumping on me and licking me all over right now? 'Oscar!' Then I hear faint barking and I immediately recognise his high-pitched squeal. Relief washes over me and I almost burst out crying. He's alive. That's all that matters.

I keep repeating his name over and over as I follow his yaps. They eventually lead me to the cupboard near my front door. I yank open the door and am met by Oscar who leaps out, licking, barking and excitedly nipping me. He doesn't care that I'm covered in blood. He's just happy to see me and I'm overjoyed to see him. I kiss him over and over, getting him covered in blood in the process. He eventually calms down and runs to the kitchen ready to be fed. Some things never change.

I feed Oscar and that's when I stand and survey the damage. My flat looks like a bomb has gone off, but then again it looked like that when I left last night, just now with the added inclusion of blood.

I walk to the bathroom, strip off my clothes until I'm completely naked and stand in front of the full-length mirror. From what I can tell I'm not hurt in any way, which means that the blood isn't mine. Oscar isn't hurt either. My next thought is that there must have been someone else in here with me last night, but where are they?

Alicia must know something about this, but until she decides to talk to me I'm on my own, so I start by taking a hot shower. Weirdly, the idea of calling the police doesn't even rate on my list of priorities right now. My first priority is to take a shower. The second is to take painkillers for my headache, put the kettle on and make myself a coffee. The next is to start cleaning my flat. I surprise myself at how calm I feel. Yes, when I woke up I had been shocked and the sight of all the blood had made me sick, but now that I've calmed down it's like I'm a different person. I calmly clean and scrub the blood out of the carpets and the relevant areas. My dress and bedding are beyond help, so they go straight in the bin. Oscar also gets a shower and a scrub.

It takes five hours until my flat is clean again. By now the sun has been up for hours and it's nearly 10 a.m. I'm also surprised that my hangover is just about gone so I make myself and Oscar some scrambled eggs, take my plate to my armchair and finally take a seat. Cool, calm and collected. That's me.

Good job Josslyn. I could not have done a better job myself.

Alicia! What the fuck! Where have you been?

Watching you. I am proud of you for not calling the police.

I should have done. I don't know why I didn't. Whose blood did I just clean up?

That does not matter right now.

But you know?

Yes, I know.

Please. I need to know what happened.

All in good time. You will know when you need to know. The fact is that you can rule out that you killed someone because there is no body.

I think for a moment. She has a point. There had been a small part of me that had jumped to the conclusion that I had murdered someone. There had been a lot of blood, so someone was seriously hurt. Maybe they ran away. But why would anyone run away from me? I'm a lovely person.

So, let me get this straight Alicia. No one is dead. Right?

Correct.

Phew! Okay, well that's a relief and a huge weight off my chest. I can now focus on my next priority, which is to find my sister.

Are you still wanting to find her?

Of course. Why wouldn't I want to find her? I need to know answers and Mum and Dad or whoever they are aren't helping me, so I'm going to find her myself.

It is a mistake.

Why?

Because she is a stranger to you. She is a nobody. I am your friend. I am your true sister. I have been with you all these years. I am the only one who has stood by your side and told you the truth.

I know you have, but maybe Alicia has been lied to as well. She probably doesn't know I exist either. I love you Alicia. I always will, but ... you're not real. She is. She's my twin. I need to find her, if only just to see her and know that she's real and that I'm not crazy.

Alicia doesn't respond for a few seconds.

It is a mistake. Do not say I did not try and warn you, but fine. I will help you find her in whatever way I can.

Thank you, Alicia.

The rest of my Saturday is spent surfing the web. I sit with my laptop on my legs, Oscar curled up beside me and trashy TV shows on in the background. I've got about fifteen tabs open online. To be honest I hit a dead-end ages ago. I've found several girls my own age with the name Alicia, but their date of birth is wrong. I've even looked on Facebook, but had no luck. To tell you the truth I have no idea what I'm doing. I don't know how to search for a person online, especially with so little information to go on. For some reason the naive part of me thought I would just type her name into Google and she would pop up out of nowhere with an address and postcode and a phone number. It doesn't help that I don't know her last name either; at least I know her date of birth, but nothing has jumped out at me. I don't know where she lives or anything.

I take a break after a few hours, feeling thoroughly discouraged and a little bit sick again. Maybe the gin hangover is back for round two. Lucy and Emma have texted me several times throughout the day, but I have ignored them. My mum has also called, so I let it go to voicemail. I sit back in my chair and stare up at the ceiling, feeling lost.

What now?

There is one thing you have not checked.

What's that?

You have been searching for someone who is alive.

Shit. You're right.

I quickly grab the laptop again and search for her name, date of birth and the word *death.* Nothing jumps out at me right away. I scroll down the results for ages, each line of text turning into a blur, but then an online newspaper article, which is several years old, catches my eye. The headline reads: *Young Hot Shot Lawyer Disappears.*

I click on it and take a read.

Alicia Phillips, age 23, a young lawyer, disappeared three days ago on the night of the 15th of June 2014. Her adopted brother has asked anyone with information to come forward. Her brother, Peter Phillips, was the last person to see her alive at a club at around 12:15 a.m. She did not return home. A note was later found from Alicia in her bedroom, saying she could not bear to live any longer. It is presumed that she committed suicide, but her body has never been found. The case has now been closed, but her brother continues to search for answers.

I re-read the article again and slowly lean back in the chair. I enlarge the picture of Alicia Phillips and study it. She doesn't look like me. In fact, she looks nothing like me. She's blonde and stunningly beautiful with a happy smile and perfect teeth, but it's her. I just know it is. Have you ever had that gut feeling that you know for a fact you're right about something, even though there's no evidence to back it up? That's how I feel right now. It's a long shot, but I have to try because I have to know for certain.

I quickly look up Peter Phillips' address online. He lives in Cambridge. It's just under a three-hour drive from here. I scribble it on a scrap of paper, pack an overnight bag, grab a few bits for Oscar and bundle us both into the car without even giving it a second thought.

Road trip!

Chapter Six

Alicia

My name is Alicia and I am a psychopath. I have always been a psychopath and I always will be one. You may be wondering why I am the way I am. To put the matter simplistically: I was born this way. I was not created, nor did I eventually grow into being a psychopath. However, I do believe that I have evolved over the years of being alive. I have had to. It is all about survival. In order to survive one must evolve. That is how it is, how it was and how it will always be. I wish to tell you my part of the story. I do not believe that you are ready to hear the entire story; not yet.

You may be wondering where Josslyn is at this time. Do not worry. She is safe – for now. Josslyn and I have an understanding, a connection, one that has stood the test of time, one that will never break. I cannot say that I love her, for I do not feel that emotion. Love is merely a word to me; it means nothing. I do not understand it, but what I can tell you is this: I do care about Josslyn because without her, I would not exist. I exist because she exists. She is me and I am her. She does not know this fact, but I came into being long before she imagined me on that day in the woods. I have always been there, inside her, watching, biding my time. I knew that one day she would sense my presence and I would become real to her. That day finally arrived and I was free.

Josslyn started talking to me as if I were a real person and I answered back. If I could feel joy then that is what I would have felt at that moment. It was a relief to be able to talk. I have watched Josslyn a great deal over the years. I can sense, even at times feel, her own emotions, but this is very rare. I do my best to avoid those types of situations. I believe that emotions make a person weak. I am not weak. I have found that she often becomes like me; cold and distant. I do believe that I am wearing off on her.

You may have many questions for me at this moment, but I cannot give you the answers. I am not willing to part with certain pieces of information about myself yet. There will come a time in the not so distant future when all will be revealed, but that time is not now. I will tell you about my past and I will attempt to explain who I really am, so you can understand me.

I am not evil, nor am I a monster. Being a psychopath does not mean you are those things. It means I am different from the average human being. A psychopath is unable to feel emotion and therefore they cannot distinguish between good and evil, between love and hate, between right and wrong. This does not mean I am automatically evil, that I hate everyone and that I always do the wrong thing. I do as I please and I do not care about the consequences, as long as things go my way. If that means that people get hurt or I must break the law, then so be it.

I started off my life as Josslyn's imaginary friend. These types of childhood friends are common, I have come to understand, and often are made up because of a child's loneliness. Josslyn has always been lonely, but I believe, deep down, she prefers it that way. She is like me in many ways. She prefers her own company and the company of animals. Again, I do not feel love for animals, but I accept them more than I do a human being. The good thing about an animal, especially a dog, is that they do not speak and they are always happy to see you. I do, however, dislike cats. They, for some reason, can see into my soul and clearly do not like what they see.

As the years went by I began to gain Josslyn's trust and she was very loyal to me. She would do whatever I asked of her, until that day when I asked her to kill Tornado. This was a defining moment in our relationship and she failed. That was the first time I took her over. She would not do as I wanted so I had no choice, but I knew I could not take her over unless she wanted me to. At least, that was what it started out like.

I started to learn that I could control her movements and actions. The first time this happened was when she started university. A girl on a night out called her a slut and Josslyn slapped her across the face, something I had thought about doing at that instant, but Josslyn did it for me. She did not know where that anger had come from, but I knew it was because of me. We were becoming one.

I began to take her over more and more to enable her to carry out her deepest and darkest desires. She was too scared to do them herself, but I was not. I do not believe in fear for it is merely a pointless emotion. Eventually she started to realise that I was not always nice and was becoming dangerous, so she began to fight me. She refused to let me take over and her mind was becoming stronger with each passing day. I knew that this was bad news for me, so now I try and keep my distance.

We still talk and I believe we have a good relationship. Some would even say we are friends, but ever since the day when I nearly strangled that piece of shit Daniel in his sleep she has been wary of me. She will not let me take over and I can feel myself becoming more and more ... I guess you would call it furious. Until tonight. I finally took back control.

Josslyn let her guard down and I was able to take her over. I only needed a split second and that was all I received, but it was enough. Her head exploded with pain at the bar but before she could comprehend what was happening, I was there.

Daniel ran up to me, obviously seeing that Josslyn was in pain, but it was too late for her. She was gone. He touched my arm and I slowly lifted my head and looked at him. I saw the smile slip from his smug face as he glimpsed something sinister within me, but I quickly put on my act, something I had been trying to perfect over the years.

'I am fine,' I said with a smile. 'Too much to drink.'

'Are you sure, Joss? Do you want to sit down, or maybe I should call you a taxi so you can go home?' I could hear the concern in his voice, but he need not have worried. Josslyn was safe; he was not.

'Yes,' I said, as I gently stroked his arm. 'Please take me home.' I saw the stupid smug smile light up his face again. There he was thinking he was about to get lucky by taking advantage of Josslyn. I would make sure that he would never touch her again. I had a suspicion he was the one who was calling her and breathing heavily down the phone, but I was not certain. It did not matter. He deserved to die.

You may be wondering what he could have possibly done to deserve to die. The answer: he was still alive. He first attacked Josslyn after being with her for only a few weeks. She had to stay late at work to do some paperwork, something I know she despised, but Daniel accused her of cheating on him, so he hit her. The next time it happened was because Josslyn defended Oscar. Daniel had tried to hit the dog and Josslyn had stepped in, so he hit her.

This continued for some time, but for some reason Josslyn would not break up with him. She was weak and I knew she needed my help, so I tried to strangle him while he slept. The plan backfired, but luckily Josslyn realised how dangerous he was and broke up with him shortly afterwards. He then, however, became extremely clingy and would often call her dozens of times in a row until she had his number blocked. This is another reason why I believe that he is her stalker.

Anyway, back to tonight.

I continued with the helpless drunk girl act all the way back to my flat. He kept touching my leg while we were in the back of the taxi and his fingers were getting dangerously high up my dress. I fought back the urge to rip his throat out with my teeth as we entered my flat. Oscar ran to greet me, but started barking hysterically at Daniel and growling. I guess he was not such a dumb dog after all. Dogs can sense evil too. For his own safety I shut Oscar away in the cupboard. He would be okay in there for a few hours.

Daniel started making himself at home immediately. He put the kettle on and gave me a glass of water as I laid down on the bed. He grinned at me as he left the room to go to the bathroom. This was my chance. I leapt off the bed and went to my dressing table. I lifted up the removable drawer and pulled out what I was looking for: a long, sharp knife. I had told Josslyn to hide it there a long time ago for her own safety. There had been several break-ins in the area at the time and I told her to make sure she had some hidden weapons just in case. I got back on the bed and hid the knife under my pillow as I waited for my prey to return.

He did return and he had taken his shirt off. He set down the cups of coffee he had made by the bed and joined me on it, laying next to me, tracing his hands over my body. I did not feel terror. I just stared at him as he spoke, my eyes locked onto his with pin-point accuracy.

'I always knew you would come back to me, Joss. We had something special, you and me. I forgive you for that night you tried to kill me. Now we can be together for always.' He stared deep into my eyes and stroked my face.

I shifted my body and straddled him. I could feel how hard he was under his trousers. I leaned forwards over him, pressing my body into his as I ran my hands up his chest and felt his heart beating. How sweet it would be to no longer feel that pathetic thumping through his chest.

He closed his eyes, clearly enjoying his last moments, but I would soon ensure that his last moments were not ones of pleasure. I gently placed each of his arms at his side so that I was kneeling on them, pinning him against the bed. I knew he was stronger than I was so I needed to be quick before he could overpower me. There was something extremely empowering about sitting on top of a man who was about to die at my own hands, especially one who deserved it. I leaned my face down so that it hovered above his and slowly and carefully slid my right hand underneath my pillow, feeling the cold blade between my fingers. I clenched my fist around the handle and with one swift movement I plunged the blade all the way into his chest until it stopped.

Then again. And again. And again. I stabbed him twenty-six times and relished every single second as I watched the blood spurt from his body and his pathetic life leave his eyes. It was a pure masterpiece. I finally stopped because my arm was tired, not because I wanted to.

I surveyed my work. The poor insignificant fool had not even had the chance to fight back. He was still pinned beneath me, a look of shock and fear on his face. The blood started to pool around me. I was drenched in it, as was the surrounding area. Nobody said that murder was pretty, but I found it enthralling.

I worked fast. First of all I cleaned the knife and put it back in its hiding place. Then I cleaned my hands and any blood that was dripping off me before I headed downstairs to Josslyn's vet practice. I unlocked the storeroom and found the items I needed: black bin bags, duct tape and a tarpaulin, which was brand new and had never been used. I carted it all back upstairs and began to wrap the body up in it. There was still a lot of blood, but once I got the body sealed up it finally stopped flowing.

The bastard was heavy and it took all of my remaining strength to drag him down the stairs and out to Josslyn's car. I somehow managed to hoist him into the boot and slam it shut. I knew I did not have the time to go anywhere and dispose of the body. That was a job for another day. I could feel myself losing grip. I needed to get upstairs quickly before I was seen. It was nearly four in the morning. I ignored Oscar's whimpers for attention and crawled into bed and shut off the light.

I believe you know the rest. Josslyn is naïve and I knew I could convince her that no one was murdered here. She was shocked when she woke up and scared at first, but then a calmness took over her. She behaved very well and cleaned up the flat like I knew she would without asking too many questions. She did not call the police because I believed that she should not. As I said, Josslyn and I are becoming closer and sometimes she feels what I feel. This, I know, will be of benefit to me in the future.

Unfortunately she now has this insane idea of finding her long-lost twin sister, but I will let Josslyn learn the hard way and let her realise why ignoring my warnings is a mistake. She will learn. She will soon understand that I am her true family, only me, and we can be together for the rest of our lives. I have always been there for her, have always protected her. She is blinded by the notion of the real Alicia. There is no Alicia. There is only me. I must protect her at all costs, no matter what the consequences. If I must lie, then I will lie. I have already killed for her. One day she will understand. One day she will be all mine.

Chapter Seven

What the fucking hell am I doing? I'm driving to a place I've never been before, to meet a man I've never met, to ask him about a long-lost twin sister I only found out about the day before yesterday. Am I crazy? Please, tell me if I am. I'm not sure why I've had a sudden surge of bravery (or stupidity), but there's a part of me that's enjoying the rush of nerves and adrenaline.

I never go anywhere new. That's specifically why I chose a university nearby, so I wouldn't have to travel far to get back to my parents' house. I've never been more than about twenty miles from where I grew up (and that was only to pick up a second-hand fridge-freezer for my flat and my dad was with me at the time). I like to stay close to home. I feel safe there. Travelling has never been on the cards and has never been of any interest to me. That was always Alicia's thing. She always said she wanted to travel and see the world whereas I'm perfectly happy to stay in one place, but today I was certainly going outside of my comfort zone, in more ways than one. Now I'm off to Cambridge!

I'm driving in silence because the CD player in my car is broken and I hate listening to the radio. Honestly, I couldn't tell you what kind of music people listen to these days. I heard Steps have made a come-back. I do know who Ed Sheeran is though – he's cool.

Oscar isn't the best road trip companion because he falls asleep almost instantly. He's probably a bit confused as usually his trips in the car last all of thirty minutes (to my parents' house and back). Whenever I slow down for a traffic light or road junction he lifts his head to check if we are there yet and then promptly goes back to sleep when he feels the acceleration of the car again. All I can say is thank God for satnavs on phones (my car is too ancient to have a built-in guidance system), but it's draining my battery and I forgot to charge it before I left. Now it's basically a race to get there before my battery goes flat and I'm left stranded in the middle of nowhere with absolutely no clue as to where I am. I guess I could follow road signs, but that's never been a talent of mine either and as for reading a map ... you can forget about it because I don't have one with me and I wouldn't be able to read it anyway.

I can't help but dwell on the situation I found myself in this morning. I woke up covered in blood – someone else's blood. It had also looked like I'd made some sort of attempt at cleaning, but then abandoned the idea. I know something bad happened. I know Alicia took me over. It's happened before, several times. She is getting stronger and more forceful. It used to be that I would need to give her permission to allow her to take me over, but she has found a way of doing it on her own.

The last thing I remember about last night was downing those drinks at the bar, and then nothing. There had been a flash of pain, but then darkness. I know something happened after that. I'm not stupid and I have a horrible feeling that I know who the blood belongs to ... Daniel. I have no proof of course, but I have a suspicion. Maybe he got what he finally deserved. A part of me isn't even sorry or worried about him, but then the normal part of me is slightly concerned. Maybe I should call him – just to check he is okay, or at least alive. Maybe I should—

You do not need to call him because he is not dead.

Then it is his blood?

I did not say that. If you call him then he will think you care about him.

True. I don't want to give him false hope. I just wish I knew what happened in my flat last night.

If it was important then I would tell you.

And you don't think that waking up covered in someone else's blood is important?

No.

Jesus, you really are a psychopath.

I really should be more concerned about all that blood, but to be honest I'm more concerned about being so far from home. I don't know where I'm going to stay tonight because I can't imagine I'll be finished with my errand and be able to get back home at a reasonable hour. The annoying satnav lady says I'm only five minutes away. I've been driving for nearly three hours. I did take a break around halfway, but now my butt is asleep and my stomach is rumbling. It's actually nearly six in the evening. Maybe I should find somewhere to stay for the night and then visit Peter in the morning. It would make more sense, but there's this nagging feeling inside me and I just can't wait any longer. I have to meet him now and find out if his sister is my sister.

I pull up outside a quaint little brick house. It's semi-detached and looks fairly old and in need of a new paint job, but the neighbourhood seems nice. Not too busy. In fact, there aren't any people wandering around at all, which is a bit weird. Cambridge is clearly a big city, but I don't think I've driven all the way through it. I must be on the outskirts somewhere. There are streetlamps and road signs showing the names of the roads, but it's hard to make them out in the dark. I have just blindly followed the satnav voice until it told me to stop.

My heart is practically leaping out of my chest as I cautiously approach the front door. I open the little metal gate and take a deep breath. I've left Oscar in the car, which he isn't happy about because he is yapping his head off and trying to squeeze his head through the small gap in the window. I press the bell and hold my breath.

Shit ... what do I even say? I haven't given it any thought. I can't just say that I'm his sister's long-lost twin, which means we are related (well, not really, but you know what I mean). I need to think ... quick. *Shit*. The door opens and the most beautiful man I have ever seen in my entire life peers out at me.

I mean ... I can't even think straight. I just stare open-mouthed at him for what seems like hours. He has a chiselled jaw line that must have been carved from pure marble and short dark hair that is slightly messy and in need of a trim. He is wearing snug fitting jeans that have seen better days and a crisp white shirt, which is unbuttoned. He has nothing on underneath it so I catch a glimpse of his tanned torso and six-pack abs. He looks like he's just finished a photo shoot for a men's fashion magazine.

He looks slightly startled for a second when he sees me, but then licks his lips, which makes my heart flutter.

'Yes? Can I help you?' he asks.

Shit. I haven't said anything yet. I drag my eyes away from his chest, which has a thin layer of hair on it and look up at him. Wow, he's tall. Oh my God his eyes ... they are dark hazel brown and so sexy.

'Errr ...' I stutter. 'Hi. Sorry. I – am ... errr.' Fuck! What's my name again? 'My name is Alic— sorry, Josslyn. I'm Josslyn.'

'Okay,' he says, looking confused. 'Are you selling something?'

'Um, no!' I yell at him, a little too loudly. 'I'm Josslyn.'

'Right, well you already told me that. I'm sorry but I have to go and ...' He turns to shut the door on me.

'I know your sister!' He stops and opens the door wider. I'm not sure what I'm going to say next, but I press on. 'I'm a friend of your sister ... from a long time ago.'

'I know all of Alicia's friends, but she's never mentioned anyone called Josslyn.'

'We had an argument, but we really were close once. I was just wondering if I could ask you some questions about how she died.'

'She's not dead,' he replies quite bluntly.

'Right, well ... about how she disappeared then.' He frowns at me and looks me up and down. I suddenly feel naked and I take a small step backwards. 'I'm sorry, I know how hard it must be for you, but I really cared about Alicia and I want to know what happened to her as much as you do. I just need to know a few things, that's all and then I'll leave, I swear.' I may sound desperate, but that's because I am. I have an overwhelming itch that I need to scratch. I must know if she is my twin sister and what happened to her.

Peter stares at me some more and then sighs heavily. 'Okay,' he says with another sigh. 'Come in ... is that your dog barking in the car?'

'Errr yeah, that's Oscar.'

'Well bring him in before the neighbours complain. I hope he likes cats.'

Oh shit. He has a cat. This could be fun.

I get Oscar out of the car and he immediately runs up to the nearest bush and cocks his leg. While I wait for him to finish what is no doubt the longest pee in history, I look up and down the road. There still aren't any people on the street, but I can see a few curtains twitching over the road. Nosey buggers.

Are you seriously going into a complete stranger's house to ply him with questions about his possibly dead sister?

I told you. I have to know.

Do you realise how dangerous this is? He could be a psychopath!

Looks who's talking! I don't care. You always tell me I need to take more risks and be brave. Well ... that's what I'm doing.

I said be brave, not stupid. Whatever you do you cannot tell him that you might be her twin sister.

I wasn't going to tell him, but why can't I?

Because it is ridiculous and is more than likely not true. Just promise me you will not tell him unless you are one hundred percent certain.

Okay, fine, I promise. Now keep quiet or you'll distract me.

Oscar finally finishes his mammoth pee and runs up to the front door, which Peter has left cracked open for me. He barges his way straight into the house and begins sniffing everything, clearly hunting for the cat. Peter walks out of the lounge which is just off to the right of the hallway where I am standing. He watches Oscar making himself at home and smiles.

'Hi Oscar. Nice to meet you.'

'Sorry,' I say, feeling embarrassed. 'He doesn't get out much.'

'I can see that. Harrison is around here somewhere. Do you like cats?'

'Uh yeah, I like cats. I'm a vet, so I like all animals, but cats don't always like me.'

'Don't worry, Harrison is a nice cat. He likes everyone.'

We shall see about that.

Harrison comes waltzing into the room. He is completely black, not even a fleck of another colour anywhere on him. He stops dead in his tracks when he sees me and then spots Oscar. Oscar spies the cat and immediately rushes up to him in excitement. Harrison looks terrified at first, but then just accepts Oscar's welcome and lets him lick his ears.

'Aww,' I say. 'Look at that! Nice kitty. Hi Harrison.' I do my best and slowly approach the cat, but he sees me again and raises his hackles and hisses, then runs away. Damn.

'Oh wow, sorry about that. I've never met a person who Harrison doesn't like.'

I shrug my shoulders. ‘No problem. Cats never like me.’

‘Weird.’

There’s an awkward silence. I glance nervously around the room, taking in the decoration. For a bloke he has quite decent taste. Everything has its own place, everything is colour co-ordinated and tidy. He clearly likes brown and cream because everything has that colour scheme and the theme is very modern. Considering that the outside of the house looks pretty run-down, the interior surprises me.

‘Do you want a cup of tea ... or something stronger?’ he asks. Considering I got completely wasted last night I should probably stick to tea.

‘A cup of tea would be great, thanks.’

‘You sure? I was about to crack open a bottle of white wine.’

‘Even better.’

You do not take much convincing.

Shut up.

I wait as he takes some wine glasses from the glass cabinet in the corner and watch as he pours the wine. I suddenly realise that he looks like he is going somewhere. His hair is slightly damp, like he's recently showered, and his wallet and keys are on the side table.

'I'm sorry,' I say as I take the glass from him. 'Am I interrupting your evening plans?'

'Sort of,' he says with a slight laugh. 'I have a date tonight, but it's not for a couple of hours.'

'I'm so sorry!' Oh my God, I'm mortified and slightly disappointed that he's taken.

'It's fine. I love my sister. She's more important. If you know something or we can figure something out then I'll do anything. Please, take a seat.'

I nod and take a seat on the lush sofa. Ooooh, it's soft and velvety. I take a sip of wine and quietly and happily breathe a relaxed sigh. Peter takes a seat next to me at the opposite end of the three-seater sofa.

'So ... what do you want to know about Alicia?'

I take a large gulp of wine to try and settle my growing nerves. ‘She once told me she was adopted. Is that true?’

‘Yeah. My parents adopted her when she was just a baby.’

‘So are you older than her?’

‘Only by a year. I don’t remember a time without her. I didn’t even know she was adopted until our parents told us.’

‘How old were you when they told you?’

‘About eight. They waited until we could understand it a bit better.’

I nod as I feel a lump forming in my throat, slightly jealous that Alicia had parents who didn't lie to her for twenty-eight years. ‘How did she take it?’

‘Better than me, but at the end of the day she’s my sister. Just because we aren’t blood related, it doesn’t change anything.’

‘That’s lovely. You’re a good brother.’

‘Thanks. Do you have siblings?’

'No. I'm an only child. I always wished I had a sister though, someone I could talk to and share things with. I was a lonely kid.'

'I can imagine.'

I'm not sure why, but I can feel tears starting to form behind my eyes. Talking to him about Alicia is making me feel emotional and vulnerable. I need to know if she knew about me, so I press him further.

'Did your parents ever tell you about Alicia's real parents? I'm sorry for all these questions, but I just have this weird feeling that if she disappeared then she disappeared for a reason.'

'Not really. Well, they said she wasn't wanted. That's all. I don't know their names. I've never seen her pre-adoption birth certificate, only the one she got afterwards with my parents' names on it.'

'Alicia never said she wanted to find out more about them?'

'Once she told me she wanted to find them, but then she changed her mind. You think she might have gone to look for them?'

'I don't know. Maybe.'

'Why do I get the feeling that you aren't telling me everything? I don't know you. I don't know how well you know my sister, but there's something ... familiar about you. I can't explain it.'

I feel myself go hot and red in the face. I would make the worst hostage (or best if you look at it from the aspect of the kidnapper) because when I lie anyone can tell straight away just by the colour my face turns. I also have trouble looking people in the eye, but then again that's just how I am naturally. I just don't look people in the eye. I always look somewhere just past them or at the bridge of their nose. Alicia, on the other hand, is an expert at staring people in the eye. It makes people nervous and I think she likes that. She has an evil stare.

'I'm not sure,' I say timidly as I take another gulp of wine. If I don't take it easy on the wine I'm not going to be able to drive later.

'Honestly, you look so familiar. Maybe I have met you before. When did you say you knew Alicia?'

Shit. I'm really not good at lying.

Let me take over.

No. Thank you Alicia, but this situation is already too complicated.

Suit yourself.

I glance around nervously and then spot a picture of a young Alicia at what looks like a summer camp. She's wearing a red Camp Bell t-shirt and a matching hat and smiling while holding a massive backpack up in the air.

'From camp,' I say stupidly.

Peter sees me look at the photo. He walks over to it and picks it up. He smiles. 'I really missed her when she went away that year. She came back ... different.'

'Different?'

'She seemed to have a lot of secrets that year. She was fifteen.'

'Teenage girls have a lot of secrets.'

'Yeah, maybe. So you two met there? She never mentioned you.'

'Like I said, we had an argument.'

'About what?'

'A boy.' Classic. Peter nods, as if understanding exactly what I meant. Then he frowns as he places the picture back on the side.

'She was always into boys. I didn't like it. I guess it was just me being an older brother, but I always felt protective of her. I always thought we told each other everything. That night when we went out to the club, the night she disappeared, she was acting weird. She kept saying that she needed to know the truth. I questioned her about it, but she refused to talk to me and ran out of the club. That was the last time I saw her. Once the note was found the police ruled it a suicide and closed the case. Her body's never been found. She didn't kill herself. She wouldn't.'

'What do you think happened to her?'

Peter shakes his head. 'I don't know. I just know that something wasn't right with her that night.'

I remain silent. He isn't giving me the information I need, but it is promising. There is still a possibility that Alicia is my twin. Maybe she found out about me that night – maybe that was the truth she needed to know. Maybe she went in search of me and something happened to her. These are all questions that I don't have the answers to, nor do I really have the ability to find out the answers by myself. I need Peter's help, but I can tell that his trust in me is fading. He doesn't know me so why would he trust me? I need to tell him what I know ...

No.

I have to tell him, Alicia. I won't tell him about you, but I should at least say that I think Alicia is my twin. It may spark a memory or he may be able to ask his parents for more information. I have to try. Please trust me Alicia.

Silence.

She's pissed off, but I can't worry about her now.

'I haven't been completely honest with you about who I am. I'm sorry. I hoped I would be able to figure things out on my own, but I can't. I don't know what to do or even where to start.'

Peter raises his eyebrows at me. 'Who the hell are you then?'

'My name is Josslyn, but I'm not a friend of your sister. I've never met her before. I only found out she existed two days ago. I grew up as an only child and everything was fine, until I found a picture in my parents' attic while I was cleaning it. This ...' I pull out the sonogram and hand it to Peter. He takes it and stares at it. I continue. 'Turn it over.'

He does and then I watch his expression as it changes from mildly confused to utterly astounded. 'I don't understand,' he says slowly. 'Josslyn and Alicia ...'

'I found out that I'm adopted and that I have a twin sister called Alicia. My parents only wanted one child and chose me. They never told me about Alicia until I found out by accident. I believe, but I'm not certain, that Alicia could be my long-lost twin sister.'

The silence that follows is very uncomfortable and I don't know what to do or where to look in the room. I want the floor to open up and swallow me whole. Peter slowly hands the picture back to me, stands up, walks over to the half empty bottle of wine on the table and picks it up. He walks back to me, tops up my glass and then tops up his. We drink in silence.

'Fuck,' he finally says.

'Yeah,' I reply with a nervous giggle. 'That's pretty much what I said when I found out. I'm not saying that I'm definitely right, but I have this feeling deep down inside me.

I can't explain it. When I look at a picture of Alicia she looks so familiar to me. You said yourself that I look familiar to you.'

'But you don't look anything like her.'

'We aren't identical.'

'Ah.' More silence. Without saying anything else he picks up his phone and starts typing.

'What are you doing?'

'Cancelling my date.'

'Oh shit, I'm so sorry I've ruined your evening. I can go if you want me to.'

'No, it's fine. I want to find out more about you.'

The fact that he is cancelling his date via a text message proves he is an asshole.

Leave him alone, Alicia. He's a nice guy.

I am warning you now. He is bad news. I do not trust him.

You don't trust anyone.

My point exactly.

Peter finishes his text message and chucks his phone on the table before taking a seat again on the sofa. He studies my face for a few seconds, which makes me feel slightly uneasy.

'You do kind of look like her you know. A little bit. Same eyes.'

'Really?' I smile, feeling quite emotional. 'Like I said, I'm not one hundred percent certain, but I thought maybe you might have some things of Alicia's that might give me some clues. I assume that your parents never told her that she was a twin.'

'To be honest I doubt they even knew themselves, but I can't be sure of that.'

'They never mentioned anything at all? What did they tell you both about her adoption? Can you remember?'

'I really can't. All they said was that she was adopted. Like I said, she once said she wanted to find her real parents, but then changed her mind. I'm not sure why. She told me that we were her real family and she didn't care about her biological parents. That was the last I heard about it. What about you? You had no idea this whole time that you were adopted and had a twin?'

'Nope.'

'Shit. How'd you take it?'

'Pretty badly. I downed three glasses of gin in the space of about ten minutes.'

'Nice.'

'Not so much the next morning.'

We share a laugh. This is so surreal. Here I am talking to a complete stranger, sharing a bottle of wine, laughing and chatting. I can honestly say that I feel so relaxed, so calm, not my usual self in a social situation. Usually when I have to talk to someone I struggle and hate every second, but I'm actually enjoying myself. I never thought I would say this about another person, but Peter is actually easy to talk to and I like him.

And you fancy him. I may be a psychopath, but I can recognise that emotion.

I don't fancy him.

Right okay. You are such a bad liar.

'Did they tell you anything about her? If they knew that you were twins, why'd they split you up? Is that even legal?'

'I guess so. They said that they chose me because I was the bigger, healthier twin. Honestly, I hate my parents so much right now. I don't know what to think. They wouldn't tell me anything else. They said it was for my own good.'

'What the hell does that mean?'

'I don't know. I ran off shortly after that and haven't spoken to them since.'

'How did you find out about me?'

'I did some research. I came across the online article about Alicia's disappearance. I used Google to find your address. Sorry.'

'No apology necessary. I'm here to help. I want to help. I want to find out what happened to my sister. Maybe she found out about you. I'm not sure, but I know she's not dead.'

'How?'

'I don't know. I just ... do.'

Well fuck me if that is not the most convincing answer I have ever heard in my life.

I didn't even know Alicia could be sarcastic, but it was so good I actually have to hide a smirk from Peter so he doesn't think I'm a weirdo.

'I guess I just need closure,' Peter continues. 'Alicia was happy. At least I thought she was. I just need to know what happened to her.'

'I know what you mean. I feel the same way. I mean, I feel this overwhelming need to know the truth about why we were split up and if she really is my twin. I've been alone my entire life, so to suddenly be told I may have a twin out there makes me feel ... I don't know ... like there's more to living.'

There's a long silence, which is filled by Oscar snoring his head off on the sofa next to me. He is lying on his back with his legs in the air.

Peter chuckles. 'Someone feels at home.'

'Honestly, he's so embarrassing,' I say with a giggle as I tickle his tummy.

'So ... I guess we should come up with a plan. What do we do now?'

'Honestly I have no idea,' I say with a sigh. 'I was kind of making this up as I went along.'

'Yeah, I could tell that. You aren't that great at lying.'

I told you.

'Yeah, so I've been told. Did Alicia keep any journals or anything like that? She must have left behind a lot of stuff.'

'Yeah, it's all in storage. My parents will still have it somewhere. They didn't throw anything away.'

'Maybe we should start by looking through her things.'

'Yeah, maybe, but I've already looked through most of it and I didn't find anything about a long-lost twin.'

'Maybe that's because you weren't looking for anything like that.'

'True. Okay, then it's settled. Tomorrow we'll go to my parents' and take a look.'

I stand up to leave. 'Great. I'll get going. I've already ruined your evening enough.'

'Don't be silly. Stay here. I can't let you drive now.'

'I can take a taxi.'

'Which hotel are you staying at?'

'Errrrr ... the one on, I mean, the one ...'

'You don't have a hotel booked, do you?'

'No.'

'Honestly, it's fine. Stay. We'll talk. Get to know each other. We could be family after all,' he adds with an awkward laugh. Something about that statement makes me feel a bit weird. *Family*. He could be my family ... and I've practically been imagining him naked on top of me the entire time I've been here.

'Okay, well ... thank you. I hope your girlfriend forgives you!'

'Oh, she's not my girlfriend. She's a blind date. Benny, my best mate, set us up. She's a girl he works with.'

'Oh, right. Well I hope I haven't ruined anything with her.'

Peter smiles as he cracks open another bottle of wine. 'This isn't how I imagined my evening to go, but I'm glad you turned up at my door, Josslyn.' He tops up my wine.

'Me too!' We clink glasses and drink.

I think you may have a drinking problem. You should see someone about that.

Trust me Alicia, if I was to see anyone about anything it wouldn't be because of my drinking problem.

Chapter Eight

Peter and I spend the remainder of the night talking about pretty much everything and anything. I find out that he and Alicia grew up in London, in an up-market suburb called Richmond. They both went to the same university; Alicia studied Law and Peter studied History and is now a teacher at a nearby boarding school for boys. They moved from Richmond to Cambridge to make a fresh start straight after university. Alicia passed her degree with top marks, but she did not go down the lawyer route. She chose, instead, a quieter career as a Legal Secretary (I think back to the newspaper article I read about her being a 'hot shot lawyer'. I guess 'hot shot legal secretary' didn't have the required ring to it). Peter also says he loves animals and he asks me loads of questions about being a vet, which I gladly answer. I don't think I've ever spent so long talking to another human being and actually enjoying it. I don't keep glancing around the room or looking for the exit. I don't keep checking my watch or my phone and I don't give him one-word answers. I actually speak to him and hold a normal conversation (at least I assume that's what a normal conversation is like). It feels ... good. Alicia doesn't say a word, other than a sarcastic comment here and there.

Before I know it Peter says it's gone one in the morning. By this point we have managed to get through two bottles of wine and half a bottle of gin (it seems that not only is he the nicest guy ever but he also loves gin like me!). It's safe to say that I'm rather tipsy, but Peter is the perfect gentleman and gives me a spare blanket so I can sleep on the sofa. He says goodnight and switches off the light. I fall asleep instantly, with Oscar curled up beside me.

I wake up to the smell of bacon and coffee. I don't have to open my eyes to know that Oscar isn't beside me – I know exactly where he is. He's no doubt begging for bacon. I crack an eye open. It's still fairly dark, the curtains are all drawn, but I can see light coming from the kitchen. I swing my legs off the side of the sofa and do my usual counting to five and then join Peter in the kitchen. Oh dear God, he looks even better this morning. He has messed up hair, overnight stubble and is wearing tracksuit bottoms and a white t-shirt ... and he's cooking. My mind automatically goes to very naughty places. He sees me staring at him and grins.

'Morning. Sleep well?'

'Err ... yeah. Like the dead actually.' What a weird choice of words that is!

'Me too. My head's a little sore, but I thought coffee and bacon would help. Want some?'

'Yes please. Thank you.'

'Take a seat.' He points to the high stool next to the kitchen counter. I shuffle onto it and watch him as he finishes cooking, while also taking in just how neat, tidy and clean his kitchen is. It's so clean I bet I could eat off the floor. Everything has its own place. Jars of staple foods such as pasta and rice are on wooden shelves and have their own labels, each one perfectly lined up. It's a little too neat to be honest. He must have some sort of OCD. No normal person has a kitchen this clean ... apart from my mum.

I never understand why people put labels on clear jars. You can clearly see that is pasta and rice, like you would suddenly forget.

Morning Alicia. Woken up on the wrong side of the bed, have you?

Thanks to you I have yet another hangover, but at least you are still alive and he did not murder you in your sleep.

Why would you even think that?

Because unlike you I actually do not believe that everyone is nice. Everyone has their secrets. They all have dark thoughts.

I don't believe that everyone's nice, but Peter just so happens to be a nice guy.

Remember what happened with the last nice guy you fancied?

I was young and naïve. Daniel was an asshole. I won't make that mistake again.

No, you will not because I am here to stop you.

'You like your bacon crispy?' Peter's voice jolts me back to reality.

'Huh? Oh. Yes. Thank you. Where's Oscar by the way?'

'Oh, he's outside having a nose around the garden. I gave him some toast cut-offs. I hope that's okay. I didn't give him any bacon though.'

I laugh. 'I'm surprised he didn't jump up on the counter and steal it out of the frying pan.'

'He did that?'

'Once, yeah! I had to treat him for burns.' We both laugh.

I tuck into my bacon sandwich while the coffee finishes brewing. It smells heavenly. He hands me a massive mug. I take it and our hands touch briefly. I swear to God I feel a jolt of electricity. I'm not sure if he feels it too, but it makes me lose my breath for a second.

'So, I've called my parents and told them I will be coming over soon to look through Alicia's things, so they are getting the boxes out of storage.'

'Did you tell them about me?'

'I told them that I would be bringing round a friend, but I haven't told them who you are ... or who you might be. I don't want to confuse them or get their hopes up that Alicia might still be alive. They have accepted that she committed suicide. I wouldn't say that they have moved on, but they have made their peace with it.'

I nod my understanding. 'It must be hard for them.'

'Yeah. It was. It still is.'

Oscar breaks the awkward silence by scratching at the back door to be let in. Peter opens the door for him and he rushes in, excitedly wagging his tail so hard that his whole back-end is shaking from side to side.

'He really is a character, isn't he?' laughs Peter. 'What's his story?'

'He was a rescue. Some guy dumped him at my vet practice when he was a puppy because he was fed up with his barking. He's my little shadow.'

'That's like Harrison. He follows me everywhere usually, except I'm not sure where he is today. He must be hiding because of Oscar.'

Or me.

'I got Harrison once I left uni and settled down here. I've always had cats.'

'So are you more of a cat person than a dog person?'

'I guess so, yeah.'

'I'm not sure we can be friends anymore.' We share another laugh.

'But I do love dogs too,' he adds as he strokes and tickles Oscar. 'Listen, if you want to take a shower then please do. It's right upstairs. First door on the left. I laid out a towel for you.'

'Do I smell that bad?'

Another laugh. 'No, but I thought maybe it would make you feel better.'

'Thanks. I could do with a hot shower actually, but the bacon was great too.' I swear I can still smell blood on me. Stupidly, I didn't pack many clean clothes, although I did pack lots of clean underwear. I scrub my skin to within an inch of its life. It doesn't help.

We arrive at Peter's parents' house about an hour later. Oscar comes along for the adventure. It's a lovely little cottage in a quaint village. Apparently, once Peter and Alicia moved away from their London home, their parents followed them a few years later. Peter said they were all close as a family, but he wished they didn't live so nearby. I could see why they would want to move and retire here after living in London for so long though. It's so quiet and remote, quite similar to my own parents' house.

My thoughts drift to them. I turned my phone off last night after the fifth call from my mum in the space of an hour. I haven't turned it back on yet. I'm enjoying the silence and the lack of social media as well, not that I post many things, but I like to flick through and look at other people's lives, see what they're up to, who they're dating, where they live and maybe once and a while like a picture of someone's dog. I sometimes find myself scrolling for hours, which is extremely unproductive, so this break will be good for me. I can focus on myself for a change. However, I do make a mental note to snoop on Peter's Facebook profile the first chance I get.

Peter's mother greets us at the door. She takes one look at me and her smile turns to shock and then a frown. She continues to look at me, which is a bit weird as she kisses her son hello. I mean, I could understand if I looked like Alicia, but I don't, so there's no reason to think that she recognises me.

'Hello. Josslyn, is it? Please, come in. Lovely to meet you.'

'Thank you, Mrs Phillips. Nice to meet you too.'

She is still staring at us.

I know, just be cool.

His mother (who is called Anne) is a very attractive woman who looks to be in her late fifties. Peter told me last night that she was very young when she had him and adopted Alicia. Anne has short dyed auburn hair (I can tell it's dyed because she has some grey roots showing) and is wearing a lot of make-up for a woman of her age. Not that older women can't wear a lot of make-up, but it just surprises me, considering that my mum hasn't worn make-up since the late 80's.

'I'm so sorry Josslyn, but I could swear I've met you before. You look so familiar. Peter, doesn't she look familiar?'

Peter and I share a knowing look. 'Uh, yeah Mum.'

'How did you two meet?'

'At the supermarket,' we both say together.

Yes, we rehearsed our answer in the car on the drive over. Peter didn't think it would be appropriate to say that we only met last night when I turned up at his door and got drunk together.

'Ah,' says Anne, although I can tell she wants to question him further. No doubt once I've left she will interrogate him like most mothers do. Mine certainly did that whenever I brought a boy home, which wasn't very often, I will add. 'Well come in. Alicia's things are upstairs in the spare bedroom. What are you looking for exactly?'

'I want to find her journals,' says Peter, already halfway up the stairs.

'Okay, well let me know if you need anything.'

'Thanks!'

Once we are both inside the spare room Peter rolls his eyes at me. 'Is your mum as annoying as mine?'

'Actually, I think mine's worse.'

'Yeesh. Poor you.'

We set to work opening up the cardboard boxes. I have a brief flash of déjà vu, having done the same thing only days ago. There are about a dozen or so, all of varying sizes. It feels weird rifling through a stranger's possessions looking for something that you aren't even sure exists. To be honest I'm not sure what I'm looking for. Everything. *Anything*.

I find a lot of books, teenage magazines, make-up, clothes and pictures. I sift through the photos one by one, taking in Alicia's face. She looks so happy in every one. She is surrounded by so many people who are also smiling. There is barely a photo of her by herself. She is always with friends and family and loved ones. I feel a pang of jealousy. Why did I turn out so ... different?

I find myself staring at a photo of her on her eighteenth birthday. In it she has long, flowing blonde hair and a tiara on her head which says *Birthday Princess* and a badge that shows her age. She also has a bottle of gin in her hand (seems we aren't so different in that area). Alicia is laughing at whoever it is behind the camera. She looks so real, so happy. I feel as if I could just reach into the photo and touch her. *What happened to you, Alicia?*

I flick through the rest of the photos from that birthday party. There are dozens of Alicia dancing, drinking, laughing, having fun, but then I come across one where she is sitting by herself; alone. I stop and study every single detail of her expression. Her face is sad; the first picture I have seen of her not happy and smiling. She isn't looking at the camera, but trying to hide away, shielding herself as much as possible. There is something in her eyes that tells me something isn't right. It intrigues me, so I pocket the photo while Peter isn't looking.

'Does Alicia have her original birth certificate?' I ask. 'You mentioned it last night that you've never seen it. Her biological parents, or at least her mother, must be listed on there.'

'To be honest, like I said, I've never seen it. Mum and Dad might have it somewhere. Let me go and ask.'

I nod as he exits the room. I'm alone in the room so I take the opportunity and search through another box. An old musty smell wafts from within. I finally see the culprit: an old doll. It's seen better days; clearly it was well-loved. I can just imagine Alicia playing with it, keeping it safe, giving it a name. I stroke the doll's ragged hair.

Peter comes back in only a few minutes later holding a piece of paper. 'Mum said that this is her post-adoption birth certificate, so she and dad are listed as the parents. She said that she doesn't have Alicia's original pre-adoption birth certificate. We would need to apply for it, but I think only Alicia can do that.'

'Oh.' I take the birth certificate from Peter and look at it, feeling disappointed. I guess to think it would be that easy to find my biological mother's name was a bit naïve.

'We might not be able to apply for Alicia's birth certificate, but you could apply for yours.' Peter's suggestion makes me feel a bit better.

'I'll do that,' I say with a smile. 'I didn't think of it before now.'

'It's a good idea.'

We continue to search the boxes for another hour. I'm completely fascinated by Alicia's life. It was so wonderful and exciting. She's been travelling abroad on numerous occasions during a gap year from university and afterwards as well. She's visited India, America, Russia and Japan and several other dozen or so countries. She made a scrapbook of her adventures and I find myself pulled into her world as I flick through the overloaded pages full of pictures and hand-written, happy scribbles. Suddenly I begin to feel a bit emotional and tears start stinging my eyes, something I am unaware of until one splashes down onto the page I'm looking at, smudging the writing slightly.

'Yes! I knew they were here somewhere!' yells Peter suddenly. I'm so alarmed by his shout that I almost fall off the bed.

I quickly wipe away my tears. 'What have you found?'

'Her journals. I knew they were here somewhere. Alicia loved writing in these. Mum and Dad bought her a new one every year. Look, there are dozens of them, each from a different year.'

Peter turns the cardboard box upside down on the bed next to me and several dozen books fall out, each one completely different in size and colour, but most thoroughly worn and used. Some are so old that the covers are falling off, while others were much newer, clearly more recent. *Bingo.*

'Wow!' I say in alarm.

I pick the nearest one up. The date printed on the front says 1998. Alicia would have been seven years old. I open it and turn a few pages. Jesus Christ, the girl could write! Every inch of each page is covered in scribbles and words. I spy a few random dates and entries and begin to read.

05 July 1998 – Peter is so lame. I hate him. He smells and is so annoying. I wish he weren't my brother. I wish I had a sister. A sister would be sooooooo cool.

18 August 1998 – It's summer! I love summer. The heat and the sun. It makes me feel happy. I'm going over to Katie's today to play in her paddling pool. I can't wait.

09 October 1998 – Mummy said that I can choose any doll I want from the store today. I'm going to get one with dark hair and brown eyes. I'm not sure why Mummy is buying me a new doll. It's not my birthday. She said it's cos she loves me so much. I wonder what I will name her.

I look up from the page and sigh. 'It's going to take us forever to go through these. I don't even know what to look for.'

'Well, let's think of some important dates, like ...' Peter pauses.

'The day she found out she was adopted?' I suggest. 'When was that?'

'Let me think ... I was eight I think, so Alicia would have been seven.'

'That's this year,' I say, showing him the journal I'm holding. 'Can you remember the date or the time of year?'

Peter sighs and closes his eyes as he runs his hands through his hair, which makes him look so damn hot that it's all I can do not to jump on him right this second. His biceps bulge as his arms bend. Lord give me strength.

'Autumn, I think. It was before Halloween because that year Alicia didn't want to come out trick-or-treating with me.'

I must have been close to the entry when I stopped reading just now. Maybe that's why her mother was buying her a new doll. I need to read more. I scan down a few paragraphs, not really taking the words in until I find one that stands out to me.

15 October 1998 – I've been very sad lately. I told Mummy and Daddy and Peter that I wasn't sad, but I am. A couple of days after Mummy bought me a new doll she told me that I don't actually belong to her and Daddy. I'm adopted. I didn't know what it meant. Mummy said that she didn't give birth to me. I know where babies come from. Mummies grow them in their tummies, but Mummy didn't grow me. Another mummy did. Mummy grew Peter, but she didn't grow me and that makes me very sad. Mummy said that her and Daddy chose me because I'm special and that even though Mummy didn't grow me I am still their daughter and they love me. I guess that's all that matters, but I can't help but feel sad about it.

16 October 1998 – Peter is being weird. He is being really nice to me. He's never nice to me. I think it's cos he feels bad about what's happened. He seemed sad at first, but now he looks like he has forgotten about it.

17 October 1998 – I had a dream last night about Mummy. Not my mummy. The mummy who grew me inside her tummy. She tried to throw me away, but Mummy and Daddy saved me. I feel better today. I realise that Mummy and Daddy told me the truth because they love me and don't want to lie to me. They always say that lying is a bad thing to do. I'm glad they told me.

18 October 1998 – Peter is back to being his old and annoying self. I hate him so much. I wish I had a sister. Maybe the mummy who grew me in her tummy grew another baby too. I asked Mummy, but she said she didn't know. I believe her because Mummy never lies to me. I guess I'm stuck with my smelly horrible brother.

I stop reading because my eyes are so full of tears that I can't see straight. Peter sees me crying and wraps his arms around me, but says nothing. I guess he doesn't know what to say either. I just cry softly, still clutching the words of my twin sister in my hands.

We stay in that position for what seems like hours until Oscar disrupts the moment by jumping up on my lap. He can always tell when I'm upset.

'Let's not read the rest here. Let's take these journals back to mine. There's nothing else in these boxes that I think will help us,' suggests Peter.

'Yeah, okay,' I say quietly. To be honest I'm actually looking forward to going back to his place. It feels cosy and welcoming there.

The remainder of the day is spent reading through Alicia's journals. Neither of us could come up with any more specific dates to look up, so we end up reading through the last year or so before she disappeared/died (whichever it is). Alicia wrote a lot less as she got older. Sometimes she went weeks without writing in her journal. She obviously had a very busy and hectic life, as she was always writing about work stresses or how she had so many meetings and appointments to keep and friends to meet. She often wrote about Peter. I could tell she loved him very much, although she always referred to him as *annoying*, but then again I guess that's what brothers and sisters are supposed to be to one another.

'Hey Josslyn, look at this.' Peter leans over to me on the sofa and moves the journal he is reading so we can both look at it. It's from 2013 – the year before she went missing. He has the page open to the 31st of May (her, and subsequently, my birthday). He points to a short passage of writing that is almost impossible to read. The handwriting is so bad, which is strange because Alicia has beautiful and clear handwriting everywhere else.

'That's weird, why is her writing so bad all of a sudden?' I ask, squinting to try and work it out.

'But look, this bit is underlined.' He's right. Three words are clearly underlined and one of them looks like ... no, that can't be right. It's looks like it says: *I found Jossy.*

I stare at Peter. 'Jossy? I-I don't ... wait ... what?'

Peter shakes his head, clearly as confused as I am. 'I don't know what to say, but it can't be just a random coincidence.'

He's right, but I can't wrap my head around it. Did Alicia somehow know about me? I quickly think back to 2013 on my birthday. I'm pretty sure I was with my mum and dad like I am on every birthday, and clearly I didn't go anywhere because I think I would remember meeting Alicia. My mind is a bit fuzzy to be honest. I can't be certain of anything.

'What does the rest of it say?' I ask.

'I can't make it all out. Her writing is so bad. Her hand must have been shaking so much. I think it says something like ... *haven't seen ... years ... she ... changed ...* and then something like ... *imaginary?* Does that look like *imaginary* to you?'

I look. Yes, it does. Oh my God, did Alicia have an imaginary friend called Jossy? Maybe I should tell Peter about my Alicia ...

Do not fucking tell him!

Alicia, this is all too weird. Maybe he can help us figure this out if he knew about you.

He does not need to know. Maybe Jossy is her fucking doll.

'What was the name of Alicia's doll?' I ask Peter suddenly.

'She never really had one.'

'The doll your mum gave her before she told you both she was adopted.' I pick up the doll I found earlier and show him.

'Oh ... I don't know. I don't really recognise it. After that day I never saw the doll again. She never played with it, not that I can remember anyway.'

Well that is a lie because the doll has clearly been played with a lot by the looks of it.

I agree with Alicia, but I don't press Peter on the matter. Instead, I grab for the 1998 journal and flick through the pages to the 9th of October and scan down the page until I see the next paragraph.

09 October 1998 – I'm so excited about my new doll, but I don't know what to name her. Oh wow, my new doll is so lovely. Mummy says I need to name my doll, but I can't think of a good enough name for her. Mummy has something important to tell me now so I must go and see her, but I have decided to name my new doll Jossy. It's a nice name and was the name of the nice girl I met a few years ago. She was very nice, but I haven't seen her since. I think maybe she was imaginary because my friend Katie said she couldn't see her even though she was standing right next to me. It's nice to have an imaginary friend, as well as lots of real ones.

Suddenly an icy chill flows through my body and I physically shiver. Peter notices immediately and actually jumps away from me in fright.

'Oh wow, what was that?'

'What was what?'

'You literally shook and I got a shock off you.'

'Oh ... I'm sorry.'

'Don't apologise. Are you okay?'

'Yes ... actually, no. I don't think I am. This is all a bit much. I ... I need to tell you something else ...'

I am warning you Josslyn! If you tell him about me I will hurt him.

Then the pain hits me. I scream and bury my head into the sofa cushions, slamming my fists into them and grabbing at my head. I can feel Peter's hands on me, trying to help, but nothing can help. All I know is that the pain is going to kill me if it doesn't stop soon. Not only is it in my abdomen, but now it's in my head.

I squeeze my eyes shut, but I can see a bright light and a face. It's her. It's Alicia. Not my twin, but the Alicia inside my head. She looks like me, but she also looks different; angry, a hard expression, dead eyes, and she is smiling. It's not a happy smile. It's horrible and twisted and is getting wider and wider and wider ...

Let me take over!

Then she screams at me and I scream louder and then it's over. The pain stops. I am crying hysterically into the sofa cushions. I can't do this anymore. I can't fight her for much longer. She wants to take over, but I can't let her. I'm not sure if I trust her.

Alicia, who are you?

You know who I am.

You can't be Alicia, my twin. Who are you? Tell me now or I'm telling Peter about you.

There is a long pause and then ...

You call me Alicia, so I am Alicia.

But you're not my twin? You're not the real Alicia?

No, I am someone else.

Who are you?

I am you.

I stop crying and push myself up into a seated position. Peter grabs me and forces me to look him in the eyes.

'Josslyn, what the fuck was that? It was like you were possessed or something. You scared the hell out of me!'

'I'm sorry. I get a bad pain in my head and body sometimes.'

'That didn't look like normal pain. Have you been to see someone about it?'

'No.'

'I really think you should.'

'I'm fine, really. I'm sorry I scared you. Please may I have a glass of water?'

Peter gives me a stern look, clearly wanting to question me further, but he eventually sighs and goes into the kitchen for my water. When he comes back I'm still breathing heavily, trying my best to catch my breath. He places the glass of water on the small table next to the sofa then takes both my hands.

'Josslyn, I'm worried about you. Please tell me what's going on. I can help.'

'No, you can't. I promise you that you can't help me.'

'But I can try.'

Do something to shut him up or I will.

I think fast. What's a good distraction? Without even thinking of the consequences I immediately lean forwards and kiss him. There's an awkward moment when he pulls away quickly, obviously thinking that it's a bad idea, but then he grabs me and pulls me into him. My body immediately relaxes and I just sink into him, feeling his warm, hard body against mine. I don't care what happens next. I just know that right now this is what I want and it's clearly what he wants, so we just give in to our urges.

Peter doesn't ask me any further questions. Problem solved!

Chapter Nine

Oh fuck, what have I done? What have I actually done? I'll tell you what I've done. I've had sex with my twin sister's brother, which I guess sounds a lot worse than it really is. I mean, obviously I know Peter and I aren't related by blood, but it's still ... icky, right? I feel ... dirty, and not in a good way. I blame Alicia. She was the one who told me to shut him up, so I did, the only way I knew how. It was the first thing that came to mind. Yes, okay, I admit it. I have a crush on Peter, but never did I think we would end up sleeping together. I've only known the guy a day! I'm not a slut. I don't do this sort of thing (okay, I had a one-night stand once at university, but who the hell hasn't?) I'm ashamed of myself (yet my inner sex goddess is grinning). I'll be completely honest here ... it was good, like really, *really* good. I'm going straight to hell.

I'm alone in bed. I pretended to still be asleep when Peter woke up and went downstairs to make coffee. I assume that's what he is doing because I can smell the freshly brewed scent wafting up the stairs. I'm hiding under the sheets, praying that last night didn't really happen. Obviously it did, but how the hell am I supposed to act around him now?

'Morning.' Peter's voice makes me jump and I peer out from under the sheet in trepidation. He's standing by the side of the bed wearing nothing except his loose tracksuit bottoms which are hanging low on his hips. His hair is all messy and sticking up in random places, but it makes him look even more yummy. I try my best to drag my eyes away from his six-pack, but it's almost impossible. I'm just imagining licking his torso all over and slowing, getting lower and lower until ...

'Josslyn? Are you okay?'

'Yes!' I shout. I quickly gather up the sheets and clutch them to my chest, suddenly realising I'm completely naked. I never sleep naked. Ever. It makes me feel too vulnerable. When I've slept with other men I've always got myself dressed into something before falling asleep. It seems that last night I felt comfortable enough to fall asleep naked next to Peter.

'Thank you,' I say a little more quietly as I take the coffee mug from him. 'I'm sorry, I guess I'm feeling a bit ...'

'Weird?' he offers.

'Yeah, weird. Do you feel weird?'

'No.'

'Oh good, me neither.' Cue awkward silence.

'Okay, maybe we need to talk.' He slowly sits down on the bed next to me. 'I won't lie Josslyn, I didn't expect last night to happen. I wanted it to happen from the second I met you, but when you told me who you thought you were then I thought maybe it shouldn't happen, but then you kissed me and then ... well ... it was pretty damn great.'

I can't help but smile. It spreads across my whole face before I even know what's happening. 'It was great.'

'It certainly was, but I have to say I feel like I've been hit by a truck.' He turns his back on me and I immediately see dozens of deep red scratches across his back. They look raw.

'Oh my God, did I do that?' I gently touch his sore skin and he flinches in pain. 'I'm so sorry! I don't remember doing that at all!'

'You don't?' He sounds genuinely shocked. 'Josslyn, you were like a wild animal, which was amazing. I enjoyed it. I've never had anyone be that ... rough with me before. It was like you were a different person.'

Oh shit.

'I ... I'm sorry. I guess I got carried away.'

Peter laughs. 'It's totally okay, but you really don't remember what happened?'

'I remember some.' It's true. I can only remember short snippets of last night and the snippets I do remember are bloody amazing, but I don't remember scratching him or being rough.

'Do you remember asking me to choke you?'

'Oh my God, what? I said that?'

'You told me to choke you and then you called me a pussy when I wouldn't do it.'

I am beyond mortified. I literally have no words to say. None at all. Peter appears to realise that I'm embarrassed.

'Honestly, don't worry about it. I've been called worse. We all get caught up in the moment, right?'

'Yeah, I guess so. It's been a while ... for me.'

'Me too.'

Cue another awkward silence. Honestly, just kill me now. This is excruciating.

'So what are we going to do about this? Pretend it didn't happen?' I ask.

'Well, I don't know about you, but I'd like you to stay around a while longer. I assume you still want to find out what happened to Alicia?'

'Yes, of course.'

'Same. I guess we still need to work together then to find out the truth and if that means spending long nights together ... then so be it.'

I smile slightly. 'Maybe we should focus on finding Alicia first ... and then see.'

Peter nods in agreement, but I can clearly see the disappointment in his eyes. 'Okay,' he says as he stands up and moves swiftly away from me.

Maybe that had been the wrong thing to say, but in my heart I feel that it was the right thing. Sex always complicates things and this situation is already complicated enough. If Alicia turns out to be alive, then how the hell would I explain this? I need to be careful and keep my distance or this could go horribly wrong. I don't want to end up hurting Peter.

'I'm going to make an early start on reading some more journals. Why don't you take a shower and join me in a bit?'

'Sure. Thank you.'

Once Peter leaves the room I immediately grab a pillow and scream into it, which actually makes me feel better. Then I quickly grab my phone and text Emma and Lucy, saying that I am away with a family emergency (which is sort of true) and could they please look after the practice for a few days. I add a few kisses onto the end of my text message for good measure. They both text back and say that it's fine and to take all the time I need. Bless them both. They are so gullible. I actually feel guilty for bailing on them the other night, lying to them and thinking bitchy things. Or maybe I don't. I don't know how to feel at the moment, but I do know one thing: Alicia has a lot of explaining to do about last night.

Alicia? Are you there?

Yes.

What happened last night with Peter?

Do you really need me to explain it to you?

Why did you take over? I know you've been doing it more and more lately. Why last night? I thought you didn't care about sex and having fun? Why would you do that?

So sue me. I got what I wanted.

Do you like Peter?

No, but he served his purpose.

You used me.

Silence.

I grit my teeth, feeling so angry and betrayed. Alicia never used to do this to me. She used to ask or be nice about it, but now she just takes what she wants from me whenever she wants it and I'm fed up. I've had enough of it. That's the second time in as many days she has taken me over without my permission. Maybe I don't want Alicia in my head anymore, especially if she's going to be a bitch to me and use me. Here's a question: how do you go about getting another personality out of your head?

What makes you think I am in your head?

There's no other explanation for it.

If you say so.

Damn her and her cryptic messages. I need to see a doctor about it though. There's no other way. I need serious help and strong medication for sure. I don't feel safe. I don't think other people are safe either. I'm really scared about what will happen if I tell a professional about her. They'll think I'm crazy, there's no doubt about that. I have to decide whether having Alicia in my head (or wherever the hell she is) is worth it or not.

Once I've showered and washed the smell of sex off me I join Peter in the lounge where he is surrounded by Alicia's journals, but he has a frown on his face.

'I can't find the year 2014, the year she disappeared.'

'That's weird.'

'But look at this one, from 2013. She talks about feeling as if someone is watching her, several times. At one point she said she was scared for her life. Then she started getting phone calls.'

This peaks my interest. 'What sort of phone calls?'

'She said a few times that she had a call from a blocked number and no one spoke. It was just silence ... and breathing.'

Holy shit. Could it be that my stalker is the same person who was stalking Alicia? But why? And who? If it is the same person then they must have known who we were and that we were twins. I'm so confused right now.

'Did the police know about this?' I ask.

'No. These journals were never looked at. There was no reason to think there was anything in them worth investigating. Her death was deemed a suicide from the start because of the note she left. The case was closed pretty much straight away. She never told me about a stalker or feeling scared. Why wouldn't she tell me?'

I shake my head because I don't know how else to answer him.

'We need to look into this more. I bet whoever was stalking her made her disappear. I don't know how, but I have an idea who the stalker might be, or if it's not him maybe Alicia would have told him about her issues.'

'Who?'

'Alicia was dating this loser called Paul at the time she disappeared. The police questioned him, but he said he didn't know anything about why she would kill herself. I always thought he was lying. There was something about the guy I never liked. Do you ever get that? A weird feeling about someone even though there is no explanation or reason why?'

'Sometimes.'

'I think we should pay him a visit.' Peter seems focused now. His facial expression has changed to one that is hard and quite determined. It seems he has a plan, so I just nod and decide to follow his lead. It's not like I'm coming up with any bright ideas of my own because my head is still fuzzy from last night.

'Can I read the journal?' I ask.

He hands it to me and points out a passage of writing.

16 April 2013 – Last night while I was walking home from work I heard footsteps behind me, but when I turned to look there was no one there. It reminded me of a horror movie I watched the day before. When I got home the kitchen window was open. I remember closing it before I left. I feel like someone has been in my house. Certain things have been rearranged or moved. Maybe I did it ... I don't remember.

17 April 2013 - I got a weird phone call today. No one spoke, but I could hear someone breathing, which got louder and louder.

18 April 2013 - Another phone call. This one lasted nearly five minutes because I didn't hang up this time. I didn't want to. The person was breathing hard again. It sounded like they were out of breath. The person grunted at the end so I know it was a man. I know this sounds gross, but it sounded like he was masturbating on the other end of the phone. Then he hung up.

Oh my God. Ewwww! I look up at Peter with a disgusted look on my face. Something is telling me to tell him about my stalker. It can't be a coincidence.

Peter has his arms folded and is staring straight at me. 'Whoever this stalker is, he's a sicko. Let's go and visit Paul.'

'Okay, I'm ready.'

I go to stand up and feel my whole body go numb and my legs give out without warning. I stumble forwards, knocking into the lamp beside the sofa. It crashes to the floor as I collapse next to it. I feel Peter at my side, quickly joined by Oscar, but I can't hear what Peter is saying. I'm fading away into the darkness, slowing sinking down and down and down. I'm trying to scream, but my voice has been stolen. Then the pain hits and I black out.

Beep. Beep ... Beep. Beep ... What the fuck is that noise? Why won't it stop? My head is pounding and, even though I feel fuzzy, I'm pretty sure it's not alcohol related this time.

I have no idea where I am. My eyelids flicker open for a second, which feels like the hardest thing to do at the moment. I close them again, processing what they have seen. I'm in a hospital room – I know that much. It's got that weird ammonia smell.

My eyes slowly open again and my brain starts working in overdrive to take in what's happening. My arm is hooked up to a machine, which is the thing that is beeping and making my head hurt. Around my bed is a blue curtain, one of those ugly hospital curtains that they use to respect your privacy. I can't see or hear any hospital staff around.

I turn my head slowly to the left, my neck screaming at me in agony. Peter is snoozing on the plastic chair next to my bed. He looks terrible to be honest. It appears that he hasn't had a shave in days, his eyes have dark shadows around them, but he looks so peaceful. I stare at him for a while, just taking in the fine lines around his eyes, the slow rise and fall of his chest. I rest my head against the cold hospital pillow and sigh deeply. I try and recall the memory of how I got here, but there is nothing, like someone has pressed a delete button and erased that portion of my memory.

Alicia, are you there?

Silence.

I guess not right now, but if I know anything about Alicia at all it's that she is always there, always watching, always listening.

I try and shift my body so that I'm propped a bit further up the bed, but I can't move. I can move my head and that's about it. My arms and legs aren't responding.

'Oh my God!' I yell out. My shout jolts Peter out of his sleep. He sits bolt upright, clearly in a panic.

'Josslyn! Thank God!' He rushes to me and presses the call button on the bed next to me. 'It's okay Josslyn, don't worry, I'm here.'

'Peter, what's going on? I can't move!'

'Just relax. It's probably just temporary paralysis from being in a coma for so long.'

'What? I was in a coma? For how long exactly?'

'I'm sorry, that was the wrong choice of words. You were only asleep for a couple of days.'

'A couple of days!'

I try to sit up again. This time I manage to move my arms, but they react so slowly. This doesn't feel right. It feels like this isn't my body. I know that sounds ridiculous and it doesn't make any sense, but that's the only way I can describe the feeling.

Suddenly two nurses appear through the curtain and they start checking the monitor beside me, then a doctor shows up and starts asking me lots of questions and looks into my eyes with a light. Everyone appears to be moving at lightning speed, as if someone has pressed fast-forward. I can't keep up. To be honest, this is all a bit much and I just stare blankly at the doctor as he talks to me. I can see his mouth moving, but the words don't make any sense.

'Hello Josslyn, my name is Doctor Jacobson. Do not be alarmed. You are safe. Can you tell me your full name?'

'I ... I'm not ... what?' I stutter.

'It's okay to be a little confused at first. Your friend Peter told us you passed out at his house. That was two days ago. Today is Wednesday the 13th of November. Do you remember what year it is?'

'Um ... it's 2019.'

'Good. And your full name?'

'Josslyn Reynolds.'

'Your date of birth?'

'31st of May 1991.'

'Good. Do you remember how you got to the hospital?'

'No. The last thing I remember is being at Peter's house. We'd just had breakfast. I went to stand up and ... that's it.'

Doctor Jacobson nods and writes something down on his chart, which he keeps hidden from me. 'Okay, that's fine,' he says in a slightly patronising voice. 'Now, I don't want you to worry, but we have run some tests in order to find out why you passed out and didn't regain consciousness.'

I frown at him. 'What sort of tests?'

'Blood tests mainly, however we didn't find anything unusual. We also did an MRI scan.' Doctor Jacobson stops and looks at Peter. 'Since you are not Josslyn's next of kin I will have to ask you to step outside while I discuss her medical results.'

Peter looks at me, clearly hoping that I would invite him to stay, but I just nod at him. He takes the hint and quietly leaves the area.

My heart is nearly thumping out of my chest. I don't know what he is going to say, but I'm pretty sure it's not going to be good. However, I never (and I mean not in a million years) expected him to say what he says over the next few minutes.

'Josslyn, we conducted an MRI scan on your brain, as well as your abdomen. Peter said that you had experienced pain there before. Your brain is perfectly healthy, however we did find some anomalies. These include a reduction in pre-frontal grey matter volume, grey matter reduction in the right superior temporal gyrus, as well as lack of activity within the anterior insular cortex. I'm sorry for all the technical medical terms. In short, this basically means that your brain is showing some of the tendencies and activities associated with being a psychopath.'

He stops and watches my reaction. To be honest I don't react at all, not at first. It's not new to me, having a psychopath in my head, but he doesn't know that. Also, this is my brain he's talking about, not Alicia's. So why would my brain have psychopathic tendencies? It's actually quite interesting. It makes me wish I had bothered to get scanned years ago, then maybe a doctor would have given me a simple explanation. Doctor Jacobson is still watching me.

'Josslyn, do you understand what I just said?'

'Yes, I ... yes, I understand. Are you calling me a psychopath?'

He smiles. 'No, I'm just saying that your brain is quite unlike many I have seen. However, there is more.'

'More?'

'We also conducted a scan on the rest of your body and found a dark shadow in your retroperitoneal space, which contains your kidneys, adrenal glands, pancreas and other nerves and lymph nodes. We took a biopsy. At first I thought it was some sort of tumour, but after discovering the results of the biopsy I believe it to be something more, something I have never come across in my thirty-year career and have only ever read about in medical journals. Josslyn, I believe this tumour is actually called a foetus in fetu. It's an extremely rare condition in which a malformed foetus is found within a living person, their twin. Less than two hundred cases have ever been reported in medical literature and, if I am correct, you are only the second woman to have been diagnosed with the condition. Usually, this is detected in males and more commonly in young babies. Only a handful of cases have ever been found in a full-grown healthy adult.'

I stare at him in disbelief, my brain trying its best to decipher what has just come out of his mouth. *Foetus in fetu.* Those three words echo around my head over and over, but they just don't make any sense. He may as well have been talking in a different language. *Foetus in fetu.* I think I need it explaining to me again.

'Doctor, can you say that again? Are you saying that I have an ... unborn twin growing inside me?'

'It isn't growing anymore. It stopped growing back in utero, but yes, the dark lump in your abdomen, I believe, is your unborn twin, more than likely an identical twin sister. It is similar to the parasitic twin theory where very early in a monozygotic pregnancy, or more commonly known as an identical twin pregnancy, in which both foetuses share the same placenta, one twin wraps around and basically envelops the other. This enveloped twin becomes a parasite. Its survival depends on the survival of its host twin. It even draws on the hosts blood supply. It lacks internal organs and any basic brain development and cannot survive on its own. Until now this parasite has gone undetected inside you, but clearly the time has now come to remove it before it does any further damage. Your body is working in overdrive to keep this foetus alive, although I use the word alive hypothetically because it is only alive in the sense that its component tissues have not yet died or been eliminated.'

Again, my brain just simply can't seem to work fast enough to understand. I'm literally lost for words. All this time Alicia has been inside me, as a parasite. She is real. She isn't just in my head. I still don't understand. If what the doctor says is true and the foetus has no brain development then how can she be talking to me?

'Doctor,' I said as calmly as I can, despite the fact that my heart is beating out of my chest. 'Speaking of hypothetical situations, can I ask you something that may sound a bit strange?'

Doctor Jacobson looks slightly shocked, but he smiles kindly at me. 'Of course. After learning about your condition I can't say I'd be surprised at anything else for a while.'

We'll see about that.

'Would it be possible that my unborn twin – the foetus in fetu – would it be possible for it to be alive inside me and speak to me, like a real person?'

Doctor Jacobson slowly shakes his head. He doesn't even pause to think about it. 'I'm sorry Josslyn, but that would be completely impossible I'm afraid. The foetus inside you is not a real human. It would have been, of course, but it doesn't have the capacity to think or feel or speak.'

Damn. Guess doctors don't know everything.

I nod. 'Of course. Thank you for explaining.'

Doctor Jacobson then lowers his voice as he says, 'Are you telling me that you do hear her and she is alive inside you? Because if that were true it would be the most unbelievable diagnosis and find of the entire century.'

I have two choices here: tell him the truth and be hooked up to machines and tested on for the rest of my natural life, or lie and pretend that everything is fine and I don't have a psychopathic identical twin in my body.

'No, I was just curious.' We lock eyes for a few seconds. 'Please can I have a moment alone?' I ask.

'Of course,' says Doctor Jacobson. 'Please let the nurses know if you need anything. I'll be back later to discuss your options, but I would highly recommend that you have the foetus removed.'

'Thank you, doctor. Oh, please don't mention any of this to my friend Peter. I'll tell him in my own time.'

'I completely understand. I would never break doctor/patient confidentiality.' And with that Doctor Jacobson leaves me alone in my hospital bed.

I take a deep breath and close my eyes. I can feel her inside me now. She is angry. She had wanted to stab the doctor with his own pen right in the jugular and watch his blood spurt out all over the clean floor – watch as his crisp white jacket soaked up the blood as he slowly sank to the floor, clutching his throat. She wanted to watch the life drain from his body, see the flicker in his eyes fade and die. It had taken all of my strength to hold her at bay. Yes, she is definitely angry and I can feel her rage increasing by the second.

Alicia. Please talk to me. Have you known this whole time?

Yes.

Why didn't you tell me?

You would not have believed me.

You don't know that.

I know you better then you know yourself, Josslyn. We were once one person. There is no greater bond than that between identical twin siblings. We share everything. You would have been scared and you would not have understood.

Maybe, but I don't understand. Who is Alicia Phillips? Is she my twin or is she just a stranger?

She is technically your fraternal twin, but I am your real identical twin. We would have been triplets – you and I as twins and she would have been the third wheel. She is our sister, but she means nothing. I am part of you and no one can ever come between us.

Of course not, but I still want to find her.

Why? Am I not enough?

Yes, but ... I just have to know where and who she is. She is alive and real. You aren't real. You're just a ...

Go on ... say it.

A parasite.

Oh shit, that was a mistake!

I am NOT a parasite you worthless piece of shit. If it was not for me you would be dead right now. I saved you! If anything YOU are the parasite Josslyn, not me!

Alicia suddenly explodes with anger and rips back the bed sheets. My arms and legs spring to life as I feel her take over my entire body. She jumps out of the bed, shoves the beeping machine against the wall, making a huge crash, and then pulls all the needles out of her hand. Her anger terrifies me and I can't seem to find my way back. She is holding me back against my will, but for the first time I am able to see her actions and feel her emotions. I am still here, but Alicia is in control now. This has never happened before. I'm scared.

Then Peter comes through the curtain. We look at each other for a beat. I can feel her rising hatred. She wants to kill him. He isn't safe.

'Josslyn, are you okay?' He can't quite work out whether to move towards me and help me or keep his distance.

Alicia grins at him. 'Never better.'

'What did the doctor say?'

'That I am free to leave.'

'Are you sure? I don't think ...'

Suddenly Alicia lurches forward and grabs his arm, squeezing it so tight she digs her nails into his skin, drawing blood. Peter flinches. He stares at her straight in the eyes, but he doesn't look afraid. He should be afraid, but he isn't. There's nothing I can do. I'm helpless.

'Okay,' he says calmly. 'Let's go.'

Alicia smiles again. 'Maybe you are not so useless after all,' she mutters.

'What did you say?'

'Get my things.'

'Yes, of course.'

Chapter Ten

I'm trapped in my own body. I can't speak or move, but I can hear everything that Alicia is saying, feel everything she is feeling and see everything she is doing. It's terrifying because I have never known her to be so cold, so heartless, so angry. Yes, she has been angry before and she has said some nasty things and probably done much worse, but this is the first time I have experienced anything like this. Usually I completely disappear when Alicia takes over. I don't know where I go exactly, but I'm not present. Yet now I am completely helpless and at her mercy.

Alicia realises after a few minutes that she needs to try and pretend to be me or she'll give the game away. She's putting on a good show for Peter, but there is a harshness to her voice and her style of movement is very unlike mine. Call me crazy, but I think Peter has noticed that something isn't quite right already because he's looking at me with a strange and confused look on his face. He believes Alicia's story that the doctor has released her and helps to collect her things from the hospital. He kindly offers to take her back to his place to rest and recover, which she agrees to. I'm looking forward to seeing Oscar. He must be wondering where I am by now. I never want him to think I've abandoned him the way his previous owner did.

I can't be sure of this, but I don't think Alicia is aware that I am still here. I can't hear her thoughts, so maybe she can't hear mine. Something has changed between us, whether it's got something to do with me now knowing what/who she really is, I'm not sure. It's a strange sensation, but it means I don't have to say or do anything, enabling me to really think about what happened in the hospital and what I found out.

This is what I know: Alicia (the voice in my head, not the *real* one) is my identical twin, or at least she would have been if she had survived and grown to term. She is some sort of weird tumour or, what was it called – a *foetus in fetu* – a rare condition where one twin envelops and absorbs the other, but not fully. She is somehow still inside of me. According to the doctor I am only the second adult woman to have this condition (that medical experts are aware of).

I wish Alicia had stayed in the hospital. I had wanted to ask the doctor so many more questions, such as: is the foetus in fetu dangerous – can it be removed completely – why does it happen?

Here's an even more interesting question – what about my fraternal twin? Is she really real or is Alicia Phillips actually a complete stranger that I have somehow fixated myself on and convinced myself that she is my twin sister? Alicia told me she was real and that we would have been triplets, but is that even possible? It seems completely impossible to me. Not only are triplets rare, but a foetus in fetu happening at the same time? Alicia and I would be famous if this turned out to be true and word got out. I would probably be part of a research study for many years. Alicia would be cut out of me and studied under a microscope, but what if I told people that she was real and alive inside me and a completely separate person? Maybe no one would believe me. Maybe I would be diagnosed as a psychopath as well as crazy and locked up and then studied.

All this scares me, but the worst part is that Alicia has known who she is this whole time and hasn't told me. Why? Is she jealous of my fraternal twin? It's almost like she has tried to become Alicia (honestly the fact that they both have the same name is getting far too confusing. I apologise, but if it's confusing for you then just imagine how I must be feeling!). Maybe I should give her a new name, just to avoid confusion, but I doubt she would go for that. She has always been Alicia to me and I have known her almost all my life. I was the one who made her up for crying out loud! I gave her that name. At least I thought I had made her up, but now it turns out that she was there the whole time, just biding her time. It's all just too confusing. I don't know what the hell is going on, but I do know that Alicia is dangerous and I need to do something about it. I don't trust her anymore and they always say that once trust is gone from a relationship then there is nothing left. Cutting her out seems harsh, but what other choice do I have? I can't control her. She can now seemingly take me over whenever she wants and that's just not cool. Not cool.

I need to take back control of my body, but I don't know how, so for now I'm being forced to watch and listen as Alicia pretends to be me. She must have picked up a few hints and tips over the past couple of decades because she does a pretty decent imitation of me at times.

'Honestly Peter, I am fine,' she says as she takes a seat on the sofa. Oscar didn't immediately rush to her when she walked through the door. He took a few moments to give her a sniff. They'd met before, but I know Oscar prefers me. He is now jumping all over her and trying to lick her face. She tries to push him away.

'I'm just a bit concerned. They released you pretty fast. What did they say was the problem?'

'It is nothing. Just low blood sugar. And a bit of stress.'

'Are you sure?'

'Yes Peter, I am sure.' I can hear the tension in her voice. Alicia has never been good at hiding her anger, which appears to build up very quickly. It seems to be the only emotion she actually has. 'Now stop asking me,' she adds.

'I'm just worried about you, Josslyn. Are you okay to continue the search for Alicia?'

Alicia sighs and rolls her eyes. 'If we must,' she mutters. It's clear that Alicia has no interest in finding her, but I'm sure she's smart enough to realise that backing out now would be suspicious.

'Okay, well good. I've been thinking about those stalker phone calls,' says Peter. 'I definitely think it's worth talking to Paul and ...'

‘I have been getting them too, you know.’

WHAT! Oh my God why would she tell him that? What’s her plan exactly? Wasn't she the one who told me not to tell him about the calls? Honestly, I can't keep up with her.

Peter stares at Alicia and frowns. ‘Y-you've been getting calls too?’

Alicia smiles at him. ‘Yes and they are very similar to the calls Alicia wrote about. I do not think they are from Paul. Why would Paul want to call me?’ Alicia stands and approaches Peter. She moves close to him, staring him straight in the face.

‘I ... I don’t know.’ Peter seems nervous and takes the tiniest of steps backwards, away from Alicia. ‘I still think he's worth checking out.’

‘Why?’

‘I’m sorry?’

‘Why do you want it to be Paul so badly?’

Peter doesn’t answer right away. I get the feeling that he is trying to figure out what to say. Alicia is a crouching lioness waiting to strike. It’s like she can sense his fear and is revelling in it. She slowly takes a few more steps towards Peter, her eyes locked on his the whole time – the evil stare, I call it.

'I just think he's worth looking into,' says Peter finally. 'Don't you? We need to rule out the most obvious suspects.'

'What about you?'

'What about me?'

'Why should I not suspect you?'

Now she's accusing Peter? Poor Peter. He's going to think I'm completely nuts. How am I supposed to rescue this situation? Peter looks genuinely upset and hurt.

'Because I loved my sister very much and I would never do anything to hurt her. Josslyn, you have to believe me.'

Alicia doesn't reply with words. Instead, she leans forwards and kisses Peter gently on the lips. I can't help but feel weird knowing that it's not actually me that is kissing him. Not that he knows, of course. It's not his fault, but a part of me is angry and jealous. I know it's stupid, but it hurts that Alicia is so callous with my feelings. I thought twin sisters were supposed to love each other. She has no respect for me, so why should I care about her? I should just cut the bitch out and be done with her. Then I'd be alone in my own body for the first time in over twenty years. Despite my annoyance at Alicia right now that fact keeps playing on my mind. Do I really want to be alone? I always said I was lonely, but I always had her. Without her I would be nothing.

Alicia pulls away from Peter, stroking his arm. 'I am sorry, I should not have done that.' Oh boy, she's too good at playing me. Plus she's also managed to completely change the subject.

Peter shakes his head. 'No, it's fine. I mean ... Josslyn, I just don't want things to get awkward or anything. I just want to find out what happened to Alicia and then ... '

'Urrgg! It always has to be about *her!*' Uh oh. Peter has clearly touched a nerve. 'Can we just not talk about her for one second!'

'You were the one who came to me for help, remember? You want to find her as much as I do. I'm sorry, but she's my sister. She's your sister too.'

'Maybe. Maybe not.'

'What?' Peter looks at Alicia in a strange way. I can feel the tension in the room. It's a mix between sexual and awkward tension, with possibly a bit of hostility too.

'I am just saying that maybe she is not my twin,' snaps Alicia. She is letting her Josslyn mask slide, clearly unable to hide her true self for long. I know she has issues with Alicia. It appears she wants me all to herself, or maybe it's just my body she wants.

'Josslyn, what the fuck! I don't get you right now. One minute you are determined to find Alicia and say she's your sister and the next ... what happened at the hospital? What did the doctor say?'

'It is none of your business.'

'Well maybe it should be. I don't see anyone else around here who cares about you and is worried about you and ...' Alicia kisses him again, shutting him right up. This time it's hard and fast and pretty damn hot.

Peter reacts almost immediately. It seems he isn't that upset with her after all. I am screaming as loud as I can, but no sound is coming out. No one can hear me. I'm still trapped and completely helpless. Alicia is in control, in more ways than one. She knows what she wants and is taking it, just like she did the other night. She says she doesn't like Peter, but clearly she does otherwise why would she keep taking me over and want to have sex with him? I'm so angry, but there's nothing I can do. I'm being forced to watch as Alicia and Peter have hot, sweaty sex on the sofa. I'm begging Alicia to stop, but it makes no use.

Alicia is ruining my life. No, scratch that: Alicia *has* ruined my life. She has done nothing but interfere, judge me, put me down and boss me around. I decide right now that I'm going to do something about it. Now I know that she isn't just a figment of my imagination it means she can be removed from my life for good. All these years I have convinced myself that I have made her up, that I have done this to myself, but she has been there all along, inside me. She may be my identical twin, but she is evil. I know that now. Alicia is no longer my friend.

I must have fallen asleep. I'm very disorientated. It's dark outside, the curtains are drawn, a lamp is on low beside me. I'm in a bed with no memory of how I got here. I hate this. I hate waking up with no memory. It's like being taken over by an alien or something. The doctor was right. She is a parasite, one that needs destroying.

I sit up and stretch. It takes me a few seconds to realise that I am stretching and moving of my own free will. I have my body back! Thank fuck for that! However, yet again, I am naked. I quickly look around and realise that Peter is laying next to me and he is looking directly at me. The sight makes me jump and, to be honest, I feel a little creeped out. How long has he been staring at me?

'Sorry, I didn't mean to make you jump,' he says with a smile.

'Were you watching me sleep?'

'Maybe. You're cute when you sleep.' Uh-huh. I'm not sure what to say to that remark, but I do know I want to get out of this bed as quickly as possible. 'Hang on.' Peter grabs me around the wrist, stopping me from leaving. I wrench my arm away from him.

'I need a shower.'

'Josslyn ... I think we need to talk.'

'No we don't!' I shout out as I run buck naked out of the room and into the bathroom. I slam the door shut and flick the bolt across. Denial. Always works, right?

Wrong.

Alicia! What the fuck is going on? How dare you take me over like that! Why do you keep doing this?

Because it is fun.

Fuck you. You're sleeping with Peter under false pretences. He thinks you're me!

I do not care. I needed to take you over. I needed to find out some things because I knew you would not do it. There is something about Peter that I find ... intriguing.

What do you mean? You never like anyone.

I did not say I like him. I am just saying that I feel a connection with him.

A connection? I'm your identical twin! If you're going to have a connection with someone then it should be me.

Now look who is jealous.

So you admit you're jealous of me.

I admit nothing. I do not feel jealousy or any emotion.

Right, yeah, I forgot. You know Alicia, I'm getting really tired of you. You don't care about anyone other than yourself. You've been a bitch to me my entire life. I'm fed up. Maybe I should have the doctor remove you via surgery.

You would really remove me, the one person who has always been there for you, always offered you advice, always listened to your whining and moaning, who has always kept you company when you were all alone? You would just cut me out? And you call me a heartless bitch.

It's not that I want to do it Alicia, but you've left me no other choice. This is my body and I should be the one who controls it. If you promise to not take me over anymore then you can stay. I would miss you, I won't lie, but I can't live like this anymore. I need to live my own life, even if I make mistakes. I'm sorry, but that's just the way it has to be.

There's a long silence but finally ...

Agreed. I will not take you over again unless you want me to, like it used to be.

You promise?

I promise.

Okay, good, thank you Alicia. Now I just need to sort out this awkward situation with Peter.

A word of warning about him, Josslyn. I do not trust him. He is not what he appears to be.

What does that mean?

I do not know yet, but just ... keep your guard up. I will do whatever I have to do in order to protect you.

Okay, thanks. Will you help me find Alicia?

I still do not see your fascination with her. You know who I am now so why bother with her?

You know why.

Because she is real. Fine, I will help you, but only so you can find out the truth so you can stop wondering where she is. I still think she is dead.

I hope you're wrong.

Chapter Eleven

What a mess I am in. I blame myself (mostly, I mean Alicia deserves some of the blame, let's be honest), but it was my idea to traipse across the country in search of my long-lost twin and track down her adopted brother, sleep with him and develop weird and uncomfortable feelings for him. I've brought all this on myself. Do you ever have those moments where you wish you could go back in time and erase everything you've done to when things were less ... fucked up? Yeah, of course you do, otherwise you wouldn't be human. We all make mistakes. Let's move on.

Now I'm about to go and visit Alicia's ex-boyfriend to question him on her disappearance with no actual proof that he even did anything. Let's face it – maybe she is dead and I'm just trying to convince myself that we will be reunited one day in some wonderful, movie-like moment and everything will be perfect. My life will finally make sense. I won't be alone anymore and things will be fantastic ...

I must seriously be deluded if I think that is ever going to happen. For a start, Alicia (my Alicia) won't ever let it happen. She wants me to herself. There will always be a constant battle going on inside my head, one that no one knows about. It's my secret to keep – my curse, but I just have to know! I can't not know what happened to Alicia. I can't explain it, but I have this overwhelming feeling that something bad happened to her and that my parents aren't telling me the whole truth. They know more. I just know it and once I'm finished here I'm going back home to confront them, hopefully with some sort of evidence to back up my case. That's my plan and I'm sticking to it.

Before I continue I'm sure you're wondering why I have suddenly forgiven Alicia for all the shit she put me through last night. I haven't. Not really, but I have to try and believe that she is on my side. Who else's side would she be on? She needs me as much as I need her. She obviously doesn't trust Peter (I'm not sure why), but I have to honour her feelings (not that she has any). Peter is a nice guy, but even nice guys have secrets. I'm just going to do what she says and keep my guard up around him (and no more sleeping with him!)

Peter and I leave Oscar and Harrison snoozing on the sofa. I feel so guilty leaving Oscar in a strange place, but to be honest, he seems fine with it. I can't ask him directly if he is okay, but I think he gets why I'm doing it. We are best buddies and we always will be. Harrison still doesn't like me (shock horror) and I accidentally surprised him by coming into the kitchen once I'd showered earlier and scared the life out of him. He hissed and ran screeching from the room and straight into a door. He was fine, but Peter did give me a weird look like I had somehow possessed his cat.

In the car ride to Paul's it's all a bit awkward (again). Peter clearly wants to talk to me about something because he keeps glancing over at me for a quick second before turning back to look at the road. He does it several times. I get the hint.

'Look, I'm sorry, okay. Last night was ...' I begin.

'Awesome.'

'Well, yes, you could say it was awesome, but it was a mistake.'

'So that's two mistakes we've made now?'

'Well technically we've done it a lot more times than ... yes, whatever. I don't know what comes over me. It's like ...' Now how do I put this without telling him that my unborn, identical, evil twin takes over my body and it's actually her he's having sex with and not me (for the majority of the time).

'Josslyn, whatever it is you can tell me.'

'No, I really can't. Trust me.'

'How can I trust you when clearly you aren't telling me the truth?'

I do the sulky thing that women are so good at and pretend to look out the window at the surrounding countryside. I can practically hear him rolling his eyes at me.

'Look,' I say finally. 'I just ... can't get into anything right now. It was fun, but ... right now I just want to find out what happened to Alicia and whether or not she's my twin.'

'And once we find out?'

'Then ... if she's my twin then it's weird because you're her brother ...'

'Adopted.'

'Right. And if she isn't then ... you're a stranger and I've fucked up your life enough.'

'Maybe I like having my life fucked up.'

I smile at him. Damn him! He's so hard to resist and stay in a huff with when he's so damn sexy and says such cute things.

'Okay, how about this,' he says. 'Let's find out what happened to Alicia and whether she is your twin. Then afterwards we can have another conversation about us.'

I raise my eyebrows at him. 'Us? Did you really just use the U word?'

'Yep. Deal?'

'Deal.'

'And in the meantime don't go jumping on me again and sending me all these mixed messages and practically attacking me out of the blue. You're the one who is initiating these ... encounters, not me.'

'Encounters? Is that what you call them?'

'Escapades?'

I laugh. 'Just so you know I didn't initiate the escapade last night.' Shit, I shouldn't have said that because he glances over at me in confusion.

'Then who did? It certainly wasn't me.'

'It was my ... hormones.'

Peter laughs. 'Right, well, tell your *hormones* to back off for a while until we get all this straightened out.'

'Will do.'

You hear that Alicia? Hands off!

Trust me, I will not be going near him again.

Finally, we agree on something.

We arrive about twenty minutes later outside a grubby block of flats in a run-down estate. Everything looks dirty, dull and grey, but that might have something to do with the winter weather. Did I mention that I hate winter? Plus, it'll be Christmas soon and that's always fun ... NOT! Don't even get me started on Christmas! It always ends the same way – me getting way too pissed on Prosecco and passing out in my parents' front garden after trying to ride the big reindeer that they put out on display every year. Then dad carries me inside, I usually throw-up and then I get tucked up in bed like a child. So ... yeah, let's not dwell on that.

I have a bad feeling about this. I decide to let Peter do the talking. I don't know Paul after all, so to suddenly have a random girl turn up at his place and accuse him of murdering her possible twin sister is probably not what he needs right now.

I follow Peter up the narrow path to the front door of the building. There's a keypad on the door with all the flat numbers and a button next to each. Even the keypad is grimy and half the numbers are faded almost completely. Peter presses the button for number eighteen and there's a loud buzzing noise that makes me jump.

'Yeah,' comes a rough voice.

'Paul, it's Peter.'

'What the fuck.' A statement rather than a question by the sounds of it.

'I've just come to ask you a few questions, that's all.'

'Yeah, right.'

'Please. It's about Alicia. I'm trying to find out the truth.'

'She killed herself. The end.'

'I don't believe that.'

'I told you I don't know anything. Go away.'

'I just need to ask a few more questions. It's important. Please.' There's a long pause and then finally the buzzing noise sounds again and I hear a loud click from the door. I guess that means he's willing to talk and that we have passed the first barrier.

After climbing four flights of stairs we reach the correct floor. I seriously need to do more cardio. I'm out of shape. Alicia always gets on at me to look after myself more, go to the gym, eat healthy food, but luckily I'm the one in control of this body (mostly) so I choose to sit and drink wine and eat takeaways instead. Once, a few years ago, Alicia took me over for at least three days. I think it was around the time I first bought my practice. During that time she went to the gym every day and when I finally regained control of my body it ached all over and I'd lost five pounds.

Peter knocks on the door to number eighteen and it slowly opens. Paul peers out at us. He is not what I expected at all. I had imagined him being a good-looking young man who dressed smart and took pride in his appearance (I'd just assumed this because Alicia was such a well-dressed, smart individual and had a decent job and therefore she'd want a man who was similar).

The man standing in front of me is nothing like that. For a start he is about forty years old (give or take) and is wearing what I can only describe as the dirtiest t-shirt I've ever seen. If I saw him on the street I would assume that he was homeless, that's how bad he looks ... and smells. He has a full beard and his hair is way overdue for a cut (try a few years overdue).

'Who's she?' he grunts in a harsh voice.

'This is Josslyn, a friend of mine.'

'She looks familiar.'

'I get that a lot,' I say.

Paul then ignores me completely and turns to Peter. 'What do you want to know?'

It looks like we aren't getting an invitation to come inside (not that I want to set a single toenail inside his flat). I can see piles of rubbish and beer cans from the door and it smells like something may be dead inside. Seriously ... Alicia dated this guy? I must be missing something. I can tell by the awkward tension in the air that these two guys don't like each other. I can understand why. I wouldn't want my sister dating some smelly, overweight, older guy who lives in a decrepit cesspool, either.

'We've found some old journals that belonged to Alicia. Did you ever see her writing in them?'

Paul hitches up his trousers and slouches against the doorframe. 'Nope. I never saw no journals.'

'Did she ever mention anything about some strange phone calls that she'd been receiving?'

'Nope.'

'Anything about a possible stalker?'

'Nope.'

Wow, this guy is literally no help whatsoever. What did Peter expect to get from him? I can feel Alicia's frustration and anger building up inside me, but I don't blame her. He is the most annoying man I've ever met.

'Paul, look, I know we haven't exactly seen eye to eye on things, but please, this is important.' Peter sounds desperate.

Paul folds his arms and grunts again. He seems to be thinking about something. 'Okay, yeah, all right, I might know something. I don't know about no journals, but the phone calls ... two nights before she disappeared she was talking to someone on the phone. I didn't hear her much, but she sounded upset. She kept getting called over and over. In the end she turned off her phone and hid it away in a drawer.'

'Did you tell the police about it?'

'Nope, didn't seem important at the time. Probably one of those scams or cold-calling things.'

'Right. Did she say anything about the calls to you?'

'Nope.'

'Did you ask her?'

'Nope.'

I try and hide my impatience as best as I can. I really want to hit Paul right now and I'm not saying that Alicia is making me want to hit him. I want to hit him myself. He is the most infuriating man ever and it seems like he doesn't care about the fact that his ex-girlfriend is missing or even dead.

'I told everything I knew to the police years ago, now bugger off. She's dead. Get over it.'

It appears that we have outstayed our welcome (not that I think we were ever welcome).

'Did you tell them about the argument you and Alicia had the night she disappeared?' continues Peter, clearly ignoring Paul's warning.

'Nope. Did you?'

'Did I what?'

Both men square up to each other and puff out their chests slightly, clearly a sign that things are starting to get a little bit heated. I automatically take a step back in case things kick off. I've never been one to get into fights, not if I can help it. Alicia on the other hand loves a good fight, but I've never been good at defending myself. Maybe I should take up boxing or something.

'Did you tell them about your argument with her?' repeats Paul with a harsh edge to his voice.

'What argument?'

Paul grins and shows his set of stained black teeth. Eewww! 'Don't play dumb with me. Alicia told me all about it.' He turns to me. 'Bet you didn't know your boyfriend here hit his own sister. Yeah, that's right, she came crying to me and told me you'd hit her.'

Peter says nothing, but those words have clearly hit a nerve. Shit, is that true? I can't imagine Peter hitting anyone, let alone his sister.

I told you to be wary of him.

Not now Alicia.

I watch as Peter and Paul stare at each other. I'm not sure which one looks angrier or who is going to speak next. I wish I had the ability to read their minds right now because Peter seriously looks like his mind is on fire. What is he not telling me? Then again, I'm not one to judge, am I?

'Go on,' says Paul in a smug voice, 'tell your girlfriend what really happened the night Alicia disappeared.'

I frown and turn to Peter. 'What did happen? Oh, and I'm not his girlfriend,' I add.

'Nothing,' says Peter through gritted teeth. 'Let's go. This was a waste of time.'

'Yeah, that's right, run away, just try and ignore the fact that your sister was on to you!'

Without warning and within a split second Peter turns and punches Paul square in the face, sending him stumbling backwards against the doorframe. Oh shit. Now that's done it. Paul regains himself pretty quickly and wipes a small amount of blood away from his nose. He lurches forward and takes a swing at Peter, who is too quick and ducks out of the way. He counteracts with another punch to the side of Paul's head – down he goes again with a thud to the floor. Both men start throwing their weight around. At one point Paul has Peter in a headlock, the next second Peter has kicked him off and has him pinned against the wall by his throat. I need to do something or one of them is going to get seriously hurt.

'Stop it!' I yell.

I do not think that is going to work.

Got any better ideas?

Threaten them.

'Stop it or I'm calling the police!' I scream. 'Did you hear me? I'm calling the police!' Both of them suddenly stop fighting. Peter shrugs Paul off and shoves him away, puffing and panting like he has sprinted two hundred metres.

'Josslyn, don't do it,' warns Peter.

'Then stop fucking fighting and tell me the truth.'

Peter holds his hand up to me and nods. 'Okay ... okay, but let's go and talk someplace else.' He wipes blood away from his mouth and starts to pull me towards the stairs leading back down to the ground floor.

'Good luck lady, you're gonna need it,' snarls Paul as he slams his door shut.

Peter practically drags me down the stairs. He has a tight grip on my right arm, so tight in fact that it's beginning to hurt. I keep trying to wrench my arm free but his grip is too strong and he seems intent on getting me out of there as quickly as possible. This doesn't feel right to me. Something is wrong. Something doesn't add up and I get the feeling that Peter is panicking and is scared. He seems lost and on the verge of a complete meltdown.

We get to the car and I finally am able to get his hand off my arm. I back away from him as I yell. 'Start talking Peter. What was that back there?'

Peter points aggressively towards the building. 'That man is nothing but a liar. Don't believe a word he says.'

'Okay, but maybe it's you I shouldn't believe. Why would he have any reason to lie?'

'Why would I have any reason to lie? He was abusing Alicia. I just know it, but I could never get any proof. She always denied it and covered things up, bruises and cuts, but I knew they were there. He's her stalker, I just know it.' Peter is seething. He's practically foaming at the mouth and spitting as he shouts at me. It's like he's turned into a different person. I know what that feels like. I can feel Alicia stirring within me. She's angry too and I momentarily have a sudden urge to grab Peter by the throat and strangle him until the life drains from his body, watch his arms go limp at his sides, watch that redness in his face turn to a ghostly white. I shake it off quickly.

'Say that's true,' I say, trying hard to quash the burning anger that's growing. 'Why would Alicia's own boyfriend at the time stalk her? He already had access to her. Stalkers usually want those they can't have, don't they? Otherwise what's the point?'

Peter takes a deep breath for a moment, clearly trying to calm himself down. 'Maybe he wanted her to be scared and enjoyed watching it.'

I decide to change the subject. 'What happened the night Alicia disappeared? The truth. Did you hit her?'

Peter frowns. 'You know what happened. I told you the night we met.'

'Tell me again.'

'Let's go back to mine ...'

'Tell me now or I'm not getting back in the car with you.'

Peter looks frantic, like he wants to explode. I feel as if I'm in danger and my guard is definitely up. He runs his hands through his hair (still managing to pull off the sexy look even though he looks like he wants to kill me) and takes a deep breath. He finally begins.

'Alicia and I had planned to go out to a club for ages to catch up and have a bit of fun. She was stressed at work, so was I. We hadn't been able to see each other or spend much time together for a while because of work and things going on in our lives, so we thought we'd have a night out together to let off some steam, get wasted, whatever.

'She rang me at two o'clock that day. We weren't due to meet at the pub – that's where we were gonna start from – until nine that night. She sounded a bit weird and said she had to cancel because she had somewhere else to be. I got angry with her because we'd had this night planned for a while and she was bailing on me and wouldn't tell me the proper reason why. Anyway, finally I managed to convince her to come out as planned, but she said she'd meet me at the club at about eleven o'clock instead. I agreed.

'She arrived at the club just after eleven and was wearing a hell of a lot of make-up, more than usual. I know that's what girls usually do when they go out, but she was also hiding the left side of her face by covering it up with her hair as much as possible. I thought maybe Paul had hit her again, but I didn't ask her about it. I just wished she would tell me about it herself. We had a few drinks, we danced, had a few more drinks. She said she was going to the ladies' room. I said I'd be at the bar with another drink. She said she'd see me in a bit ... and that was the last time I saw her. I started to get worried after about ten minutes when she didn't return and after twenty minutes I asked a female bouncer to check the ladies' room. She said she wasn't in there. I searched around the club, but she was nowhere to be seen. Her jacket hadn't been checked out of the coat room.

'I called the police just after one in the morning. That was when the investigation started and eventually the note was found in her flat. All of her stuff was still there and everything was neat and tidy. It was almost immediately deemed a suicide and the case was closed a few weeks later.'

Peter finishes his story and looks at me intently, probably able to see the suspicion on my face.

'That's the story Josslyn, I swear. Paul is just trying to pin the blame on me. I never hit her. He had this idea that I was abusing Alicia and she committed suicide to finally get away from me, but I think she ran away from him, to get away from him because she was scared. Please, you have to believe me. I'd never hurt my sister. I loved her. I still love her. Please ... please.'

I feel so confused right now. I don't know who to believe. I want to believe Peter, I do, but there's this nagging feeling (also known as Alicia) inside me that just won't accept his story. I don't know Paul (in fact I don't know Peter either) and I want nothing more than to nod and say that I believe him, but I don't. I just stare at him for what seems like an eternity until he finally says, 'Do you believe me?'

I sigh. 'I don't know.'

'Okay, fine, you don't believe me, but I bet I know how to make you. We need to search his place and I promise you I'll find proof that he was the one abusing her.'

'Are you serious? He won't let us in after what you just did to him.'

'No, that's why we're going to wait here until he leaves.'

'And break in? Are you crazy?'

'It's the only way I know how to make you trust me. I'll find proof and then we'll find out what happened to Alicia once and for all.'

I can't help but roll my eyes at him. It's a juvenile move I know, but honestly he's being so ridiculous. Who does he think I am? I'm not a law breaker. I don't do things like this!

'Fine! I believe you, you happy?'

'No, you don't.'

'Okay, no I don't. I don't know you, Peter!' I shout. My anger is starting to rise again, but it feels so damn good so I just allow it and go with the flow. 'I don't know you! You're a stranger to me. For all I know you killed your own sister and buried her body somewhere.' I may have shouted that last bit a little too loud. The words echo around the car park and the surrounding buildings.

'I can't believe you just said that.' Peter sounds genuinely hurt.

'I'm sorry, I didn't mean that.' Maybe I went a bit too far.

'Yes, you did. You know Josslyn, you can stand there and accuse me all you like of not telling the truth, but you're lying too. You lied to me the first time you entered my house and you've been hiding things from me this whole time, like about the fact you have something medically wrong with you. That pain you experienced is not just from low blood sugar and stress. You're lying about the fact that for some reason you seem to turn into a completely different person whenever we have sex and you're lying to yourself about not having feelings for me.'

'I do not have feelings for you,' I state, my voice much quieter than it had been a few seconds ago.

'There you go again. Lying to me. You're hiding something. Admit it.'

'Are you seriously trying to turn this all on me? This is about you, not me.'

Peter suddenly moves towards me and pins me against the side of the car. The wing mirror is wedged into my back, which is quite painful. His body is pressed very closely against mine and I can feel his hot, sweet breath on my face. Part of me is raging with anger, but the other part is seriously turned on. I have another mental flash of kicking him in the groin and then grabbing the nearest hard object (which happens to be a cinder block) and smashing his head into a pulp, watching as his brain gets smashed into the concrete and blood splashes over myself and the car. The next second I imagine straddling him on the car bonnet, ripping his jeans off and riding him like my life depends on it. I close my eyes tight shut, refusing to look at him.

'Tell me the truth, Josslyn,' says Peter in a calm, controlled tone. 'What are you hiding?'

My eyes fling open. I am no longer me. I am Alicia, but it's only for a few seconds, just long enough for her to say, '*Get the fuck off her or I will kill you.*'

Her voice is hard, unwavering and I'm pretty certain that Peter can tell that it's not me who just spoke. My tone of voice is different, my body language is different and he knows, I'm sure he does, but he doesn't say anything else. He slowly backs off me and steps away.

Chapter Twelve

Alicia says what she has to say and then I'm back in control. Peter is looking at me with a confused look on his face. He has, luckily, backed away from me and it's a good job he did because I have a feeling that Alicia was ready to kill him. I don't get her. One minute she's scratching his back in the heat of passion and the next she's ready to choke the life out of him. I guess that's what psychopaths are like. One thing is for sure – she is very unpredictable right now, which makes her dangerous.

I stand up straight so that I am away from the car. It still hurts where the wing mirror was jammed into my back. 'Look ... let's just ... take a moment and think about this.'

Peter nods, but doesn't say anything. He looks a little shaken to be honest and a bit white in the face, like he's seen a ghost or something that has really frightened him. I reach out my hand to touch him to show that everything is okay, but he moves away from me.

'I promise to tell you everything soon,' I say quietly. 'But this isn't about me right now. Or you. This is about Alicia and finding out what happened to her, so can we please just put everything else aside for the time being and focus on her?'

Peter nods again and clears his throat. 'Yes, of course. I'm sorry ... Josslyn.' (Is it just me or did he say my name in a really weird way?) 'But please can you trust me about Paul? Let me prove to you that he did something bad to Alicia. We need to look in his place for evidence.'

'If we do that we're breaking the law, Peter.'

'I know, but ... I just have to know, and so do you. Aren't you willing to do anything to find out the truth?' Damn him. Yes, I am, but I wasn't expecting to be breaking into someone's home. I have standards.

Do you really?

Yes!

Get over yourself and just do it.

It seems Alicia has no issues with breaking rules.

'Okay, yes,' I say reluctantly, 'but I don't know anything about breaking and entering.'

'Well, the first thing we need to do is to make sure he's out when we do it.' His attempt at a joke to break the tension makes me smile. He smiles back. 'Come on, I'm gonna move the car so he can't see it and we'll wait for him to leave. No doubt he'll run out of beer soon.'

'It's eleven in the morning.'

'Exactly.'

Peter manoeuvres the car so it's out of sight from the front of the building, but we can just about see the front doors and the car park. If Paul leaves, we'll see him. I hope there isn't a back door to the building, otherwise we're stuffed.

We settle down and watch and wait. We don't have the radio on, nor the heating as we can't risk Paul hearing the running car when he comes out, so not only are we sat in an awkward silence, but we're also freezing our asses off. What a perfect situation to be in!

So many things pop into my mind it's difficult to make sense of them. I can feel Peter's burning questions being seared into the side of my head as he looks at me, but he keeps quiet as is the deal. We have to work together on this. He needs me and I need him. We both want the same thing at the end of the day. It's just that ... well, neither of us trust the other, that's perfectly clear. I think the chance of he and I having sex again is out the window (not that I was thinking about having sex with him, of course). He also seems scared of me now thanks to Alicia threatening to kill him if he touched me. It's actually a relief that he doesn't want to come near me because I still want to kill him and jump him at the same time. These conflicting feelings are very inappropriate.

After what seems like hours (time really drags when you're on a stake-out) Paul finally emerges from his rat-infested home. His left eye is bruised and swollen from Peter's fist impact and he's hunched over like he is in pain. He's holding a beer bottle, which he quickly chugs the dregs from and then throws against the building wall. He is clearly drunk, but that doesn't stop him from wedging himself behind the wheel of his beat-up old car, turning on the ignition and driving off, swerving to avoid a road sign. Looks like the coast is clear.

'Let's go.'

Peter gets out of the car. I follow him, nervously glancing around, convinced that someone is watching us, but I'm pretty sure that's just my paranoid brain giving me grief. I'm not a criminal. I've never done anything against the law (Alicia on the other hand ... let's not go there), but the point is I've not done anything *knowingly* illegal and this is definitely making me nervous. Okay, so there was this one time while I was at university when I stole this girl's bag because she was being mean to me. It had all her notes and work in it. I guess that wasn't technically illegal, but it was a horrible thing to do, even though I did feel pretty smug when she failed her exam. I'm not really making myself look any better here, am I?

I think Peter can tell I'm nervous because he takes over everything and fumbles around in his pocket for a piece of thin metal, which he just so happens to have on him. Yes, it's suspicious, but as per our deal I hold my tongue and just allow him to work even though I want to ask him why he is carrying around the perfect tool to break into someone's home. He fiddles with the lock on Paul's front door for a few seconds before it suddenly pops open. I raise my eyebrows, both impressed at his skill and concerned at the ease with which he has just accomplished it. He smiles at me, looking all cute and innocent.

Oh dear God, the smell in this flat is just horrendous. I immediately gag, unable to control the reflex, but quickly compose myself.

'Seriously Peter, what did Alicia see in this guy?' I cover my nose and mouth in the hopes that it will help; it does not.

'Don't even get me started, but to be fair to him back then he wasn't such a loser. He was actually a decent looking and well-dressed man with a good job. He used to be married, but he divorced his wife a year or so before meeting Alicia. They met at some fancy law function and hit it off, but things went bad at his law firm I think, and he lost the company a lot of money. They fired him, then Alicia disappeared and I guess he's just a depressed alcoholic now.'

'I guess that explains it a bit, but still ... who can live like this?'

'Why don't you start looking in the bedroom? I'll check the lounge area.'

'Do I have to?' I moan as I pick my way over piles of soiled washing, empty beer bottles, cans and numerous dirty plates, as well as rubbish. I'm trying to place each foot directly onto the floorboards rather than onto something else, but there is barely any clear floorboards left.

I watch Peter disappear down the end of the hallway and into the lounge. I can see the bedroom just off to the left so I slowly make my way over there. The sight makes me cringe. More piles of dirty clothes, an unmade bed with bedding so dirty it probably hasn't been washed in years and piles of porno magazines. I shudder with disgust, but immediately get to work searching the room because the sooner we find something the sooner we can get the hell out of this hellhole.

I don't even know what I'm looking for and I'm not wearing any gloves to protect myself from the filth (or to stop from leaving any fingerprints) so I'm as careful as I can be when I move things. I'm pretty sure Paul wouldn't notice if something wasn't where he had left it, so I don't bother picking up the pile of dirty socks that tumble down off the chair in the corner when I accidentally knock into it.

After five minutes of searching I decide that there's nothing of interest in the bedroom. Although I did find a few pictures of Paul and Alicia back when they were together. Paul has his arm around her shoulders and they are staring into each other's eyes, smiling. They look happy together. I immediately feel a pang of sympathy for Paul having lost someone he obviously cared about, but I suppose photos can be deceiving. Behind Alicia's smile was a secret and sadness and I am determined to find out what happened to her. I feel I owe her that much.

I haven't heard from Peter yet, but every now and then I can hear a cupboard door opening and shutting and his feet scuffing on the floor. I decide to go and join him.

'Any luck?' I ask.

'Not yet, but I haven't checked that TV cabinet yet or that side of the room. Do you mind?' Peter nods in the general direction. I glance at the TV. It's at least forty inches, flat-screen with surround sound.

'He may live like a slob, but he clearly has money to afford a TV that size.'

'Or he stole it.'

'You really don't like him, do you?'

'Nope.'

Peter returns to searching the pile of rubbish on a small table. I pick my way over to the cabinet and open it. Inside are various papers, DVDs, random cables (everyone has random cables somewhere in their house, right?) and also books. I pull a load of papers out, briefly glancing at a few, but they are mostly bills and dirty magazines. A lot of the bills are overdue, but then something catches my eye. It's right at the back of the cabinet and I would have missed it had I not spotted the glint from the shiny clasp holding the pages together.

It's a journal.

I pull it out. It's fairly new, not well-worn; the date on the front is 2014. My heart suddenly does a few flips in my chest as I open it. Oh my God ... it's Alicia's missing journal from the year she disappeared. It has her handwriting inside. It's unmistakably hers. I excitedly begin to flip through the pages, unsure what I'm about to find, but I certainly don't expect to find a birth certificate. It's folded neatly between two pages. As I open it I scan it quickly. It's ... mine.

Josslyn Marie Daniels

Born on 31st of May 1991 at 15:02

At Salisbury hospital

Mother: Jane Daniels – Father: Unknown

Wait ... this is ... my original birth certificate before I was adopted. What in God's holy name is it doing in Paul's flat? I've never even met the guy! He did say I looked familiar when he saw me, but it didn't seem like he knew who I was. That is my first thought. The next sudden realisation hits me with a thud to the chest – I'm staring at my mum's name. My *real* mum's name. No, stop it Josslyn. Amanda Reynolds is your real mum. She raised you, cared for you, fed you, nursed your illnesses and gave you unconditional hugs.

Jane Daniels. The name means nothing to me. She's a stranger, but something inside me is drawn to the name and I can't stop staring at it. It's sucking me in. I wonder what she was like, what she looked like, where she lived. Why didn't she want Alicia and I? Was she a young teenage mum being forced to give us up by her pushy parents or were we a mistake that she had to rectify? Despite the fact that I don't know her, I wish I knew the answers to these questions. I've always wanted to know the ins and outs of everything (in case you didn't know that already). I feel incomplete and lost if I have unanswered questions floating around in my head.

My original name is Josslyn Marie Daniels. That sounds so weird. She's a complete stranger to me as well. I wonder if I would have turned out differently had our mum kept us. Who would Josslyn Marie Daniels be now? My eyes brim with tears as I stare at one of the most important pieces of paper I have ever held. Then I realise something else – something that is extremely important to our search for Alicia. My pre-adoption birth certificate was in Alicia's journal, which means that despite the journal now being in Paul's possession, Alicia once owned it. She had my birth certificate. She *knew* about me. I'm momentarily stunned and I struggle to take some deep breaths.

'P-Peter?' I stutter weakly. I start flicking through the journal while he joins me.

'Oh my God! Is that ...'

'Alicia's missing journal ... yeah. I also found this.' I show him my birth certificate. He stares at it, studies it, then the truth dawns on him.

'What the fuck? Is this yours?'

'Apparently. It was in the journal, which I found in there.' I nod towards the TV cabinet. 'Peter ...' I turn to him slowly. 'Alicia knew about me.'

'Shit,' he said. 'Also ... is that the time of your birth?' He points to the time next to the date.

'I guess so,' I answer. 'Why?'

'Alicia was born at 15:05 on the 31st of May 1991. I mean, the time of birth isn't on her post-adoption birth certificate but Mum told us the time she was born.'

'So I'm the oldest,' I say, more of a statement rather than a question. 'So there's no doubt. We're twins.'

'I guess so. Also, only twins have the time of birth on their birth certificate. Just one of those random facts I've picked up over the years. Are you okay?'

'Yeah.' That's all I say because the truth is, I don't know if I'm okay. The fact is that Alicia knew about me, but yet we never met, so something happened to her before she was able to track me down. That is, if she was planning on tracking me down. Maybe she found out about me, but didn't care. It was possible, but something was telling me that that wasn't the case. If Alicia knew she had a twin she would want to find me, I'm sure of it.

'Can we get out of here now?' I ask. The smell is beginning to make me feel nauseous and I want to be able to read Alicia's journal without the fear of Paul walking in and finding us.

'Of course, let's go. I think the journal should hold the answers we need.'

I clutch the journal and birth certificate close against my chest as we leave. I can't bear to even hand them over to Peter. The moment I get into the car I immediately open it and start reading the few pages at the end, several days before she stopped writing and disappeared.

10 June 2014 – I keep getting these random calls. My stalker is becoming even more obsessed with me. This morning before work I found a note on my car that says 'I love you.' I asked Paul about it and he said it wasn't him. The handwriting looks familiar. I think I've seen it before.

11 June 2014 – Peter and I had an argument today. We have arranged a night out to catch up in a few days. He keeps wanting to see me, but I don't want to see him. The last time we saw each other we argued. We always seem to argue these days. He keeps telling me that Paul is bad for me, but I love Paul. He's a decent man, but Peter is driving him away by being jealous and overbearing. I need to tell him to stop and give me some space. I know Peter loves me and he is my brother, but ...

I turn the page but there is nothing on the other side relating to the end of that sentence. There are torn shreds of paper attached to the inside spine of the journal.

Someone has ripped out a page from it. The next page has a new date, so I read on.

14 June 2014 – I don't really know how write this. I can barely believe it myself. I think I have a sister. A twin sister. I received an anonymous package this morning and inside was a birth certificate. Her name is Josslyn Daniels and she was born only three minutes ahead of me. I've never seen my original pre-adoption birth certificate, but I'm almost certain that we are twins. I have to meet her. I have to know. I don't know who sent me the package, but I don't care. I'm not going to tell Mum or Dad and definitely not Peter. I can't believe it. I'm so excited but also nervous. I've looked her up online. She is Josslyn Reynolds now and she lives in Ringwood. I'm going to leave tomorrow, but I need to cancel my plans to see Peter. He won't be happy, but I can't wait any longer.

15 June 2014 – I'm packed and ready to leave, but Peter has convinced me to meet him later tonight. I'll have to leave tomorrow morning instead. He wasn't as angry as I expected. He said he was going to come over and pick me up and then we'd go to a pub and then clubbing. I haven't been clubbing in years. I feel far too old now, but Peter has always been a party boy.

I'm so scared right now. I think there was someone outside my house. I saw a dark shape outside my window. It looked like a person, a man. I think I'm being watched.

Another phone call. This time I heard the man speak. It was a distorted voice and I didn't recognise it. He said he was going to kill me. I have to leave tonight. I'm not going to tell Peter. I'm just going to leave as soon as I can get away from him. I feel like I'm in danger.

I turn the page but there's no more writing. The page is empty, like an unfinished novel; it's infuriating. Those were her last words that she wrote in her journal. *I feel like I'm in danger.* I stare at them, each one burning into my brain. I glance over the rest of the paragraph and one word stands out from the rest: *Kill.* Someone said they were going to kill her. Is this person the same person who has been calling me? Come to think of it, I haven't received a weird phone call since I've been here. Not that I'm counting on getting one of course, but who would want Alicia dead? Was it really Paul? He did have her journal and my birth certificate in his flat, after all. It's pretty damn suspicious. Where else would he have got them from if not from Alicia herself? I doubt she would have willingly given them to him. She would have taken them with her so that she could show me the birth certificate. Another horrible thought suddenly hits me ... Alicia never found me. Therefore ... she must be dead. I turn to Peter.

'Find anything?' he asks me. He has been driving us back to his place while I have been reading the journal.

'Yeah ... I think Alicia is dead.'

'Why would you think that?'

'She found out about me. She writes that she was going to find me and was going to leave that night, the night she disappeared, but she got a phone call from a man who said he was going to kill her. She never found me, Peter. I never met her.'

Peter doesn't reply, clearly not willing to accept this news. 'Are you sure?'

'I think I would remember if some random woman showed up and said she was my long-lost twin.'

'But you've had blackouts before. When we slept together you said you didn't remember it. Maybe you blacked out again.'

Holy shit! He's right. Alicia!

Alicia ... did you meet her? Did she make it to see us?

Yes, I met her.

Oh my God. You did it. You killed her, didn't you?

Alicia doesn't answer me, but she doesn't have to for me to know the answer. My whole body suddenly turns icy cold and I start to severely shake all over. Pressure starts to build up inside my head and my heart feels like it's sandwiched between two heavy iron slabs. I can't catch my breath. I think I'm having a panic attack.

Luckily Peter has just pulled up into his parking space and is able to get out, run around to the side door and open it, letting in the cool, crisp air, but it's not enough and it doesn't help. The air burns my lungs and feels like thousands of tiny needles in my throat. I'm gasping for breath, but it's gone. I'm going to die. I know it. It's all I can think about. That and the fact that I killed my own twin sister without actually realising I was doing it.

I can hear Peter's calming voice somewhere in the background, but I can't seem to focus on it straight away. His voice gets louder and louder; eventually it's ringing in my ears.

'Josslyn! Josslyn! Breathe! Just breathe!'

I grab his arms and squeeze them as tight as I can. I lock my gaze with his as he reminds me over and over to breathe. I'm probably cutting off the circulation in his arms, but if I am he doesn't try to loosen my grip.

It seems like hours later that I'm finally able to draw sweet oxygen into my lungs, but it still hurts. Everything hurts, but things are starting to come back into focus. My head stops spinning, the weight from my chest is releasing and I start to see things clearly again.

'Josslyn, are you okay? Was that a panic attack or the same pain you had before?'

'P-panic ...' but that is all I can get out. Any words that come into my mind are completely lost by the time I open my mouth. Peter seems to understand and just nods.

'Put your head between your legs. I've heard it's supposed to help.'

I do as he says and close my eyes while my head is dangling upside down. I attempt to steady my breathing by doing that thing I learnt in yoga (the one time I went). Breathe in for three and out for three. In through the nose and out through the mouth.

I'm interrupted by Oscar who is trying his hardest to jump on me and lick my face. I hear Peter come running over.

'Sorry, he escaped between my legs when I opened the door. I went to get you some water.'

I start laughing weakly as Oscar plants wet, sloppy doggy kisses on my face. He is yapping with excitement and squealing like a little pig. At least he still loves me, despite all the horrible, unimaginable things I've done. Then Oscar decides that he's showered me with enough love and wanders off towards my parked car, which is just behind Peter's. He cocks his leg on the wheel. I'm still sat on the passenger side seat so I get up slowly and watch Oscar, keeping an eye on him to make sure he doesn't stray into the road. He doesn't. In fact, after his pee, he makes a beeline directly for the back of my car and starts sniffing around. Ah, I know what he wants. I always keep a few dog toys in the boot in Oscar's emergency doggy bag. It's got a bowl, treats, toys and spare food, as well as a bottle of water. I guess he deserves a toy after all he has been through over the past few days. He's been left alone in a strange house with a moody cat while I've left him to hang out with another human. I owe him.

I struggle to my feet and shuffle over to the back of my car. I always keep my car keys in my coat pocket so I pull them out and click the car open. Oscar is jumping up and down with excitement because he knows what's happening. I open the car boot and am met by a wall of stench so bad that I automatically gag. There's a large object in the boot of my car wrapped in a tarpaulin. Without even looking inside I can tell what it is. It's a body.

My day is just getting better and better.

Chapter Thirteen

Alicia

Hello. Yes, it is me. I am sure you have a million questions for me again, but I cannot answer them all. Not right now. It is still not the right time.

The first thing I will say is that Josslyn is safe. She is sleeping. I took her over in the hospital because she pissed me off. How dare she say I am not real. I am more real to her than anyone else. I need to find out some information and to do that I need her body. I enjoy being able to talk and move like a normal human being. I hate being cooped up inside her.

Rather than explain what happened when I took her over in the hospital (as you already know what happened), I thought I would tell you a story. The story of how I met Alicia – the other Alicia. I feel like you should know what happened so you can understand why I did what I did. You may not like me. You may think I made the wrong decision, but I stand by my actions and I would do it again if I had to. That bitch was going to cause trouble and get in my way and, as you already know, if something or someone gets in my way then I remove them. Nothing and no one was going to stop me from carrying out my overall plan.

Let me take you back six years to the year 2014 on the 16th of June when Alicia Phillips walked into our lives out of the blue.

Josslyn had just moved into her flat above her vet practice, except it was not a business yet. It was an empty shell of a building, run down and mouldy in places. I had severely disagreed with her about buying it because I knew it would ruin her eventually. She was in thousands of pounds worth of debt already because of going to university, but now she was adding to that debt by getting an enormous loan to buy this dilapidated pile of bricks. I had not been able to change her mind and she had signed away her life in a matter of seconds. Her father had agreed to help her renovate the building to a state good enough to set up her vet business, but at the time it had just been her and me; not even Oscar was around at the time. He appeared a few months later.

We were standing in the middle of the room, which would eventually be the reception area. It was a blank canvas, dusty and dirty. Loose bricks were piled in one corner. A broken table was wedged against the left wall and the front door was practically disintegrating before our eyes, but Josslyn had a huge smile across her face and was explaining to me exactly where everything was going to be once she and her father had finished decorating. She planned to open her practice in two months' time. She had a lot of work to do, but she seemed determined. I knew Josslyn very well, better than she knew herself. I knew she would do absolutely everything possible to make this small business a success. I could not doubt her enthusiasm. I had never seen her this fired up about anything before.

Now, before I go any further, I must tell you that I already knew about Alicia Phillips and who she was, so when Josslyn saw her briefly out of the corner of her eye (too briefly to make a lasting memory) I immediately recognised her. I shall reveal how I knew about her another time. Be patient.

Alicia was walking towards the building from across the street. I reacted instinctively and immediately. I took

Josslyn over. She did not even know what had hit her. One second she was explaining how the reception desk would run along the left wall and the next she was asleep, never to remember a single moment of what happened next. I felt it best that she did not know about the woman walking towards me with her bouncy blonde hair and perfect smile. This stranger did not deserve to know us and would only complicate our lives, so I did what was best for the both of us.

Alicia stopped outside the building and peered through the open door. 'Hi,' she said nervously. 'I'm sorry to disturb you.'

I did my best to put on a polite smile even though I was seething inside. How dare she come here. 'Not at all. What can I do for you? Come in.'

Alicia stepped across the threshold and glanced around at the mess. 'Have you just bought this place?'

'Yes, I have.' She did not need to know any more than that. I decided to keep my answers as brief as possible. The whole time I was planning on how I was going to get rid of her. I never meant to kill her, not at first, but she was determined to put her nose in where it did not belong – my life. I did not need her. I did not need anybody, not even Josslyn.

'It looks like a bit of a do-er up-er,' she said with a laugh.

'Nothing I cannot handle. Now who are you?' I decided to play dumb. I, of course, knew perfectly well who she was. I was aware that I was coming off as slightly rude, but this was no time for niceties, nor sisterly bonding.

'I'm so sorry,' stuttered Alicia. 'I – I don't really know how to put this without sounding like a complete crazy person.' She fiddled with her hair, a nervous trait that I had often seen Josslyn do. 'My name is Alicia Phillips. That's my adopted name. I think my original name was Alicia Daniels. I was born on the 31st of May 1991 at 15:05. I was adopted and I believe I had a twin sister and we were separated at birth. I have this ...' Alicia fumbled around in her handbag, pulled out a birth certificate and handed it to me.

I glanced at it and saw that it belonged to Josslyn Daniels. I frowned and returned it to her, not even reacting to the certificate at all. 'You are mistaken. My name is Josslyn Reynolds. I am not adopted.'

'Are you sure?'

'Perfectly.'

Alicia looked severely disappointed. I can only assume that she was hoping that we would meet, find out that we were long-lost twin sisters, hug, cry and then become best friends, but that did not happen; nor was it ever going to happen.

'But ... I'm sure it's you. We have the same birthday. We were only born three minutes apart.'

'A strange coincidence,' I stated bluntly.

'But ...'

'Listen, Alicia. My parents would never lie to me for my entire life. They would never hide something like this from me. I am not your long-lost twin sister. Now, please leave or I will have to remove you.'

Alicia opened her mouth to speak, but then abruptly closed it when I glared at her and took a step towards her. She shuffled back towards the door.

'I-I'm sorry to have wasted your time,' she whimpered, as tears began to fill her eyes. 'Please ... just take my number in case ...' She did not finish her sentence as she nervously handed me a business card.

I took it from her and watched as she exited the building, glancing back over her shoulder one last time before she disappeared from sight. I took a deep breath.

'Oh Alicia, you are not going to give up, are you?' I said to myself. 'Why did you have to come here.' It was a statement, not a question.

I glanced around the room and spied a claw hammer laying in the pile of tools Josslyn's father had brought over. I picked it up and walked outside, following the route that Alicia had taken. She had walked down the street and then turned left down a smaller side alley – no doubt her car was parked down there somewhere. I spotted her hurriedly walking towards it, her heels clicking on the concrete. She was about to open her car door when I shouted.

'Alicia, wait!'

Her face transformed from a tear-stained mess to a relieved, beaming smile. The poor, pathetic creature. I just wanted her to feel some sort of happiness, like there was a chance for us to be sisters, before I snapped the claw hammer across her pretty face. Her jawbone exploded, her teeth shattered and she fell to the ground at my feet, groaning. I looked around, but there was no one to be seen. That part of the town was very quiet and not overlooked either. There she was, bleeding at my feet. She was not dead, but she was in a great deal of pain and close to passing out. I bent down, grabbed a fist full of her pretty blonde hair and pulled her face so she could see me. She could not talk, merely able to make some spluttering and choking noises. Her eyes were wide with fear and pain. I revelled in it.

'Dear Alicia,' I said calmly, as I stared at her in her bright blue eyes, which slowly widened in shock and fear as I spoke. 'If only you had not come to find me. You may not know this, in fact, there is no way you would know this, but I am not Josslyn. Yes, I am in her body, but I am not her. My name is Alicia. I am the real Alicia. You are nothing. You should have never been born. I should have been born, but alas, I was not. You and Josslyn were the strong ones and I was left to be absorbed. That was a big mistake. For now, I have a plan to become whole again. I must bide my time and be patient. What is that saying? Good things come to those who wait. I will wait, Alicia, but you will be gone. You will not stop me.

'You may be wondering how I came to find out about you when you have only just recently found out about me. I have always known about you, ever since I could think for myself. I could sense you. I knew you were out there. I was hoping you would have the good sense to stay away. You were not a threat to me, not until today. Silly girl. Now look what has happened. You are about to die and Josslyn and I are free to live our lives. Goodbye, Alicia.'

And then I snapped her neck.

I worked quickly after that. I loaded her dead weight into the back of her car and picked up the keys from the ground, which she had dropped when her jaw smashed open. There was some blood on the pavement, but not too much to arouse suspicion. I would come back and deal with it later. The body must disappear forever and I knew the perfect place to lay it to rest.

Forty minutes later I stopped Alicia's car in a tiny lay-by on the narrow road through the woods. I managed to get the car only one hundred metres from her final destination: My Place. Yes, I had gone back to where it had all started. The hollow tree where Josslyn first encountered me seemed like such a poetic place to bury Alicia's dead body. No one would think to look for it there. She would be alone forever to decompose and be absorbed by the earth, just the way it should have always been.

I managed to drape Alicia over my right shoulder and started to make my way slowly over the uneven ground and through the thick trees towards My Place. She was heavy and I struggled to keep my legs from buckling. I told Josslyn over and over that she should go to the gym and lift weights, to get stronger, fitter, but she was fucking lazy and weak. If this was my body I would train it to be strong, healthy and fit.

Finally, I staggered towards the tree and dumped her on the ground, relieved to be free of her crushing weight on my shoulder. I was out of breath and out of shape, but I quickly composed myself and jogged back to the car to fetch the claw hammer and a shovel, which I had also taken from Ronald's tool collection.

I began to dig at the base of the tree, which was surprisingly easy due to its rotten roots and soft earth. I needed to ensure the hole was fairly deep though, so I spent at least an hour digging to ensure it was suitable. I did not want it to rain and the earth to melt away and reveal her rotting corpse. It did not look like this tree was visited by any children anymore to be used as a den, but I could not take that risk. The hole ended up nearly five feet deep and was almost directly under the old tree roots, in an empty cavern which had eroded away over the years.

Alicia's final resting place was eventually ready. I dragged her body towards the hole, manoeuvred her over the entrance and then shoved her inside with one good kick. She landed in an awkward heap, her limbs twisted unnaturally and her head lolled backwards at an angle. Her eyes were still open, lifeless and bloodshot, no longer the pretty blue they once were. I covered her over forever with shovel after shovel of dirt until she was completely gone and all that was left was a patch of earth at the base of the old tree.

I was exhausted, not just from carrying her and digging her grave, but also from holding back Josslyn. She was pushing against me, even though she would not be aware of it. I needed to sort things out, tidy up and change my clothes. I was filthy, sweaty, and blood-stained. I also needed to get rid of Alicia's car. I knew of a massive reservoir about ten miles away, which would be suitable to dump it in, but that would have to wait. I drove back to the flat, parked the car at the back of the building in an unused car park and went upstairs to have a bath in Josslyn's bathroom.

The hot soapy water soothed my sore body as I gently lowered myself into the tiny tub. The water was so hot it made my skin develop goose bumps, just for a few seconds, before it gradually became used to the temperature. The blood and dirt was slowly being erased from my skin, the grime floating on the surface of the water, which was dull pink from the blood. I relaxed and closed my eyes, enjoying the silence and the solitude. For once I was myself and I did not have Josslyn's annoying voice in my head. This was my body now for as long as I could keep it.

To my surprise I was able to hold Josslyn at bay for nearly three days, which was enough time to send Alicia's car to the bottom of the ravine and clean up the side street where I had smashed her jaw to pieces. The claw hammer and the shovel were cleaned and returned to Ronald's tool kit. I enjoyed the irony.

I, of course, had to spend those days pretending to be Josslyn. After over twenty years of living inside her head I believed I knew her well enough to convince people I was her. Her parents were none the wiser, but eventually she pushed back and returned to her body, complaining at how much she ached, which was partly due to digging the grave and partly due to visiting a gym a few times. She had even lost a few pounds, which she was grateful for, but soon piled it on again by devouring takeaway after takeaway.

So, there you have it. The story of how Alicia disappeared forever. You may be thinking that there is more to this story, and you would be correct. You may be wondering who sent Alicia the birth certificate. I believe that story can wait, for I now have more pressing matters to attend to.

I am currently laying in bed next to Peter who is sleeping soundly after what I can only describe as ferocious sex. Yes, even psychopaths can enjoy sex. Not the intimate type, but I cannot deny that I do not enjoy the feeling of control and domination. Peter did not put up a fight. He appears to like being dominated by me.

I glance down at his sleeping figure. He is completely naked, laying on his back, the bed sheet covering his sizeable modesty. I watch as his chest moves slowly up and down and fantasize about straddling him and choking the life out of him, feeling as his body stops writhing beneath me. I know it would not be possible. Peter is strong, much stronger than I. He would overpower me, but the thought is enough to satisfy me for the time being.

Peter intrigues me. I have mentioned this before, but there is something about him that I do not trust. I hope I can convince Josslyn to be wary of him, but she seems infatuated with him. I wish I could tell you why I do not trust him, but I cannot. I do not trust anyone, but Peter is different and I am unwilling to believe anything he says. I am sure the time will come when I find out the truth, but for now I must bide my time. I am tired of waiting, but it will be worth it in the end. I am sure of this.

I push back the bed sheet and walk naked into the en-suite, switching on the light. I look at the body I am using in the mirror. Josslyn, despite her love of wine and takeaways, is still in decent shape. She does carry a bit of body fat in the usual places and she is not strong. I long for a fit, strong figure with muscle and curves. I study the body in the mirror, feeling the soft skin underneath my fingertips, running them over a few tattoos that I can see.

I hear Peter stirring behind me. He comes into the en-suite, all sleepy-eyed and drowsy and stands behind me, gently stroking my body.

'You are beautiful,' he whispers into my ear. I resist the urge to grab his cut-throat razor which is laying tantalisingly on the sink and stab it into his jugular and watch as his blood spurts all over me and the walls.

I smile at his reflection in the mirror. 'Thank you,' I reply.

'What are you doing up?' he asks, nuzzling my neck.

'I had a bad dream.'

'What was it about?' The truth was that I dreamt about snapping his sister's neck.

'Nothing in particular, just strange shapes and sounds.'

'Why don't you come back to bed and I'll make you forget all about it.' He spins me round so that our naked bodies are pressed right up against one another. I feel him rise to the occasion. I suppose one last bit of fun would be sufficient.

Chapter Fourteen

I have to peel back the tarpaulin to check who the body belongs to because my inquisitiveness is just too strong. A blood-curdling scream escapes from my lungs as I realise who it is. The smell that wafts from the decomposing corpse is enough to turn even the strongest stomach. Thank goodness it's the depths of winter and not the height of summer or the decomposition would have been ten times worse. Even though it's Daniel's lifeless eyes I am staring into right now I still feel afraid because, yet again, Alicia has lied to me. I killed him. No, *she* killed him ... in my own flat. I knew there had been too much blood! Why did I believe her when she said that no one was dead? Of course someone was dead! I'm so naïve. His body has been rotting in the back of my car this entire time and I've driven to bloody Cambridge. I feel sick. I don't know what to do, but before I can attempt to cover the body back up Peter appears at my side, no doubt startled by my ear-piercing scream.

'Josslyn, are you ... what the fuck! Josslyn! What the fuck!' Peter grabs me and pulls me away from the back of the car, holding onto my arms. 'Why is there a dead body in the back of your car? Who is that? Josslyn ... answer me!' He keeps trying to get me to look him in the eyes, but I'm intentionally avoiding his gaze. I can't bear to look at him. I'm so ashamed. Oh God, he's going to find out about my Alicia. I can't hide it any longer. He may have skeletons in his closet, but mine are even bigger and more ... complicated. I'm not crying (surprisingly), but I do feel very confused and upset.

Let's think about this rationally. Yes, Daniel is dead. Yes, he was a dickhead and yes, he was a bad man, but did he really deserve to die?

Let me put it this way, Josslyn. You would not be here right now if I had not intervened. At the time, I believed him to be your stalker. I was wrong, I will admit that. It seems there is another asshole out there who is infatuated with you, but I do not regret my decision to kill him. He was dangerous.

So what you're trying to say is that you saved my life by killing him.

Yes.

I could have taken care of myself.

Could you really?

I ... Yes. I think so, but now Peter and I have to get rid of the body and we are the ones who will get in trouble if the body is ever found. You never think about the consequences of your actions, do you Alicia? You never—

'Josslyn? Are you okay?' Peter's voice interrupts my train of thought and I finally lock eyes with him.

'Yes, I'm ...' I look at the body. I'm tired of lying and trying to be strong all the time. Fuck it all. 'No!' I say harshly. 'No, I'm not fucking okay. I keep saying I'm okay, but I'm really fucking not okay. That is my ex-boyfriend Daniel and I killed him, but I also didn't kill him. It's really hard to explain and what I really want right now, more than anything else in the world, is for you to stop looking at me like I'm a crazy person and just listen to me.' I stop for a moment, expecting Peter to shout 'murderer!' or 'I'm calling the police' or something, but he doesn't say a word. Time ticks by as if the world is in slow motion. It almost looks as if he's waiting for me to continue.

'Aren't you going to say something?' I ask him.

'You wanted me to listen, so I'm listening.'

I narrow my eyes at him. 'Why are you being so ... weird?'

'I'm being weird? I catch you with a dead body in the boot of your car and you're accusing me of being weird?'

'But ...'

'I tell you what, why don't we close the boot ...' (he does) 'and let's go inside. I'll make us a cup of tea—'

'Gin.'

'A cup of gin ... and you'll talk and I'll listen and then we'll see where we are, okay?'

So that's exactly what we do. We leave the body of my ex-boyfriend to decompose some more, go inside, take off our coats and Peter pours us a large tumbler of gin each. It's barely past lunchtime and already I'm drinking. When this is all over I really think I need to cut back on alcohol.

I have been telling you to do that for years.

Shut up, I'm not talking to you right now.

Peter and I sit next to each other on the sofa, not unlike the first time we met and had a conversation, take a big gulp each and then sit in silence. I guess he's waiting for me to speak.

This is it – the moment I tell someone else about the Alicia inside my head. It could all go wrong. Peter may call the local mental institution and have me committed. He may call the police and I'll be arrested for murder. I don't know what will happen, but I know I've reached the end of my tether. I cannot continue with this charade and all these lies any longer. Alicia always told me never to tell another soul about her and probably for good reason. However, I've come to realise (very slowly) that I can't trust her anymore and I need to start taking some risks if I am to be free of her control. So this is me ... risking it all.

'Okay,' I say at last. 'This is going to sound crazy, so just don't interrupt or ask any questions until I'm done, okay?'

Peter nods. 'Okay.'

'Okay,' I say nervously.

'Stop saying okay.'

'Okay.' Damn it! I crack a smile, as does he. Maybe this won't be so bad. And I begin.

'When I was seven years old I had an imaginary friend, except she wasn't imaginary like the normal kind of imaginary friends that kids have. She was ... real ... and in my head.' Jesus Christ, this is the first time I have tried to explain *what* Alicia is out loud and it's extremely difficult, much more difficult than I thought it would be. 'Her name is Alicia,' I add.

At the mention of her name Peter shifts in his seat. I can see the questions trying to force their way out of his mouth, but he stays quiet as I continue.

'I went through my entire life thinking she was something I made up in my head. We would have full conversations and everything, but from time to time she would ... take me over. I would never remember what happened. She sometimes made me do bad things, which I didn't like. I thought I may have a split personality, but it was more than that. She was never just a split personality. She was real, but I never knew what she was exactly, until I woke up in hospital the other day.

'The doctor told me that I have a tumour in my abdomen. He called it a foetus in fetu. Alicia is my unborn identical twin, yet somehow she is alive inside me and takes over my body. She killed Daniel ... and ... I think she killed Alicia ... your Alicia. She is getting out of control and I don't know what to do about her anymore. She's evil, but she's also the only friend I have ever had. I'm scared, Peter. I don't know what she'll do next.'

I finish my story by downing the rest of the gin in my glass in one gulp, screwing my face up in disgust as I swallow the burning liquid, but it feels so damn good because it almost immediately warms my insides and starts making my body feel fuzzy and numb all over.

Peter seems amazingly calm considering the utterly impossible story I have just told him. I wish I could read his thoughts. The silence between us is terrifying, yet also I feel such relief that I want to cry.

'So ...' he says at last, clearly having trouble getting his words to form. 'My sister Alicia ... is not your twin?'

'I think she is, yes. We would have been triplets.'

Peter nods and raises his eyebrows. 'Wow. That's ... insane.'

'Yeah. Do you believe me?'

'I do and do you know why I believe you? Because I've met her. Alicia. Your Alicia. That's who gave me those scratches down my back, isn't it?'

Oh God! Trust him to bring that up. I instantly feel myself flush bright red, my face so hot it feels like it's on fire.

'I'm so sorry. She took me over. I couldn't control her.'

Peter continues. 'That's who told me she'd kill me if I didn't get off you earlier, isn't it?' I nod my answer. Peter lets out a long sigh. 'Wow, she's ... interesting, I'll give her that. So let me get this straight – what you're saying is that you don't have a split personality, but she's actually a real person, or would have been a real person, inside you.'

'Yes. I think so. I think she's jealous of your Alicia for being real. She wants to take me over completely, I know she does. She's become very dangerous ever since ... well, she's been dangerous for a while now, but I've been able to hold her at bay. Sometimes I let down my guard and she takes the opportunity to control me. I really think she killed your Alicia. I'm so sorry, Peter. I swear I didn't know until recently. She never wanted me to tell anyone about her, but things have got so messed up that I just had to tell someone. I'm glad it was you.'

Peter smiles at me and places a hand gently on my leg. 'I'm glad you told me too, but I had kind of already figured out that you had some sort of personality disorder a few days ago. Alicia is a bit scary, isn't she?'

I laugh. 'Yes, she is.'

'So my Alicia really is dead.'

'I think so. I'm so sorry.'

We sit in silence for a few seconds absorbing this information. I can't imagine how hard this must be for Peter to hear and accept. I've only known about and been searching for Alicia for a few days. Peter has been searching for the truth for years and now, after everything, he has found out that she is dead, killed by her own twin sister.

I take a deep breath. Even though the news of Alicia's death is weighing heavily on us we now have to address the next big issue.

'Now, about the body in the back of my car. His name is Daniel Russell. He's my ex-boyfriend. Alicia killed him six days ago in my flat. I woke up covered in blood, but there was no body. I assumed something bad had happened, but I cleaned up the mess as if it didn't bother me. Alicia must have put him in my boot before I woke up, but she didn't have time to clean. I don't know what happened between them, but Alicia never liked him. She hated him and often had thoughts of killing him. He used to abuse me and one day Alicia took over and tried to strangle him. He wasn't a nice man, but he didn't deserve to die.'

'Sounds to me like he got what he deserved,' says Peter in a cold, calm voice.

'Maybe,' I whisper. 'What are we going to do about him?'

'I'll get rid of him and I'll put him somewhere that you don't know about. That way if the police ever ask you where he is you'll be telling the truth.'

'You don't think we should call the police?'

'And say what – you just happened to find a body in the back of your car? Josslyn, your fingerprints will be all over it. We need to get rid of him. I'll do it. You don't have to do anything.'

'You'd do that for me?'

'Of course. I'd do anything for you.'

Peter leans towards me and tucks a stray piece of my hair behind my left ear. I'm not sure why, but I suddenly get an eerie feeling and it freaks me out. I hold my nerve, determined not to let my anxiety show. Surely no normal human being would react in such a calm way to the startling news I had just shared. Who would offer to get rid of a dead body for someone they barely know? I certainly wouldn't. I hate to admit it, but I could really use Alicia's help right about now, but she is continuing to remain dormant.

I need some advice and maybe it's finally time to go back home and face my parents. I have achieved what I originally set out to achieve: to find Alicia. I haven't exactly found her, but at least I know what happened to her. Therefore, it's time to leave. My parents don't deserve the hell I have no doubt put them through over the past few days and, despite my usual insistence that people keep their distance from me, I could really use a hug from my mum and dad. I owe them the truth. I'm going to tell them about the foetus in fetu, but I'll leave out the fact that my unborn identical twin sister is taking over my body and killing people (there's just some things that parents won't understand).

'So,' I say finally, 'about Alicia. I think ... I think she needs to go.'

Peter looks confused. 'What do you mean?'

'I mean, the doctor at the hospital said that she can be removed via surgery. I think if I have her physically removed, maybe she will get out of my head. What do you think?'

Peter smiles. 'I think it's a good idea, but I doubt she will go easily. I'm sure as hell that she's been listening to all of this. She's not going to be happy with you, but can I just ask for one favour?'

'Of course.'

'Can I speak to her?' Those words completely throw me and I can't do anything to hide my shock.

'Why would you want to talk to her?'

'I want to ask her where she buried my sister.'

'Oh.' Well, that's fair enough I suppose. However, again, I get the same eerie feeling. It runs throughout my body and makes me go icy cold, but I don't shiver. My heart seems to stop for a moment and sinks all the way to the bottom of my chest. Why am I getting these feelings? Why does Peter suddenly make me feel so nervous? All I can think about right now is getting the hell out of this house, grabbing Oscar and driving back to the safety of my home.

'I'll see what I can do,' I say. 'Maybe I can ask her myself.'

Peter nods. 'Okay.' He stands up. 'Right, I'll go and dispose of the body.'

'Thank you, Peter. Listen, I ... I really appreciate everything you have done and for helping me over the past few days, but once Daniel is gone I think ... I think I'm going to go home. I'm going to call my mum in a bit and tell her I'm coming back. My parents must be so worried about me. I'm also going to call the hospital. Alicia made me leave in such a rush so I need to talk to the doctor and schedule the surgery back home. I think I've done everything I can here. We've found out what happened to Alicia. I'm still not sure why her journal was in Paul's flat, but ...'

'He was her stalker,' says Peter, matter-of-factly.

'Are we sure about that? It still doesn't feel right. I mean ... it doesn't make any sense.'

'It makes perfect sense. He may not have killed her, but he was still obsessed with her and must have taken the journal and your birth certificate from her house at some point before she left to find you.' I bite my lip to stop myself from arguing with him. This isn't the right time. There are things that need to be dealt with first. I must keep looking at the bigger picture, but my defences are up. 'And listen, once I get back, I'm coming with you back to yours,' adds Peter.

'You ... what? Why?'

'You need someone to look after you and I want to make sure you're okay. If I remember correctly there's still a stalker out there who is after you, too. I won't let the same thing happen to you like it did Alicia, even though it was you who ... you know what, it's too complicated. I just want you to be safe. I feel it's my duty.'

'Thank you, but I can look after myself.'

'I'm coming with you. End of story.'

I really did not expect Peter to want to come home with me. It's the last thing I want to happen. If I bring him home then my mum will get the wrong idea and think he is a new boyfriend and things will get overly complicated, especially when I attempt to explain what has happened. Well, not everything.

I can tell that there is no way I will be able to change Peter's mind, so I just accept my fate.

Chapter Fifteen

Peter returns two hours later. I don't ask him where he has dumped the body and he doesn't bring it up. He merely switches the kettle on and goes upstairs for a shower, like he has just come back from the gym, not just buried (or whatever he's done) a body. He seems weirdly calm, so I allow him get on with things. He packs a small bag and puts some food and water down for Harrison, leaving the cat flap unlocked so he can come and go as he pleases. I packed up all my stuff while Peter was out, secretly wishing I could just get in my car and drive away while he was gone, but he had taken my car.

Finally, we are ready to leave. Oscar is mega excited, but when Peter takes a seat in the front of the car he soon gets in a strop. He stands on the back seat and barks at Peter for the first ten minutes of the journey. Eventually, he realises that he is destined to be in the back so he curls up in a ball and goes to sleep. I'm not sure if it's the fact that I know there was a body in my car for six days or not, but I can still smell decomposing flesh. Peter said he had cleaned the boot, but the smell is still lingering and probably always will. I think I'm going to have to sell this car and when the new owner asks what the weird smell is I'll just smile and say 'what weird smell?', like it's no big deal and hardly noticeable, even though I'll be trying my best not to gag the whole time. At one point on the journey I have to open my window and let some fresh air in.

Peter and I don't talk a great deal during the drive and Alicia is staying quiet as well, so I find myself alone with my thoughts for the first time in a long while. I don't like it because my mind immediately goes to very dark places and starts over-thinking everything. The thought of telling my parents about the real Alicia is worrying me and I'm not sure why. They know about her, so I shouldn't be worried.

I spoke to the doctor I saw at the hospital earlier on the phone. He was not happy that I had left without being discharged, but he agreed that I was in no immediate danger. He said he would contact Bournemouth hospital and arrange the surgery there. I would get a letter in the post in the next couple of days with the date and time and what I would need to do to prepare. I begged him not to make a big deal about the whole thing. He really wanted to have me in to run tests and do all sorts of other things to find out more about the foetus in fetu, but I refused and said I wanted it removed as quickly as possible and I didn't want anyone to know. I said I didn't want to be studied like a lab rat. I just wanted her gone. He kept repeating that it was such a fascinating case, which got me annoyed in the end, but I managed to hold my tongue rather than start an argument with a medical professional.

Alicia has become such a thorn in my side. I see that now. She is evil. I have spent all these years convincing myself that she is my friend, but true friends don't murder your own sister. In fact, Alicia was *her* sister too, but she saw her as someone who needed to be removed from my life. She never even gave us a chance to meet. I feel so betrayed. Alicia has stolen my life from me and it's time I claimed it back. This is my body and my life and I don't want to share it with her anymore. Plus, she may have ruined my chance with Peter, who at first I believed to be a decent guy, but now I find him slightly odd. There's just something about him that doesn't sit right with me, but I do feel bad for him. His sister is dead. However, he hasn't actually looked sad since I told him ... which again is ... odd.

While I have my thoughts to myself I may as well try and ask Alicia about where she buried Alicia's body (honest to God I wish I'd given her another name!)

Alicia. Are you there? I really need to ask you something.

Silence.

Please. I know you've been listening.

Silence.

Fine, I'll ask anyway and ...

I know what you are going to ask me. You want to know where I buried her body so you can tell Peter.

Yes, I do. It will give us both closure.

I will never tell you.

Why not?

Because your DNA will be all over her body. I may be a psychopath, but I am not an expert at getting rid of bodies and evidence. If her body is found then you will be the main suspect once they find your DNA. The police will also find out that you are related, which will look even more suspicious. I am doing it to save you. You should be thanking me.

Thanking you! Are you fucking serious! Why are you always going on about protecting me and saving me when it's you who has been fucking up my life this whole time? If it wasn't for you I wouldn't be in any danger. If you had kept Alicia and Daniel alive then there would be no bodies to hide or evidence to cover up. Why kill them?

To protect you.

You mean to protect yourself.

Same thing.

Fuck you, Alicia. I'll be glad when you're cut out of my life.

I shall see you on the other side my sister. Goodbye.

Goodbye? Wait. Is this it? Is this the last time you're ever going to talk to me?

Silence.

I guess so.

My mum is a sobbing mess when I pull up into the driveway. I sent her a message earlier to say I was on my way and that I had some things to tell her. I also mentioned that I'd be bringing along a friend (although to be perfectly honest to call Peter a *friend* is a bit of a stretch, but I went with it anyway). Mum was undoubtedly happy and relieved to hear from me and she said she couldn't wait to see me.

There she is standing in the doorway to the house, red in the face, her eyes puffy from crying, but she has a massive smile on her face as soon as she sees me. I notice her throw a quick glance at Peter as we both get out of the car. Oscar bounds up to the house like always, making a quick pee stop by the potted plant on the way, then pushes past Mum and into the warmth. I give Mum an awkward hug.

'Hi Mum. This is my friend, Peter.' I do the general introductions.

'Hello, Mrs Reynolds, lovely to meet you.' Peter politely extends his hand and she shakes it. If her eyebrows were any higher up her forehead they'd be in her hairline. No doubt I will get a million and one questions about him later when we are alone.

'Lovely to meet you! You know, I've not heard anything about you, but I'm so glad you're here. Please come in. Your dad's just making a pot of tea.'

We follow Mum into the house where I proceed to introduce Peter to my dad, who mimics my mum's shock, confusion and raised eyebrows. If we hadn't have had an argument recently I'm pretty sure they would be asking Peter lots of questions and being exceptionally awkward and embarrassing, but it seems that my parents are on their best behaviour, as they keep their thoughts and questions to themselves.

There's a horrible silence while we all take our seats and Dad hands out the tea and puts a milk jug and a sugar pot on the coffee table, as well as a plate of chocolate caramel digestive biscuits (my all-time favourite biscuits, which means they are feeling sorry for themselves and are trying to get me to forgive them. Fun fact for you: I once ate two whole packets of these biscuits and then proceeded to curl up into a ball on the floor complaining I felt sick for the next two hours. Good times).

It's my mum who decides to start the conversation. 'Darling, I just want to say how happy we are to see you and whatever it is you want to say to us we will listen and answer any questions you have. You deserve to know the truth. I'm so sorry about how things ended last week.'

'Thanks Mum, that means a lot. Before I start I'll just reassure you that Peter knows pretty much everything, so there's no need to hide anything from him. I only met him a few days ago, but he's important. Actually he's ... Alicia's brother.'

My parents let out an audible gasp at the same time. 'Oh my goodness!' my mum exclaims.

'Adopted brother,' Peter corrects.

'How wonderful!' she exclaims. I can't help but notice the slight disappointment in my mum's voice. I can tell she was hoping that Peter was my new boyfriend, but now I expect she realises that it would be weird to be in a romantic relationship with your twin sister's adopted brother (hence why I shall be leaving out the fact that Peter and I have slept together on numerous occasions over the last few days. I warned him not to mention it to my parents while we were in the car on the way over).

'You found her?' asks my dad.

'Not exactly,' I say sadly. 'I found Peter and we talked and he told me that Alicia disappeared five years ago. The police ruled it as a suicide, but her body has never been found.'

'Oh my goodness, I'm so sorry, Peter. That must have been an awful time for you.' My mum sounds genuinely sympathetic. She's always been like that, so caring and thoughtful. She is nice to everyone.

'Thank you, Mrs Reynolds.' Peter proceeds to complete the story. 'I was convinced that she was still alive. I never gave up hope. Then your daughter turned up at my door and told me that she was Alicia's twin sister. I was shocked, obviously, but together we decided to find out what really happened to my sister once and for all, but unfortunately ...' (at this point Peter flicks his eyes briefly towards me and then back to my mum) '... we found out that she is dead.'

My mum covers her mouth with her hands in shock. 'You found her body?'

'We believe so,' says Peter. A slight white lie, which we concocted, but it's for the greater good.

'I'm so sorry,' my mum says again. 'Josslyn darling, I'm so sorry.' She takes my hand, squeezes it rather hard and starts to cry. 'I'm so sorry you never had the chance to meet her. It's all our fault. I can't even begin to tell you how sorry I am darling. Is there anything I can do, anything at all, to make you forgive me?'

'Yes Mum, actually there is.' This was what I had been hoping for. 'Please can you tell me the real story about how and why we were separated as babies. I know you didn't tell me the whole story. I want to know.'

My mum nods almost immediately. 'Yes, of course darling. Anything.' She clears her throat, as if ready for a big speech. 'Well, you already know about the fact that your father and I found out that we couldn't have children. We told you that bit, which was true. We decided that adoption was the best route forward for us. The truth is darling ... is that your mother was ... abused by your real father. He ... sexually abused her. They weren't in a relationship.'

I take the reins on this one because I get the feeling that she is having a hard time saying the actual words. 'Mum, are you saying that my biological mum was raped by a stranger?'

My mum nods frantically. 'Yes, it's so horrible isn't it? That's what the adoption agency said was the reason why she wanted to give you up. We agreed to adopt you very early on in her pregnancy, but then we found out she was having twins. The adoption agency told us that they would find a suitable home for the other child. We thought about adopting her too, but there were issues ... '

'What sort of issues?' At this point my heart is racing and beating so hard and fast that I'm barely able to take a breath, but I'm much more calm and controlled than last time.

My mum continues. 'They told us that one twin had limited brain function or something like that and that her brain was different to a normal person's.'

'So ... what ... you ... decided to adopt the healthier twin, like you said?'

'No darling. We chose you. You were the one who was different. We thought that you might be harder to adopt because of your issues, so we adopted only you. Your mother named you Josslyn and Alicia. We kept the name and obviously so did the other family, which is lovely I think.' My mum stops talking, but I get the feeling that she isn't done yet.

'Mum,' I say quite sternly. 'Do you know where my real mother is?'

'Oh darling,' my mum sniffs. 'Your mother died during childbirth.'

I'm momentarily stunned. I open my mouth to speak, but no words come out so my mum continues on.

'The agency told us this after you were born. We held you in our arms and you were so perfect, but they told us that there had been complications during the birth.'

'What sort of complications exactly?' I don't know why, but I have a horrible feeling of dread, like I know something bad is about to happen. Yeah, *that* feeling.

My mum glances at my dad briefly before continuing. 'Something went wrong while your mother was in labour. She started bleeding heavily. During your birth while your mother was pushing you got stuck and you were starved of oxygen for longer than is deemed normal. They eventually had to deliver you via caesarean, but by then it was already too late for your mother. She continued to bleed and she eventually died. It was a tragic situation, but I'm afraid it left you with ... complications. You had been starved of oxygen a little too long, but the doctors and midwives were able to save you. They told us that due to the lack of oxygen to your brain you may have health issues later in life, as well as the different brain function, which they couldn't really explain properly. They also found some sort of shadow in your abdomen, but they told us it was nothing to worry about.'

At this point I look at Peter, who appears to be holding his breath, desperate to say something. 'Are you saying that I was the cause of my mother's death?'

'No darling, not at all. It just happened. No one knows why these horrible things happen. They just do, but you were saved and thankfully you never showed any sign of any health issues as you grew up. You are perfect.'

If only she knew the truth, but the real truth would destroy her. To think that if the doctors back then had been a little more thorough they could have realised what Alicia really was and I would have lived a normal life.

'So this ... shadow they found ... it was nothing?' I press on.

My mum nods. 'Yes, that's right. You never had any problems so we never had you checked over by any other doctors. It was a miracle!'

I lean back against the sofa cushions and sigh heavily. How do I even begin to explain this next part? My mum is going to be so confused.

'Okay, look. There's something else I need to tell you both. It may be difficult to hear. You remember that severe pain I had after I found out about Alicia last week?

Well, I've had a few of those types of episodes, severe pain in my abdomen and sometimes all over my body. While I was with Peter I had a severe episode and I blacked out and woke up in hospital a few days later.' At this point my mum gasps, but allows me to continue speaking.

'The doctor at the hospital said he had conducted some tests and scans on me and found a dark tumour in my abdomen. Mum, calm down, it's not cancer or anything.' She starts crying hysterically, but then gathers herself once I reassure her. Honestly, she's such a drama queen.

'After more tests and scans the doctor found that the tumour is actually a ... foetus in fetu.' I stop talking and allow those strange words to float in the air and sink in, but my mum and dad look seriously confused. I'm not surprised because the phenomenon is so rare that I doubt many people have ever heard about it.

For the first time since this conversation began my dad speaks. He clears his throat first, as if to announce his presence. 'Are you saying you're pregnant?'

My mum gasps again. Honestly, she is so annoying!

'No! Oh God no! I'm not pregnant. It is a foetus, but it's not mine. It's ... well it's my twin, actually it's my identical twin.' For obvious reasons I leave out the part about her having a name and that I've been having full conversations with her inside my own head and she takes over my body ... oh, and that she's evil and has killed people, my fraternal twin sister included.

Again, it seems to be almost impossible for my parents to comprehend this news so I continue and try to explain it as best as I can, although I don't use all the fancy words that the doctor had (mainly because I can't remember them).

'It's extremely rare. The doctor said I'm possibly only the second woman who this has happened to and the fact that I have a fraternal twin is even more unusual and seems almost impossible, but it's true. I would have been one of triplets had we all survived, but very early on in the pregnancy, apparently I absorbed my identical twin inside my body and it has been there ever since. It hasn't caused any issues until now when I started getting severe pain. The doctor who I spoke to said it can be removed safely via surgery. I am waiting for my scheduled operation now to have it removed.'

My mum finally takes her hands away from her mouth and takes a deep breath. 'Well, I ... I'm glad you are okay,' she says slowly. She then gets up, moves closer to me and wraps her arms around me in a tight hug. I'm slightly taken back by this gesture, but I return the hug. It feels good to be friends with my mum again. I never meant to hurt or push her away, but now I've had time to process everything I know that she and my dad are the most important people in my life. They may not be my biological parents, but that doesn't matter to me. They are my parents and I love them.

'That's incredible,' says my dad. 'It's like something out of a movie.'

I laugh slightly. 'Yes, it is quite amazing to be honest that something like that can happen, but I just want you both to know that I am okay. You did nothing wrong by not taking me to any other doctors to have me checked over. It's just one of those things. It's crazy, but I'm okay. I promise. I'll let you know when I hear from the hospital about my surgery.'

My mum has more tears in her eyes and is clearly worried about me. I know her well enough to know that she wants to bombard me with questions, but she doesn't. She just smiles.

'Thank you darling. Whenever it is we will be there right by your side. And Peter ...' She reaches over and squeezes his hand. 'Thank you for looking after our Josslyn. We are eternally grateful.'

'Not at all, Mrs Reynolds. I'm glad she turned up at my door. Josslyn means a great deal to me. We are, after all, family.'

My mum beams a smile, but I feel physically sick. Why did he have to go and say that? It makes me feel really ... icky. I mean, he's seen me naked. I've seen him naked. We've done stuff ... stuff that makes me blush just thinking about. Yet here he is acting like it never happened and acting totally fine.

'Please, call me Amanda,' says my mum.

Urggg ... now they are on first name terms!

Chapter Sixteen

Peter and I leave my parents' house about an hour later after my mum has plied us with more tea and biscuits. She wanted us to stay for dinner, but I explained that we had to go because I wanted to check on my flat and catch up with some work stuff (a complete lie because Lucy and Emma have said that everything is under control, but I do plan on going to work tomorrow).

It is now Thursday evening. It feels like a lifetime ago that I first found out about Alicia, but it's been less than a week. My mum finally lets us leave after I've reassured her for the hundredth time that I will call her the minute I get my surgery date or if anything remotely bad happens to me.

I drive on auto pilot back to Ringwood. The weather is wet and windy and downright miserable, rather like my mood. All I want is to be by myself, but Peter is still tagging along and I really need to try and get rid of him. I don't understand why he's sticking around. We've solved the case. Alicia is dead. What more does he want? I'll let him stay the night and then politely tell him to go home, saying that if I need him I'll call him. I just want to be alone; that's all.

I unlock the door to my flat, walk in and immediately smell bleach, but at least there's no blood left and the place looks fairly clean for once, so I'm not too embarrassed when I invite Peter inside. He does the polite ritual of nodding and saying, 'I like what you've done with the place,' which actually means 'it's better than nothing.' Oscar immediately runs to his water bowl, which is empty, so I refill it and flick the heating on. It's colder than the bloody Arctic in here.

'You want a pizza?' I ask Peter. I have no energy to cook any food.

'Always.'

'I'll order in.'

'Sounds perfect.'

'What do you want?'

'Can't go wrong with pepperoni.'

I call the pizza place. They answer by saying, 'Hi Josslyn! Long time no speak.' Clearly they have my number on their phone as I'm a regular customer. Usually I always order a large Mexican chicken pizza with stuffed crust and sweet potato wedges and onion rings on the side. 'Same as usual?' the man asks me.

'Um, no, actually, yes, but can I also add a large pepperoni please.'

'Feeling extra hungry or do you have company?'

'Not that it's any of your business, but I have company.'

'Hey, this job sucks ass, so I always like to gather any gossip I can. Is he cute?'

'Yes, very.'

'Have you shaved your legs?'

'Okay, listen buddy, I'm pretty sure you're only paid to take food orders, so please can you just do your job?'

'Sure.'

There's a silence on the line.

'No, I haven't shaved my legs.'

'Best get on that, love.'

Once I've finalised the order I feed Oscar. Peter makes himself at home on the small sofa and flicks on a football game. I go and take a shower because I smell so bad and these clothes are in desperate need of a wash. Once I'm in some clean jeans and a white t-shirt I join Peter in the lounge area while we wait for our pizza.

'So,' says Peter, turning the volume down on the television. 'Do you remember our deal?'

'What deal?'

'The deal we made in my car. Once we found out the truth about what happened to Alicia we would talk about us.'

Ah shit, the *us* talk. I had been hoping he would forget about that.

'Cup of tea?' I say, immediately getting to my feet and exiting the room. He follows me into the kitchen.

'Don't try and get out of it.'

'I'm not, but if we're to have *the us talk* then I at least need of cup of tea.' Or a large gin, but I really need to make a conscious effort to cut back on my drinking. 'Want one?'

'Sure,' he says with a hint of a smile as he leans against the side of the kitchen cabinet.

'Actually, while you make the tea I need to ask you ... did your Alicia say where she buried ... my Alicia?'

'Um, no, she didn't. She wouldn't tell me anything. I'm sorry. She said that she can't risk the body being found as there is my DNA on it and it will put me at risk.'

'Of course. I understand that, but once you have your surgery there won't be another chance to find out. I won't tell anyone. I just want to know where she is so I can have closure. Can I talk to her?'

'Alicia? She doesn't want to talk to you. She won't even talk to me right now.'

Peter eyes me up and down, as if scanning me for a malfunction. 'Why doesn't she want to talk to me?' His voice sounds serious and has dropped down an octave or two.

'I don't know. She doesn't like talking to anyone.'

Again he stares at me and then cracks his knuckles. I feel a cold shiver run down my spine, which gives me goose bumps all over. It only lasts for a second, however it's enough to set my teeth on edge. Peter finally nods.

'I understand. She's quite complex, isn't she?'

'That's one way of putting it.'

'Will you tell me about her?'

'You don't want to talk about *us* first?'

'Do *you* want to talk about us first?'

'Not really.'

'Then tell me a bit about Alicia. I'd love to hear some stories. When did you first notice her? Has she always been evil?'

Yeesh, everyone always wants to know about Alicia. The sooner she is gone the better, then I can finally start to live my own life, not that I'd change anything, but at least I wouldn't have her voice in my head. Although, I must admit that she has been very quiet lately and I have sort of missed her. Soon she will be gone forever and I won't be able to undo it. I had better get used to the silence.

'She first appeared when I was seven, as I said. I made her up. She was my imaginary friend. I gave her the name Alicia because it was a name I had always felt a deep connection with. I suppose that's because of your Alicia, like a part of me knew she was out there somewhere. Alicia first took me over when I was eight and killed my childhood cat, Tornado. Cats don't like her, which means they don't like me.'

'Ah, so that explains why I haven't been able to get Harrison to come inside for the past few days.'

'Yeah, sorry about that.' I do feel bad that the poor cat has been freezing outside because he wouldn't come in while I was there.

'He'll get over it.'

'So anyway, after she killed Tornado she disappeared for two years. I thought for a while that she was gone completely, but then she came back. I was ten and I was playing by myself as I always did. I had lots of plastic animals, which I would pretend to heal and make better and one day she just said, 'Hello Josslyn, did you miss me?' And I screamed. Once I calmed down she apologised for killing Tornado and then we became best friends again. It was great to have her back. I didn't feel alone anymore.

'We did everything together. Over the years as I became a teenager I noticed that she wanted to disobey and misbehave a lot more than I was comfortable with. Whenever my parents would ask me to do something, like feed the animals or do some chores, she would answer back to them rudely in my head. It got worse and worse. She slowly started to change. I don't know if she was always a psychopath or if she turned into one, but I was nearly eighteen by the time I realised she was ... different. She has no feelings, no emotions and doesn't care about anyone except herself, but she did care about me – at least I thought she did. She was always there to protect me and back me up, like she had my back. She always had an answer for everything.

'I started university and that's when things got really serious. She took me over and beat up this girl who called me a freak because I preferred to study by myself rather than hang out with anyone. She didn't even have to take me over sometimes. One time I just punched this guy clear in the face because she told me to do it. I was becoming more and more like her every day. That's why I always want to be alone: because she wants to be alone. She says it's better that way.' I stop talking, finish making the teas and hand him a steaming mug.

Peter takes it calmly. 'It's fascinating.' That's all he says.

'Yeah, to you maybe. You have no idea what it's like to have a psychopath inside your head telling you to kill people all the time.'

Peter doesn't answer. He merely smiles sympathetically. 'No, I don't. You're right. I'm sorry. It's just ... the fact that she would have been a real person is ... unthinkable. Just imagine if it had happened the other way around – if Alicia had absorbed you and you were her inner voice.'

'I am sometimes. Recently, when she's taken over my body, I've been able to see and hear what she's doing. It's never happened until now. It's terrifying.'

'I bet.'

We're still standing in my tiny kitchen, clutching our mugs of tea, taking a sip once in a while. Honestly, it's so easy to talk to Peter sometimes, yet I feel a general uneasiness around him now. I still find him unbelievably attractive, but I learnt a long time ago to be wary of extraordinarily good-looking men. They may look pretty on the outside, but inside they aren't always nice (by the way

I'm aware I'm making a very broad and sweeping rationalisation here. I'm sure there are plenty of extremely good-looking men who are also very lovely, but I just don't happen to know any).

Peter clears his throat. 'So ... about *us*.' I can't help but mentally roll my eyes. Right, I guess he isn't giving up. It's time to break his heart. I know I'm doing the right thing.

'Peter, listen ... there is no us. Yes, we slept together and it was ... great, but the whole Alicia thing, your Alicia and my Alicia. It's just too complicated and to tell you the truth I'm just not looking for anything serious right now ...'

'If you say *it's not you, it's me* I'm going to have to slap you,' he teases.

I smile. 'Sorry,' I say quietly.

Peter takes a deep breath. 'It's okay. I knew it was coming. You've made it pretty clear that you don't want anything serious, but you can't deny that we had something.'

'Are you sure that wasn't because of my Alicia?'

Peter doesn't answer straight away. He lets those words hover in the air a few seconds. 'I won't deny that she was ... fun, but Josslyn, you and I have a connection, can't you feel it? It's you I ... like, not Alicia.'

Why did he just pause before he said *like*? Oh my God, was he about to say he loved me?

I look at him, like really look at him. I can honestly say with one hand on my heart that, apart from the fact that he makes my private parts tingle when he stares at me, I don't feel anything else towards him. Something has changed. Something about him isn't trustworthy. Maybe I should do some snooping on him – check his Facebook profile, that sort of thing. Maybe even check his phone. I spy it laying on the kitchen counter next to him. That would be a good place to start. I'm already mentally flicking through his phone trying to find some piece of evidence that's good enough to give me an excuse to make him leave. Why do I always do this? Why do I push people away even though they've done nothing wrong? It's Alicia, I'm sure it is. She's the one who has changed me and made me more paranoid. Now she isn't even talking to me and is leaving me to create my own mess and clean it up.

'I don't know what you want me to say, Peter.'

'Just say the truth, that's all I ask.'

'I've told you the truth already. I don't want anything from you. We can be friends, but that's it. We can't ever be any more than that.'

'Okay, I understand. I mean, it hurts but ... I'll get over it.'

We share a smile. Was it that easy to break his heart? Maybe I hadn't even broken it. He appears to be taking this break-up (not that it actually is a break-up, because we were never together, and you can't break-up from someone you aren't with) rather well.

'I think, if it's okay with you, I'll head back home tomorrow. I don't want to crowd you and become a burden. You said it yourself that you like your own space. I shouldn't have come with you. I guess I was just hoping ... you know what, I don't even know what I was hoping, I just know it's better if I leave you alone for a bit.'

Part of me wants to jump for joy and happily slam the door behind him as he leaves and another part wants to rush forward, grab him and never let him go.

'I'm sorry Peter, I didn't mean to lead you on or anything.'

'You didn't. Honestly Josslyn, it's fine. Please, don't worry, but I'd appreciate it if you can tell me when your surgery is so I can maybe come and help you out, you know if you want me to. I really do care about you.'

'Thank you. I know you do. The pizza will be here soon, so let's eat, then in the morning I'll take you to the train station.'

'Thank you.'

My plan is in motion. The pizza arrives, we eat, chat some more (not about us or Alicia, but just general friend stuff) and then go to bed (he on the tiny sofa with a duvet and me in my own bed). Yes, it's slightly awkward, but we get through it like the mature adults we are.

I finally turn off the light and breathe a sigh of relief. I now need to stay awake until I know that he is fast asleep. While I wait for him to drift off I take out my phone and start scrolling. I type his name into the search bar of Facebook. Unsurprisingly a lot of names pop up, so I go through them one by one, discounting them as I go. I get to the end of the list. He's not there. He's not on Facebook. That's ... weird – everyone who's anyone is on that bloody site. I try all the other social media apps. Nope. Nothing. He doesn't exist on any of them. The only place he exists online is in the newspaper articles about his sister's disappearance, the yellow pages site I got his address from and on the website of the school where he works. None of which actually help me at all. Okay, it looks like that part of my plan has failed.

It's nearly one in the morning. My flat is so small that I can hear his soft snores from the other room. It's time. I climb out of bed as quietly as I can (not forgetting to lift my feet up and count to five), leaving Oscar, who is taking up most of the space, to sleep soundly. I peer through the darkness at his sleeping form as I gingerly creep forwards. The light from the moon is doing a good job of lighting my path and my eyes immediately fall on his phone, which is laying tantalisingly on the floor beside him.

I mustn't. It's wrong. I know it's wrong and even though I can't actually hear her, I know for a fact that Alicia would be telling me to take it and look through it. It's now or never. Without even thinking any more about it my body automatically lurches forward and snatches the phone off the floor. I retreat into my bedroom and close the door. My heart is racing, as if I've been caught with my hand in the biscuit jar by my mum. It doesn't occur to me until it flashes up on the screen that he would have a password. Of course he uses a password to protect his phone. Everyone does!

I type in 'Alicia'. Nope.

I type in 'Harrison'. Nope.

Shit. One more chance. It couldn't be. Could it?

I type in 'Josslyn'.

Bingo.

Okay, slightly creepy, but I quickly brush past the weirdness and start snooping. I immediately go to the text messages and WhatsApp messages. Nothing jumps out at me. Just messages from his mum, someone called Frank Master and a girl called Rebecca. I don't know why but I'm rushing to get this over and done with as quickly as possible. The sooner I find something (or nothing) the sooner I can replace his phone and go to sleep.

I quickly open up the recent phone calls and start scrolling. That's when I see my name on the screen. I press on the recent calls and a list of dates and times come up before I'd met Peter, before I even knew who he was. The last call was on the 7th of November at 17:30 – the exact date and time of my last suspicious phone call from my creepy stalker.

Oh. My. God. It's him. It's Peter. He's my stalker!

Chapter Seventeen

My mind is working overtime to try and figure everything out, but it's all jumbled together and nothing makes any sense.

Peter is my stalker.

He's the one who has been calling me and being weird and creepy and by the look of his maps app I can tell he has also visited this area recently (the bright lights in my rear-view mirror on the way to my parents). He already knew my address, my parents' address, God only knows what else he knows about me. Has he actually been inside my flat? Has he been through my things?

Suddenly I feel afraid. I don't know this man at all, not even a little bit other than the fact that he likes it when I bite his chest during sex. Oh my God! I've had sex with my stalker! If he wasn't already obsessed with me now he probably thinks we're in love or something and I've just turned him down. Maybe he's planning on killing me before he leaves tomorrow ...

I immediately lunge for the drawer beside me and fumble around hastily for the sharp knife I know is hidden there. My hands are shaking, my mouth is dry, even my vision is going blurry. The darkness feels like it's closing in around me. I don't know what to do ... wait, I need to call the police. No, I shouldn't. Ahhhh! Okay, let's think about this rationally for a second. I am alone in my flat and my stalker is asleep in the next room.

What would you do?

I could creep up on him and stab him in the chest, which basically wouldn't solve anything and I'd be left with another dead body to clean up.

I could call the police ... and say what? I've never called the cops and told them about the suspicious phone calls, so they'd have no record of them. I have no proof to show them other than his phone call list, but how can I prove that we didn't know each other when he called me? I can't, that's the problem.

I could wake him up, hold him at knife point and force him to tell me the truth and risk being killed by a mad man.

Out of those three options I decide to go with option three. Let's face it, if Peter wanted to kill me he's had plenty of opportunities to do so over the last week, so I decide to give him the benefit of the doubt.

I keep the knife grasped tightly in my shaking hand as I slowly get out of bed. I am so caught up in recent events that I momentarily forget about doing my counting routine – there are more important things to worry about now. The room feels cold and I'm shivering slightly because I'm only wearing a thin top and tiny spotted shorts. I should really invest in some winter thermal pyjamas, especially since on more than one occasion the heating has stopped working during every winter I've lived here and I've almost frozen to death. I peer around the door and into the lounge area. He's still snoring softly and laying on his back, his left arm draped casually above his head. It's now or never – time to be brave. I wish Alicia was here ...

I creep forward, stop once I'm standing over him and slowly point the knife against his neck. I press firmly, just breaking the skin, which jolts him suddenly from sleep. In the moonlight he sees me above him and freezes.

'Josslyn? What the fuck!'

'You,' I say quietly, a mere quivering whisper. 'It's you.'

'What?'

'You know what.'

'Josslyn, please just get the knife away from my throat and talk to me. What the hell is going on?'

I lift up his phone to show him, which has been clutched in my other hand as a makeshift torch. He sees the screen, which I've left on the call list. It takes a few moments before it dawns on him what I've found.

'Okay, listen, I can explain ... whatever it is you think you've seen, it's not true.'

'You're a liar! You've been lying to me this whole time!' I shout. 'You knew exactly who I was when I turned up at your house and you led me on and used me! You've been stalking me this whole time!' My eyes are brimming with tears, but not sad tears, angry tears. The kind of tears that make your blood boil and your whole body shake with rage. It's usually Alicia who acts like this, but now it's all me.

Peter has his hands up in a defenceless manner. 'Josslyn ... please, just put the knife down before you hurt yourself. Can we put the light on and talk?'

'I am so goddamn sick of talking!'

'Okay, so let me talk ... please.'

I take a few steps away from him, still grasping the knife as tight as I can, using all the strength I have left to hold it up like I am pointing a gun; a barrier between him and me. I back up until I get to the main light switch and flick it on. The room lights up and blinds us temporarily. Peter slowly sits up, rises to his feet and goes to step forwards towards me.

'Stay back!' I shout. I'm backed up into the corner of the lounge. The only way out of my flat is to get past him to the door, but there's no way I can do that. He'd grab me before I got half-way. 'Don't take another step!'

'Josslyn, we both know that you don't have it in you to hurt anyone, that's Alicia's job.'

'Just fucking try me!'

'Can you just lower the knife so I can talk without the threat of being stabbed?'

The blade of the knife is shaking quite forcefully. I can't seem to control my own body. Fear and anger have taken over, but I need to be sensible about this. He's right. I do need to calm down because it's the only way I'm going to be able to get out of this situation. I need to make him think I'm calm and I need to get the hell out of this building so I can make a break for it. I momentarily think of Oscar, who is still snoozing on my bed. It seems nothing, not even a knife confrontation in the next room, will wake him. I need a new guard dog.

'Okay,' I say slowly. I lower the knife to my side, but I don't loosen my grip, not even for a second. 'Talk.' I feel like a coiled spring ready to explode.

Peter sighs and I can noticeably see him relax his shoulders and body. 'Okay, so ... yes, I know who you are, Josslyn. I knew who you were when you showed up at my door. I can't say that I wasn't a little bit surprised. I never thought you would find out about me or Alicia. You startled me. I didn't really know how to react so I just played along with your story, knowing full well that it wasn't true. You're so cute when you lie, or at least try to lie. There's always a tell-tale sign. You blush bright red.

'I know you so well, Josslyn. I know you hardly ever brush your hair. I know you wake up every morning, place your feet on the floor and then bring them up and count to five. I have no idea why you do that, but it's intriguing. I know you are lonely. I know you tell Oscar you love him more than you tell your parents. I know about your Alicia. I didn't know exactly what she was until you told me, but I know she gets in your head and makes you believe things that aren't real. I know you crave someone to love you. I know ...'

'Stop it!' I shout. My breathing has become rapid and I'm struggling to catch it. I have that heart sinking feeling again, like it's about to drop out of my chest and onto the floor.

'I'm sorry, but I do know you better than anyone else in the world.'

'I-I had no idea who you were until a week ago. How? How did you find out who I was? Tell me everything or I'm calling the police.' I show him his phone, which is on the dialling screen and the numbers 999 have already been entered. All I need to do is touch the call button.

'Okay, I'll explain. It all starts with Alicia. My Alicia. I loved my sister very much. We were very close and I loved being with her all the time. She made me happy, but she felt that our relationship needed boundaries as we got older and she started to push me away. I felt so empty and lonely without her, so I started keeping an eye on her without her knowing. Just things like checking to make sure she got to work okay and what she was doing on a Saturday night when she said she didn't want to hang out with me. You see, I didn't just love my sister, I was *in love* with her. I don't know how it happened, but I wanted her more than anything. I became obsessed with her. I hated every man she dated and made any excuse I could to try and get her to see me, but she was happy living her own life without me. She didn't need me, but I needed her more than anything else in the world. I couldn't function without her. That's when I had the idea about pretending to be a dangerous stalker, so that she would come running back to me, saying that she was scared and that she needed my help. However, my plan backfired because she never told me about the phone calls she was getting. She never confided in me. I was very hurt and so I continued to watch her and call her.

'That's when I found out about you. I entered her house and read her journals, which I did on a weekly basis. She wrote everything in those damn things, stuff she would never talk to me about. It was the only way I could find out what she was really thinking. She had her suspicions about me, that's for sure, but she had no idea what I was really doing. I had a key to her place, which she had given me, so I wasn't breaking and entering. She wrote about you and she had your birth certificate, which was sent to her by an anonymous person. I was shocked, stunned, confused. My Alicia had a sister, someone who I had never met, someone she had never met, but who was a part of her. And so my new obsession was you, Josslyn. I knew I had to meet you, to learn more about you, but I had to be patient. I didn't want to ruin things, but then something happened that I wasn't expecting and it shattered my very soul. My Alicia disappeared.

'You have no idea just how much I truly suffered after she went missing. I couldn't function, I couldn't breathe. I needed something else to distract me, *someone* else. I'm telling you the honest truth here. I did not know what happened to Alicia, but I knew it had something to do with you. Before I called the police I went into her house and I planted the fake suicide note, took her journals and your birth certificate. I was determined to find out what happened to my sister on my own. I didn't want help from the police or from anyone else. It was me who planted it in Paul's flat to try and persuade you to think that he was Alicia's stalker, but you didn't seem convinced. You are very clever Josslyn, more so than you give yourself credit for.

'I tracked you down. According to her journals, Alicia had gone to find you and then disappeared, but I couldn't find any evidence of where she went. I watched you for days, weeks, months ... years. I've been watching you this whole time, learning about you. Obviously I had to live in my own house and go to work. Sometimes weeks would go by where I wouldn't be able to see you, so I'd call you. I easily found your mobile number from some paperwork at your vet business. I know how much debt you are in. I know a great deal about you.

'My love for you grew and I knew I had to have you in my life for real. Thoughts of my Alicia lessened as I fell in love with you. If I couldn't have Alicia then I was determined that I'd have you. One day I went to see you again. It had been a while, too long and I missed you, but you were ... different. You were acting differently, you spoke differently to people and even walked differently. It looked like you, but it wasn't you. I was so confused. You were definitely a different person. I needed to find out who this person was. She fascinated me more than anyone I had ever met, more than Alicia and even more than you, Josslyn, but I just didn't know who or what she was. My obsession grew. I had to find out what was going on, so I was patient again and watched and waited. You became more than an obsession to me. You became my whole life.

Nothing else mattered to me. And then ... you showed up at my door.'

The whole time Peter was talking I had been trying not to hyperventilate. Every word that came out of his mouth made me wince and want to run away. I feel betrayed, violated and sick. This whole time he has been watching me and I knew nothing about it.

I know I need to speak because he finished his speech about twenty seconds ago and there is now a devastating silence. He makes another move towards me and that's when I automatically raise the knife again.

'Stay back! You ... I don't understand. You're a freak! You're an absolute crazy person! You should be locked up. You've admitted that you were in love with your own sister, which is just ... eww, and then became obsessed with me and then ... I can't even ... how do you expect me to react to this?'

Peter takes a step backwards. 'I'm hoping that by telling you the truth you will understand and learn to trust me when I say that I love you and I've always looked out for you. You never have to feel alone ever again because I will always be there for you. Always. Please just give me a chance to prove it and ...'

'You seriously think that I'll just forgive you and let you be a part of my life after what you just told me? You're sick! You need help and I don't mean just any type of help, I mean professional psychiatric help.'

'Look who's talking.'

Okay, well I guess he has a point there. I am the one who has another person living inside her who kills people.

'I should call the police right now!'

'Go ahead. Do it. I dare you.'

'Is that a threat?'

'No, it's a warning. You won't do it Josslyn because, believe it or not, you do have feelings for me.'

I burst out laughing, but it's not a real laugh, more like one of those hysterical fake laughs. 'You really are deluded, aren't you?'

'You're the one who's deluded, Josslyn.'

We stare at each other for what seems like hours, neither of us saying another word. I have an actual crazy person in my flat.

'Peter, please leave,' I say in as stern a voice as I can muster, but in actuality I'm terrified and want to back myself up into a corner and cry for four days.

'I'm not leaving you, Josslyn. Not until you understand.'

'Even if you stayed forever I will never understand. How do you expect me to trust you now? How do you expect me to even like you? You've been stalking me for years! You've lied to me. You've taken advantage of me. Surely you can see why I can't have you around anymore. Now, please leave. The next time I ask you it will be followed by a phone call to the police.'

Peter stares at me, his left eye twitching. His jaw is tight and his body tense. He looks as though he's about to launch himself at me any second. My grip on the knife tightens just in case I need to use it. Not that I know how to use a knife to defend myself properly, but I assume the stab and swipe method would do the job in this situation.

'Okay, I'll go.' My whole body sighs with relief, but I still keep the knife at the ready. 'But Josslyn, there will come a day where you will come looking for me again. I can guarantee it.'

'And I can guarantee that if I ever see you again or catch a whiff of you being anywhere near me, I will call the police and file a restraining order. You've been warned. Have a great life. Now get the fuck out ... NOW!'

'Goodbye, Josslyn.'

Chapter Eighteen

Thank fuck for that. Peter is gone. He can find his own bloody way to the train station or can even walk back to Cambridge for all I care. I double bolt the door to my building and the door to my flat. I can't be certain that he will actually leave the area. If he's capable of watching me for years without me knowing about it then I'm pretty sure he has the capability to continue to do so.

I'm alone in my flat. Oscar is still asleep on my bed – honestly, he is utterly useless. I could have been stabbed to death by a crazy man and he would have still slept through it. I don't feel safe in my own home. I feel like I'm being watched. My skin is prickly due to my hairs all standing to attention. I really wish I had a triple lock on my door, but I don't, so instead I wedge a chair under the door handle, but that doesn't make me feel any safer. I draw the curtains. Nope. I still have that lingering feeling of dread and pure terror that Peter is going to break in and stab me in my sleep.

I'm standing in the middle of the lounge still holding the knife. I have no idea what to do. It's nearly 2 a.m. There's no way I'm going to be able to go to sleep. There's only one thing that will dull this horrible feeling in my chest: gin. Lots of gin, more pizza – and maybe another shower. I feel dirty again.

I leave the knife resting on the side by the sink while I take a shower, hoping it will rid me of the awfulness of what has just happened. It seems to be clinging to every part of me. God, I wish I was normal. I wish I was a normal girl who lives a boring life and who goes to work every day and gets on with normal, everyday stuff. Why is that so much to ask? Why do I have to be some ridiculously rare miracle and have an identical twin living as a parasite inside of me? Why does she have to be evil and kill people? Why do I suck so much at meeting decent men? Why does every man I sleep with turn out to be a psycho? All these questions and more buzz around my head like flies. It feels as if I'm shouting them at myself. It's so loud; in fact it's deafening.

I scream at the top of my lungs while standing in the shower, the water running into my mouth. I keep screaming because, believe it or not, it feels good to let out my pent-up emotions, and trust me, they are plentiful. I lean against the tiles, allowing the hot water to completely cover my face until I'm gasping for breath. I stop screaming, realising that my screams could probably be heard from across the street and I really don't want anyone calling the police because they heard a woman screaming.

I eat some leftover pizza (Peter didn't eat all of his – what a loser. Who leaves pizza?) and pour myself a large tumbler of gin. I've skipped the tonic (because I don't have any) and drink it straight. I continue to do so until I feel the wonderful fuzziness in my head. The alcohol dulls my brain function just enough so that I can stop over-thinking and worrying that Peter might be waiting outside my door to kill me when I next step outside. Yes, I am aware that not a mere few hours ago I said that I would cut back on my drinking, but that was then and this is now. Things have changed since then.

I enjoy my pizza and there just so happens to be a serial killer documentary playing on some random late night horror channel. Bad idea. I quickly switch over when they start talking about psychopaths and how they have no emotions, and how some have that overwhelming urge to kill. I flick randomly through the channels until I land on a repeat of Love Island. Fuck it. Time to lose my Love Island virginity.

An hour later I'm four gins down and crying hysterically when the winners are announced and, for a flicker of a moment, I think that maybe there is someone out there for me ... somewhere. Who the fuck am I kidding?

The next day I stumble around at work like I'm high on drugs. I naturally fall back into my routine, my body remembering exactly what to do and where everything is, but my mind is blank. There is literally nothing inside my head except a blank space. Lucy and Emma do their best to talk to me in their high-pitched excited voices, asking me where I've been, but I just give them one word answers. I can't help it. I'm numb. I don't know what or how to feel. All I know is that I'm lost and more alone than I have ever been in my whole life. I explain to my colleagues that I'll be going into hospital for surgery soon, to which they respond with total shock, but refrain from asking further questions. They agree to continue to run the practice while I'm out of commission. I feel like hugging them both because, despite my coldness towards them, they still would bend over backwards to help me. I don't deserve them.

My hospital letter arrives the next day. My surgery is scheduled for seven days' time on the 22nd of November at 9 a.m. I'm filled with an overwhelming surge of fear and panic, but also pure and utter relief. Alicia will be gone soon. It will be over in seven days. I just keep repeating this in my head over and over, yet I also have so many other things rattling around in there. Things like: what will happen after the surgery, will life be normal for me, will Peter finally leave me alone? I wish I knew the answers so I could know if things will be better than they are right now. Then my mind could relax and not feel like it's functioning at a thousand miles an hour.

I spend the next week in a haze. Work is work. Mrs Smith comes in again with her cat saying that it hissed at her and therefore there must be something wrong with the animal. Part of me snaps and I tell Mrs Smith that maybe she should stop trying to force love upon the poor cat and leave it the hell alone. I actually have more respect for cats now more than ever. They only want to be left alone to live their lives, hunt mice, sleep and do whatever they feel like. That's what I want. I want to be alone and safe, away from anything that could possibly hurt me.

The day of my surgery draws closer and my thoughts turn to Alicia. She hasn't spoken to me for days, which I know I need to get used to, but it's very disconcerting knowing she is there and is aware of everything I am doing, but is refusing to talk. She's making no attempt to stop me from having her removed. It's like she doesn't care. I hate to admit this because it goes against everything that I've recently learned and been through, but ... I miss her.

It feels like I've lost a limb. She was, no *is,* a part of me and I know she is there. She's been a security blanket for me over the years. If anything ever went wrong or I needed help or advice, Alicia was always the first person I spoke to about it. Not my parents. It was always Alicia because she understood me, or at least I thought she did. I don't even know her anymore. I don't know who she is or who she's been pretending to be all these years. Did she ever care about me at all? Has she always only been out for herself? There was once a time we swore to be best friends forever and would grow old together and always have each other's back. What happened to the Alicia I used to know? Back when we were children, even after she made me kill my cat, after those two years of being absent, she came back and we were stronger than ever.

It's a drizzly cold Wednesday night. My surgery is the day after tomorrow. I'm in the bath, the water so hot my skin is bright red, but I like it that way. The steam from the water is burning my nostrils as I breathe it in. It's a rather pleasant feeling. My eyes are closed as I think back to a happy time when I was with Alicia.

We were doing home-schooling at the dining room table in the old farmhouse. I was twelve years old. Mum was supervising at the other end of the table, reading a book. My head was buried in a maths book; the symbols and numbers looked like jargon to me. Nothing made sense. Even to this day I don't think I've ever had to use fractions in my everyday life. I always hated maths. It was my worst subject, but Alicia appeared to be really good at it. She was always much smarter than me. I envied her in a way. We used to joke that I had the body, but she had the brains (in a sense).

Come on, Josslyn. Think. You know the answer.

No, I don't. I'm so stupid. Please, just tell me.

At least give it a try.

Wouldn't it be easier if you just told me the answer? Why do I need to learn this stuff when I already know it because you know it?

There may come a time when I am no longer around.

Then I'll use a calculator.

The two of us shared a giggle, which escaped my lips.

My mum looked up at me. 'What's funny, darling?'

'Nothing, Mum,' I said quickly, then held up the book in front of my face so she couldn't see me grinning.

After another minute Alicia finally agreed and told me the answer to the sum. It may seem like an insignificant memory, but it was a good one, a happy one. It was a time when Alicia and I were as one mind and laughed and enjoyed each other's company. I can't help but dwell on the comment she made about her not being around one day. Did she know that the truth would be discovered one day and she would be cut out of my body like a tumour?

Another memory pops into my head seconds later. Another happy one. I'm older and I had just started university. I remember creeping into my very first class on the first day, nervous as hell, shaking with fear. I'd never been around so many people my own age before. Everyone was talking amongst themselves, sharing laughs and stories of how wasted they had been the night before. I overheard how many boys this one girl had kissed in one night. I was horrified. I was so naïve and completely clueless when it came to talking to boys. I hugged my study books as I took my seat, glancing around and hoping to God that no one noticed me or talked to me. Alicia had told me to act confident and if anyone caused me any trouble then she'd step in and handle it. I remember her not being thrilled that I was going to university, but it was my dream to be a vet so she didn't have any other choice in the matter.

There I was, completely terrified and completely alone. No one introduced themselves to me or glanced in my direction, but then Alicia said the most beautiful words to me in the whole world. I don't know why she said them, and she never said them again, but in that moment they were exactly what I needed to hear. They gave me the confidence to get through the rest of the class and even answer a question.

I am proud of you, Josslyn.

A tear comes to my eye while laying in the bath and it trickles down my already damp cheek. I close my eyes and dunk my whole head under the water, the heat of it stinging my eyelids. I can't hear anything except for the slow thud of my own heartbeat. I do that thing where you try and slow it down, but it continues to race. I feel disconnected from my body under the water. Nothing else matters.

While I'm holding my breath another memory appears – this one not so nice. It was at a time in my life when I was in a very dark place. I was still with Daniel and he had hit me again. I don't remember why, but he never needed a real reason. I was crying in the university toilets, the ones that were hardly ever used because they were in a secluded part of the main building. I was staring at myself in the mirror, tears running down my cheeks, my eyes puffy and red, a purple bruise forming around my left eye. I looked at myself and then Alicia spoke to me.

You are so weak, Josslyn. I am ashamed to be a part of you. You need to stand up for yourself, sort your life out, break up with that asshole, but instead you do nothing and just expect things to sort themselves out on their own. Take control Josslyn, or I will.

I can't.

WEAK!

I'm not weak!

You are weak and you always will be.

Shut up!

And then I punched my fist through the mirror. To be fair to Alicia it wasn't long after that that I did take control of my life and broke up with Daniel, really knuckled down and got on with my studies.

My eyes open under the water and I come up gasping for air. Here I am again, at a dark time in my life, but now I'm taking control all by myself. It's time to get rid of that bitch.

The day finally arrives. My parents allow me to stay at their house the night before with Oscar, as he will be staying with them while I'm in the hospital. They have also planned that I will go back with them so they can look after me while I recover. I don't try to argue with them because, to be honest, I think I'm going to need the help. From what the doctor has told me it's a fairly big operation. They will have to open me up and cut out the tumour. Apparently it's in an awkward position and quite close to a major blood vessel and a bunch of nerves. The doctor asked if they could do a study on me and run tests on the foetus once it was removed, but I refused. I don't want to be a human guineapig, nor do I want Alicia to be cut open and studied under a microscope. It just isn't right.

I'm a bag of nerves as we walk into the hospital. My stomach is in knots and my head is pounding. We find the ward, speak to the nurse and I get settled in my area and on the bed. My mum sets up her station on a nearby chair; she's brought a book and some food. She hasn't said a lot, which is very unlike her. Normally she bombards me with ridiculous questions and tries to control everything, but today she is calm and collected, not like me who is trying to run a mile inside my own body. Everything feels tight, my breathing, my chest, even my skin feels like it's trying to squeeze the life out of me. Is this my body trying to tell me not to go through with this or is it Alicia trying to send me a warning? The doctors have reassured me that although it's a serious operation there should be no risk to me and after a few weeks of recovery I will be back to my normal self (whatever the hell that means).

My mum and I listen carefully and intently as the doctor talks to us about the surgery. He explains exactly what will happen, which is very nice of him, but honestly the way he keeps referring to Alicia as 'the tumour' is making me uncomfortable. She's more than that. She's a person, maybe not a person with feelings and emotions, but she's still a person. I can't tell the doctor that – he wouldn't believe me anyway. Neither would Mum. They would automatically think I was mentally unstable, which there is a strong case for, but I know the truth.

The doctor (who is called Doctor Hastings) finishes by asking if we have any questions. He's quite young and fresh-faced with jet black hair and a tiny bit of stubble, no doubt on a long shift. He is friendly and attractive and does put me at ease somewhat.

Mum looks at me and smiles weakly. 'W-what will be done with the, um ...' She can't seem to bring herself to say the word.

'Tumour,' adds Doctor Hastings.

'Yes.' My mum looks a bit embarrassed and awkward.

'We will dispose of it properly and safely the way we would do with any normal tumour.' The thought of Alicia being *disposed* of in any way makes my stomach turn.

I want to say something, but what can I say? I can't very well ask to keep it and have a proper burial, can I? Maybe this is wrong. Maybe it's not too late ...

'That's fine,' says my mum. 'And will Josslyn suffer any side effects from its removal?'

'Not at all, other than hopefully not having that awful pain ever again, so that's a good thing.'

'That's great,' says my mum again. We look at each other and I send her my best 'stop asking stupid questions' face, which she appears to understand. 'Thank you, doctor.'

'Are you happy, Josslyn?' Doctor Hastings asks me.

I open my mouth, but then abruptly close it.

'She's just a bit nervous,' adds my mum.

'Of course. Well, if you have no more questions then I'll be off. I shall see you in theatre. The anaesthetist will be along shortly to go over things and then the nurse will get you in your gown for surgery. Try and relax. It will all be over before you know it.'

I manage to give him a pathetic smile and then he walks away.

I'm laying in my hospital bed in my ugly gown. Mum has gone to get a coffee and sandwich, so I'm alone behind the blue curtain that surrounds the bed. I don't have a private room, but there isn't anyone else on my ward at the moment, which I'm grateful for because I hate being around sick people (or I guess any people for that matter, as you well know by now). This means I am alone with my thoughts, which is not a good thing. My brain is in fast-forward, everything is moving twice as fast as usual. It's a strange sensation and it does nothing to calm my already over-stimulated nerves. I take a deep and steady breath and then ...

Hello, Josslyn.

I almost jump out of the hospital bed. I grip the edges so hard my knuckles turn white.

Fuck me, Alicia. You scared me half to death!

That is ironic. You once asked me if I was afraid of death. The answer is no. I am not afraid. Are you?

I-I don't know. Why the fuck are you talking to me now? What about everything that happened with Peter?

Aren't you going to say that you were right all along about him?

I have nothing to say about him.

Why are you talking to me?

I wanted to say goodbye.

I'm momentarily stunned into silence. I literally have no idea what to say to that.

I-I'm sorry it had to end this way, but if you hadn't killed people and lied to me then I wouldn't be having you cut out of me. I can't live like this anymore. I hope you can understand that.

I understand.

That's all you have to say?

Yes.

You aren't sorry for the hell you've put me through all these years and what you did to our sister?

I am not sorry. I did it all for you, Josslyn, to keep you safe. I have done all I can now. The rest is up to you. I wish you well. You are my sister, now and forever.

Tears fill my eyes.

I'll miss you Alicia.

Goodbye Josslyn, my sister ... see you in another life.

Chapter Nineteen

Alicia

I am walking through thick, white fog. It surrounds me, engulfs me, appears to swallow me whole. I cannot see through it, so I feel my way, my arms stretched out in front of me, trying to find something to grab on to, anything. There is nothing but an empty void of space. The fog is endless and I am trapped.

There is a bright, white light ahead. I do not know what it is, but my gut instinct tells me to head towards it, so I do. I walk for what seems like forever. On and on and on. The light never gets any bigger, nor does it get any smaller. It is a constant reminder of something that is there giving me hope, yet also never yields its existence. The light is endless and I am trapped.

There is a noise coming from somewhere. I do not know what it is or where it is coming from, but I turn automatically towards it. My body aches and I am weary. It feels heavy, but it is mine. I move cautiously through the white fog towards the noise, but it keeps changing direction. I stop and listen as intently as I can, but all I can hear is the beating of my own heart.

Thud. Thud. Thud.

Beep. There is that noise again. Beep. It appears to be getting louder now. Beep. It is closing in on me. No longer am I following the noise, the noise is coming to me. BEEP!

My eyelids flicker open. The effort it takes to open them uses all of my concentration and energy. My vision is foggy and all I can see is a white light. It is blinding me. I close my eyes to block it out, but it still burns through my eyelids. Every part of me hurts. The beeping noise is close now and is pulsing at a steady rhythm in time with my own heart.

I am alive. It is me. I am here.

The air is warm and the smell of chemicals fills my nostrils. I know exactly where I am, but it is very disorientating. This is the first time I have been alone in this body and in complete control of it. Every minuscule movement takes effort, but it feels glorious to finally be here. In my real body.

Yes, it is me. Alicia.

My plan has worked and I have gotten what I have always wanted: my body. I have always been the real host. Josslyn has merely been along for the ride, but for some reason she has had control of my body instead. The only way I knew how to claim it as rightfully mine was to have her cut out. Josslyn was unaware of this, of course. Had she known the truth she would have never gone through with the surgery. Unknowingly, she has removed herself from my body, but it was the only way. I could no longer allow her to ruin my life and my body. She has used it for nearly thirty years. It is my turn now.

Do not get me wrong, I did care about Josslyn. She was, after all, my identical twin sister and twins share a bond that is unlike any other. We were once the same person, but she was weak and I am strong, yet somehow she was the one who played host while I merely had to watch. I bided my time and was patient. Very patient. I took control when I could, but I knew that the only way to get complete control was to get rid of her, the tumour inside of me.

When Josslyn found out about the tumour I knew it was the perfect opportunity to start my plan. I needed to turn her against me, to make her think that I hated her, that I was evil. Yes, people died, but it was a small price to pay for my eventual freedom. Josslyn had her chance with her life and this body. Now it is my turn. I do not regret what I did. I would do it again in a heart-beat if it meant I could be alive.

'Josslyn, darling? Can you open your eyes?' I can hear the soft voice of Josslyn's mother, Amanda.

I slowly open my eyes and there she is, hovering over me, a pathetic look of worry over her face, which soon lights up with a smile when she sees my eyes open.

'Oh darling, you gave us all a fright for a while, but you're here now and everything is okay.' She starts stroking my hair and face like I am a pet.

Amanda steps back and allows the nurse and doctor to check the monitor I am hooked up to. My mouth is dry, so dry that I cannot form words. I lick my lips.

Amanda seems to pick up on this and lifts a glass of water to my mouth. I sip on the straw and wet my lips and mouth.

'Thank you,' I say quietly.

'How do you feel darling?'

'Weak, but not for long.' Amanda frowns at me.

Yes, I am aware there is a harshness to my voice, very unlike her daughter's tone. If I am to fool her into thinking I am her daughter I know I must do a better job at pretending to be Josslyn.

'I am okay Mum, just tired.' I have learnt from Josslyn over the years that she never calls her mother anything other than Mum and so I must do the same, even though it feels alien to me.

'Of course, darling. Your father's here. He just popped out to put more money on the car. They charge a fortune in this place for parking.' She awkwardly smiles at the nurse, who then turns to me.

'Everything went well Josslyn, except we had a hard time bringing you round. You seemed to want to stay under. The only thing I will say is that the doctor had to leave a very small piece of the tumour inside. It was wrapped around a nerve and blood vessel and was too dangerous to remove, but since it has been separated from the main bulk of the tumour it should eventually be absorbed by your body. If not, then it will just stay in there, but won't cause you any further harm. You need to rest for a few weeks, no lifting heavy objects or anything like that. You will have a small scar where the incision was, but it will fade over time. You are on a lot of pain medication, which should help you relax. Do you have any questions?'

'No,' I say bluntly, then I realise my mistake. 'Thank you,' I add with a smile.

The nurse smiles at me awkwardly and then leaves. It is just Amanda and I. She is staring at me, studying me. I look at her.

'What is it, Mother?' I ask with a slight impatience to my voice.

'Nothing, darling. Why did you call me Mother and not Mum?' Fuck. This is harder than I first thought. 'Are you sure you're okay?' she adds.

'I have never been better.'

Annoyingly, I am told that I am required to stay in hospital for another day and a half as my blood pressure is very low and I keep nearly passing out whenever I attempt to stand. My body is frail and weak, but my mind is strong. I will soon train this body to be as strong as my mind. I will become better than Josslyn ever was, but first I must endure the torture of other people helping me. I do not like to rely on others, but I have no choice. The nurses bring me food and change my dressings, as well as check my vitals every few hours. Amanda sits by my side and reads to me. She also shows me videos of Oscar dancing about in the garden, which Ronald has taken for me on her phone. I have to show her how to work the phone however, because she is so incompetent at using technology. I feign interest in all of this, often using the phrase 'I am tired' as an excuse to be left alone.

Amanda brings me a massive bar of Josslyn's favourite chocolate (Cadbury's Dairy Milk) and I turn it down. I explain to her that I will no longer be putting unhealthy food into my body. It shall be nourished with nothing but healthy food, vegetables and lean protein to help feed my recovering muscles. Amanda looks at me as if I have just spoken another language, but then appears happy and pleased that I am finally going to start looking after myself properly. The hospital food is as good as poison, but I must endure it for a while longer until I can get out of here. I must continue to be patient.

I was due to leave on Sunday, but apparently there is some ridiculous rule that patients cannot be discharged on a Sunday, so I have to endure another night. Finally, the moment comes when I am allowed to leave this hellhole. I am strong enough to stand and walk by myself now, albeit a slow shuffle. I move cautiously towards the exit, refusing the wheelchair they have brought for me. Amanda and Ronald hover at my side, determined to help me, but I decline. I still have to go and live with them until I am able to commence regular activity. It was what Josslyn agreed to do, so I must keep up appearances as best as I can. Already I am forming a plan for the coming days, weeks, months and years. I will succeed.

Oscar greets me at the door like he has not seen me in years. He jumps up and down with excitement, but then stops and tilts his head as he stares at me. I know he can tell I am not Josslyn, even though I look like her. He does know me. We have met quite a few times, but I am aware I am not his favourite person in the world. His favourite person is gone and Oscar will have to accept that.

I gingerly crouch down to his level and hold out my hand to him as a peace offering.

'It is me Oscar,' I say calmly. He sniffs my hand and then proceeds to lick it. It seems it may take some time, but he will come around.

'That's strange,' says Amanda. 'Usually Oscar goes crazy when he sees you. Must be all the strange smells from the hospital.'

'Must be,' I reply.

Amanda helps me walk upstairs to the spare bedroom, which was Josslyn's old room. It still bears some resemblance to her, but has now been taken over by wooden furniture and a flowery bedspread. There is an old teddy bear propped up on numerous pillows on the bed. I pick it up slowly and stare into its dead eyes for a long time until I am jolted back to reality by Amanda's voice.

'Darling, did you hear what I said? Do you want a cup of tea?'

'Yes, I will have a cup. Thank you ... Mum.' Amanda smiles awkwardly at me and leaves the room. It is difficult to speak like Josslyn when we are (were) so different. There are many things I must learn if I am to keep up the charade of being Josslyn, but it will not be for long. When the time is right I shall leave this place and never come back. I do not belong in this life. I am destined for other, greater things.

I spend the next week at Amanda and Ronald's home. I know the place very well, but I do not feel comfortable here. I attempt to engage Amanda in the normal mother and daughter conversations, like Josslyn used to, but I can tell Amanda is suspicious of me. Obviously she has no idea of the truth, but there is a look in her eyes which suggests her daughter has changed. She does not hug me, nor does she make any attempt to. I can tell our relationship is strained so I do not waste any more time attempting to comfort her.

Ronald is much easier to interact with because he does not talk very much. He prefers to sit in front of his television and watch football. Even though I despise the game I take up residence on the soft sofa and watch it with him. Josslyn never enjoyed football either, but she did enjoy her father's company, so this is what I am trying to emulate. Oscar curls up beside me and rests his head on my lap, finally accepting that his owner will not be returning. I gently lay my hand on his fur and stroke him, which causes him to lightly wag his tail.

Ronald looks at me. 'Do you want to watch something else Jossy?'

'No, I am perfectly fine watching this ... game.' I do not think I will ever understand football or why people insist on it being exciting.

'It's nice having you home,' says Ronald. If he keeps up this infernal talking I will have to leave sooner.

'Thanks ... Dad. It is nice to be home.' And that is all we say to each other.

A full week after my operation I am feeling much stronger. I still have pain in my abdomen where they cut through the muscle and in the area of my scar, but it is slowly beginning to heal. I can lift a full kettle and put some light dishes away in the kitchen. I decide that while I am living with Amanda and Ronald I may as well earn my keep and help Amanda in the kitchen. She has wanted to make me lasagne all week, which was Josslyn's favourite meal, but I decline and ask if I can have something with less cheese and fat. I tell her it is nothing against her cooking and that it is delicious, but I remind her I want to eat healthier now, so she makes me some lemon chicken with sweet potato wedges and green beans. I eat it gladly, determined to fuel my body so it can repair itself as quickly as possible. I intend to return to my flat very soon.

I have been in contact with Emma and Lucy while I have been away from the practice. Despite my hatred towards them they have been very diligent and told me that everything was under control and that they cannot wait until I return. Little do they know that I plan to sell the practice. I decide that now is the time to break the news to Amanda and Ronald. I call them both into the lounge.

'Mum, Dad,' I say solemnly. 'Thank you for looking after me during this past week. It means a great deal to me that you have so graciously done so, but the time has come to move back into my flat. I believe I am strong enough to look after myself now. I shall, of course, still take things easy and not overdo it. I still have another week off work.'

'Are you sure, darling? You are more than welcome to stay a while longer,' pleads Amanda.

'No, thank you, but I believe I feel ready to return home.'

'Is it just me or do you talk differently since your operation?' asks Ronald with a slight laugh. 'You sound so ... posh and formal.'

I smile at him. 'Oh come on Dad, I am just messing around.' Amanda and Ronald look at each other, but say no more on the subject. I take a deep breath. This next part is going to be difficult for them to hear. I must prepare myself for a lot of questions.

'Mum, Dad ... I must also tell you something else. I have thought long and hard about this, but I feel it is what is best for me. I have decided to move away. I do not know where yet, but I will be selling the vet practice and moving away to start a new life elsewhere.'

In the silence that follows you could hear a pin drop. Maybe it was too soon to drop this bomb on them, but I do not wish to hang around any longer than I need to. They will understand in time. It is Amanda who speaks first.

'B-but ... darling ... I don't understand. Why?' She appears to be close to tears, which is understandable considering she has had her daughter close by since she first came into her life.

I attempt to explain. 'After my health scare with the ... foetus ... I have decided that I want to fully live my life and do something different. I am no longer happy where I am. You must have noticed how desperately lonely I have been. I feel a change of scenery will do me the world of good. Once I have fully recovered I shall be moving. I am sorry, but my mind is made up.'

There is another silence, but this time it is Ronald who speaks.

'I'll help you sell the practice and make sure you get a decent profit. We will, of course, help you out with money if you need it until you are on your feet again.'

'Thank you, Dad. That is very much appreciated.' I could have turned down their generous offer of course, but I am not so stubborn that I wiii refuse help if I genuinely need it. The money will come in handy, as will the assistance of selling the practice.

'We'll miss you Jossy,' says Ronald.

'And I shall miss you,' I say, but only because it is considered polite to do so.

Amanda appears to accept the news fairly quickly for she does not ask me any further questions or try to talk me out of it as I expected. I do, however, hear her crying in her room an hour or so later. I stand by the door and listen. It is not my intention to hurt Josslyn's parents. I do, in a way, think of them as my own. However, in order for me to remain strong, I must leave them and fend for myself, something I had wished Josslyn had done many years ago.

The next day Ronald drives myself and Oscar back to our flat. He helps me carry the small amount of luggage I have upstairs without a word and then proceeds to give me a stiff hug before he leaves. We have arranged to meet later in the week to discuss plans for selling once I have broken the news to Emma and Lucy. I am sure they will be devastated about losing their jobs, but that is something that cannot be helped. They are both hard-working individuals and I no doubt expect they will find decent jobs in the near future.

Also, as it is nearly December, I have agreed to stay until after the festive period is over, however I do plan on spending as much time away from Amanda and Ronald as I can, although the formality of Christmas dinner will be upheld.

Once Ronald has left my flat I am finally left in peace. Just the way I like it.

Chapter Twenty

Alicia

The next two days are spent in agony. Without the help of Amanda I am forced to do all the normal jobs like cooking and cleaning, but I can feel my body getting stronger each day, so I push through the pain threshold. I attend my scheduled hospital check-up and the doctor says I am recovering well, but to continue taking it easy for another few weeks. It is very frustrating, but I know that in the long run it will be worth it. I take short walks with Oscar each day, which is strangely liberating. I enjoy our one-on-one time and, even though my weak body cannot throw the ball as far as usual, Oscar does not seem to mind. He apparently enjoys my company as well.

I have considered giving Oscar to Josslyn's parents to look after indefinitely. I do not know where the next phase of my life will take me and having a pet is going to be quite an inconvenience, but as I look into his sad and somewhat calming eyes I realise that I am unable to part with the beast. Maybe a part of Josslyn has worn off on me. I feel a strange maternal instinct towards Oscar, like I need to protect him with my life. He is all I have left of Josslyn now, so I will continue to protect and care for him as long as he lives.

Once I am strong enough to drive my car I decide to pay someone a visit. It is long overdue and I need to ensure all the loose ends are tied up before I make my final departure in the new year. I drop Oscar at Amanda and Ronald's house early, saying that I will be back later tonight. I tell them I am going to check out some new houses to rent, but in actuality I am driving to visit one man. Peter Phillips.

It took me a while, longer than I care to admit, but I finally realise who he is. He is like me; a psychopath. However, we are vastly different. He appears to need to focus his attention on another human being in order to survive. I call it weakness. No person should have to depend on the acceptance of another. He has a strange obsession with me that I cannot understand. I must ensure that we are on the same page. He told Josslyn that he wanted to speak to me properly. Well, today he will meet the real Alicia and will finally get his wish.

I arrive at his house. I have not messaged him to warn him of my arrival so I am expecting him to react shocked. We have a lot to talk about, but I do not intend to stay long. I am merely here to say what I need to say and leave.

I knock on the door and he answers almost straight away. I am slightly taken aback by the state of him. His beard is well overdue for a shave, his hair is messed up and tangled, his eyes are deep set and hollow, his clothes unwashed. He is a pathetic excuse of a man.

'Josslyn!' he exclaims. He attempts to rush forwards and embrace me, but I immediately block him by holding up my hand.

'No,' I say darkly.

He stares at me blankly for a few seconds. 'A-Alicia?' he stutters.

'I believe you wanted to meet me in person.'

'I ... Yes! I don't understand.'

'You will. May I come in?'

'Of course. Please.' His demeanour has changed slightly now that he knows it is me. His guard appears to be up, clearly aware that I am the person responsible for his sister's death, yet he also once admitted to being fascinated with me. 'Would you like a cup of tea? You look good.'

'Spare me the pleasantries. I require no tea. I am only here to ensure that you never come near me again. If you do, I will kill you. Likewise, if you ever inform anyone of what I have done, I will kill you. Do you understand?' It feels good to be able to talk like myself, rather than pretend to be Josslyn.

Peter stops and faces me squarely. 'That sounds like a mighty big threat from someone I have barely met. We aren't so different, you and I. You're clearly a psychopath, as am I. We could make a great team. We don't need to be enemies, Alicia.'

'We do not need to be, yet we are. You stalked Josslyn for years without either of us knowing about it. You lied to us. I cannot trust you.'

'I would never have hurt Josslyn. You must believe me. I love her.'

'If you were a real psychopath you would know that we cannot feel that emotion. I believe that what you say you felt for Josslyn was nothing but power. You liked the fact that you were in control – the same with your sister. You like making women feel weak and inferior. You crave their attention. You want them to crave you the way you crave them. That is not love.'

Peter smiles at me and takes a small step towards me. 'Maybe you are right. Let's say I do want to control women, but some women like to be controlled.'

'No woman should be made to feel afraid for her life by a pathetic excuse of a man. I killed Daniel because he was a danger to women. What makes you think for a second that I would not kill you too?'

'Because a part of you knows that we have a connection, no matter how much you try and resist it. My sister and I had a close bond, but it faded. Josslyn and I had a bond, but it again quickly faded when she became suspicious of me and that was all thanks to you. You could see the real me, even though you didn't know exactly who I was. You and I ... we have a bond that will never break because we are the same.' Peter has been taking small steps closer and closer to me during his speech so he is now only a few feet away. I hold my ground.

'You are pathetic,' I spit angrily at him. 'I am nothing like you.'

'No Alicia, you're worse because you have actually killed people. I have never killed anyone. You killed my sister. Don't think I have forgotten about that. I loved her.'

'And Josslyn? What about her? Are you going to grieve for her as well? She is dead, Peter. I am going to let you in on a little secret of mine. Josslyn was the one who was cut out of this body, not me.'

At this Peter straightens up and shakes his head. 'But I thought Josslyn had you removed. I assumed that she had changed her mind and not had the tumour cut out.'

'No, she removed herself instead.'

Peter laughs. 'Well fuck me! You sneaky bitch. I guess that means that it's not Josslyn's body I fell in love with ... it's yours. Tell me, Alicia. Why can't we be together?'

'Because you are weak.'

Peter suddenly lunges forwards, grabs me by the neck and lifts me a few inches off the floor, just enough so that I struggle to breathe. It seems my body is still weak and

I am unable to loosen his grip on my throat, but I do not panic. I merely stare at him while he attempts to strangle me.

'Looks to me like you're the weak one.' He releases his grip and I stumble slightly as I regain my balance.

'Not for long,' I say with a gasp. I clutch my sore throat. 'This body will soon be strong.'

'You know Alicia, you're a fucking liar. You say that you don't care about me, but in case you have forgotten, we've had sex several times, which means that clearly you do want me, if only in a physical way.'

'I admit that you were a welcome distraction in some areas and I had my fun with you. I also used you to turn Josslyn against me. She liked you from the start. She liked you a lot and when she realised that I had taken her over and we had engaged in sexual intercourse she became jealous. She started to distrust me. She started to distrust you. Slowly but surely you started to show your true colours. I helped her along, of course. I did not want you anywhere near her. I was a fool for not seeing what you really were until it was too late.'

'I liked Josslyn. She was so innocent and pure, but I could also see a darkness inside her, which intrigued me. Yes, that was you. It was you I was drawn to Alicia, not her. I just want you to love me the way I love you.'

I throw my head back and laugh. 'No one will ever love you Peter, just like no one will ever love me. That is just who we are. We are not meant to be loved.'

'Josslyn loved you.'

I stop and grit my teeth. Despite my best efforts to ignore his comment, something inside me twinges. It affects me more than I care to admit. Yes, Josslyn did love me as a sister even long before she knew who I really was. She told me many times over the years. I have never said it back to her, never been one for expressing my emotions because I have none, so it has been difficult to connect with anybody, Josslyn included, but I must admit that over time I have grown fond of her.

'Josslyn hated me,' I say solemnly. 'She hated me because I turned her against me. That was the plan all along. She was never supposed to meet you. I did my best to stop her. I killed people to protect her. Daniel. Alicia. I killed them for her because I needed her safe. I needed to keep her safe until the time was right.'

'And you used me,' says Peter, shaking his head.

'Of course I used you. You mean nothing to me. You were an inconvenience that got in my way.'

'Tell me where my sister is. That's all I ask.'

I grin, not because I am happy, but because Peter still cannot let his sister go. He is more twisted and lost than I ever thought possible and I revel in his pain.

'I will never tell you where she is. She will continue to rot in the ground where I buried her and you will continue to mourn her, just like you will mourn Josslyn. You do not deserve to know the truth.'

'Just tell me why you killed her. The truth. You say she got in your way. What does that mean? You owe me at least an explanation for that.'

'Fine. I will tell you why I killed her. She came looking for me, for Josslyn. I admit, I was shocked when she told me who she was. I had not been expecting it, so I knew I had to act fast. I told her to leave. I followed her to her car. I broke her jaw with a claw hammer and then I snapped her neck.'

Peter's eyes turn dark, his fists clench at his side. He wants to hurt me, maybe even kill me, but I know he will not because I am the last remaining piece he has of his sister and of Josslyn. Without me they are both gone forever. We are all connected and always will be. Peter knows this.

'You're lying,' he says. 'You knew who she was when she came looking for you. You were the one who sent Josslyn's birth certificate to her, weren't you? You wanted her to find out and come looking for you. You planned it all along. Why? Stop lying and tell me!' His loud, angry voice echoes around the living room.

I breathe out a satisfying sigh. I am in control. I always have been. My life was stolen from me by my own sisters. They had no right to be happy and to find each other. I deserved a chance at life. I suppose that means I must have one emotion: envy. Yes, I envied my sisters for living while I was trapped inside my own body like a prisoner.

Alicia was happy, thriving and alive. Josslyn was ... well, let me just say that she was living. She may not have been completely happy, but she was the one who was holding me hostage. It took me a long time to figure out the truth. When Josslyn first met me I was as clueless as her. I did not know who I was or why I was there. How could I? However, I was smart and I figured it out over time. It was me who found out I could control Josslyn. It was me who realised that this body was truly mine and not hers. It was me who found Josslyn's birth certificate one day while I was going through some of her old things. It was me who saw the time of birth on the certificate and deduced that only twins have their time of birth recorded. I did it all and I planned it all.

I planned for Alicia to disappear and come and visit me. Then I killed her. The only thing I did not plan for was Peter. He got in my way. I was blind. I should have recognised the signs. I should have realised that he would be a nuisance. I knew Alicia had an adopted brother of course, but I did not realise he was a psychopath like me. I did not know he was in love with his own sister or that he had found out about Josslyn, but once I knew I quickly altered my plan to include him. We engaged in physical contact because I knew I could control him. It was easier than having him as my enemy. He tried to convince us that someone else had killed his sister, but he failed pathetically. His true self was too difficult to conceal, but luckily Josslyn was very clever. She managed to figure out the truth about him by herself, just like I knew she would. I believe I had taught her well. She was stronger than she realised.

My overall plan was to get rid of Alicia and Josslyn and to have my true body back, which I have accomplished and now it is time for Peter to go as well.

I take several steps towards Peter, gradually getting closer and closer until my face is a mere few inches from his. Then I speak very calmly and simply.

'You may hate me for what I did to your sister and to Josslyn, but really you should be thanking me. They made you weak. You were addicted to them. People like us deserve to be free from distractions and addictions. Now you are free. Now I am free. You can either say thank you and never see me again, or I will kill you. Maybe not today. Maybe not tomorrow, but I will kill you if you ever even look at me again. Do you understand?'

There is a silence that falls, one that is fraught with tension. This, I know, could go one of two ways, but I remain strong. I stare at Peter as if staring into his very soul and I know that one day he will come for me. He cannot stay away from me. I am his weakness and obsession now. One day I will need to fight for my life and I must be ready. He will never stop. I should kill him where he stands right this second, but something stops me. I must be patient, as I have been all these long years.

'Thank you,' he says slowly. 'I promise I will leave you alone forever.'

I smile and back slowly away from him. He is a bad liar. 'Goodbye, Peter.'

'Goodbye ... Alicia.'

Goodbye Alicia, indeed.

Chapter Twenty-One

Alicia

It has been a year and a half since I last saw Peter and I have never looked back. A great deal has happened during that time and many things have changed, myself included. I am a new person. I have a new identity, a new body, a new life. I am no longer Alicia. She is gone. I decided that if I was to be completely free from my old life then a new name would be required. It has also served the purpose of hiding from Peter. I am not afraid of him, but I do know that it is only a matter of time before he finds me and then I will have to do whatever I can to stop him. I am ready now. It has taken me a year and a half, but I am finally ready.

As soon as I was completely recovered from my surgery I began to work on my body, which was weak and soft. It was difficult at first, but it slowly began to change into something different, something better. I ceased eating junk food and drinking alcohol. I did not miss either of those things. They were her vices, not mine. I fuelled my body with the correct amount of carbohydrates, protein and fat, never eating to excess, but enough for what my body needed to heal and grow. My body fat melted away and I started gaining lean muscle. My arms and legs slimmed down and my torso became tight.

I began to exercise in some form every day whether it be running, lifting weights, yoga, boxing or Taekwondo. I attended classes whenever I could, but mostly I have taught myself via online videos and other training aids. Each physical activity has its own benefit to me. Running improves my cardiovascular system and helps me clear my head. When I run nothing else matters and I always return home feeling more in control and clear. I was slow and cumbersome at first, but eventually I became faster and could run for longer. Lifting weights has made my body and mind strong and has enabled me to develop muscle and improve my physical appearance. No longer is this body soft. I use Yoga to improve my flexibility, as well as helping to clear my mind. I remember when she tried Yoga once. She said it was stupid and that she could not clear her head because I was in there. Now there is no one inside my head except for me. Boxing allows me to release any pent-up anger or frustration as well as teaching me to defend myself. I feel this is very important, as I know he will come for me one day. Finally, Taekwondo balances my mind and enables me to learn more about self-defence, adding to my skill set. I have worked hard, never taken a day off, always been moving forwards, always striving to be better and to improve myself. I am determined to continue to do this.

Along with my body I have also altered my hair and general appearance. I have light-blonde hair and have had it cut short into a mid-length bob. It frames my face better. I keep it neat and tidy. No longer do I look like her, but like me, who I was always meant to be. I have a rigorous skin-care routine. She did not look after herself and the stresses of her daily life had started to show even though she was barely thirty, but now my skin is brighter, tighter and more youthful. I regularly give myself facials and ensure my nails are neat and filed. I wear make-up, not every day, but on the days I wish to look more presentable.

Not only have I changed physically, but also my career and living arrangements have altered. I told Amanda and Ronald that I would be moving away and that is what I did in early 2020. I sold the vet practice with the help of Ronald and was able to pay off a few debts and loans with the money. I then began to make plans to travel the world for a year because I had been unable to decide where I wanted to settle. For years I had dreamed of seeing the world, but then something happened that I did not anticipate. A virus started spreading around the globe at an extraordinary rate. It was very unfortunate timing for me, but I wasted no time in moving to Italy before the United Kingdom was locked down in March. However, Italy was very badly hit by the pandemic, but I was lucky and moved to a very remote region in Tuscany and shut myself away from the outside world while it fell to its knees around me. The lockdown in Italy enabled me to hide away for a few months. I used the time wisely. I bought a small villa, built a home gym, renovated the entire building, planted a vineyard and started planning to open up my own business for when the virus had finally run its course.

I decided to open a wine bar. Yes, a wine bar. You may think that is slightly contradictory to my no alcohol rule and you are partly right. I did not drink alcohol for nearly a year while I worked on my body, but now I do enjoy the occasional glass of wine. Not the cheap swill that she used to drink at less than £4 a bottle, but local and expensive wine, the grapes grown right here in Tuscany. My vineyard is still young, but eventually I intend to make my own wine and sell it in my bar. I call it *A Slice of Paradise* and I enjoy sitting on the balcony overlooking my vineyard as the sun sets with Oscar on my lap, taking in the spectacular views. The sky seems to bleed so many different colours, all smashed together to form the most beautiful sight. Even my psychotic mind can appreciate the beauty in something like that. Feeling the warmth of the setting sun soak into my skin each day gives me life, gives me a purpose. It may not be the plan I had in mind when I started, but it is a perfect situation to find myself in.

You may be wondering how I can afford this lifestyle. Well, that is an unfortunate story, but one that must be told. Before I tell you I must insist that you do not blame me or accuse me of any wrong doing. It was not my fault, but I admit I did not do anything to stop it from happening. Sometimes things are out of your control and there is nothing you can do but sit back and watch as they unfold. The virus took a lot from me, but also gave me so much more than I could have anticipated.

A few months into last year the virus took over Amanda Reynolds. She fought it hard, but she was one of the unfortunate souls who succumbed to its poison. She died slowly and quite painfully, I am told. Ronald told me that she was already weak and her heart was broken because I had moved away. She mourned the loss of her daughter. I could not tell them where I was living, even though I assured them I would, because it was too risky. I avoided all contact and any communication until Ronald left me a voicemail saying that Amanda had died. By this time I was living in Tuscany and everyone was living in a full national lockdown. I was unable to attend the funeral. It was a difficult time for all of us. I was in two minds about how to handle things, whether I should stay away or visit Ronald to help and support him. I chose to stay here. I did not wish to cause him any more pain and I could not risk showing my face again.

Unfortunately there was worse to come. Ronald died in a freak car accident during the autumn of 2020. It was very sudden. I was told it was a tragic accident, but a small part of me did not believe that. I do not wish to make false accusations, but I am aware that a certain person may wish to get my attention or try and trick me into coming back home. I know he is capable of anything, so I cannot let my guard down. He does not know where I am as far as I am aware, but I know he will never stop looking for me.

A few weeks after the death of Ronald I was contacted by his solicitor. He informed me that I was the sole recipient of Ronald and Amanda's last will and testament. I had inherited their whole estate, including all of their savings and possessions. The house took a while to sell due to the lockdown, but, thanks to the stamp duty being cut, it finally sold and I was able to use the money to renovate my villa and start my wine business. Naturally things were slow to start with, but I did not mind. I found myself enjoying the process. I had a roof over my head, I had food in my cupboards and I had everything I needed in one place. I did not have to worry about other people in my life. Her parents were gone, but they had provided me with the best possible opportunity to start my new life. They may have been her parents, and they did not know the full details, but I believe they would have wanted her to use the money to improve her life. I believe I have done just that.

I am currently sitting in my favourite place: my balcony looking out over the vineyard. It is not sunset, but the middle of the day. The heat of the June sun is gently warming my body. Things have almost returned to normality. My wine bar is finally open for business and is bringing in a steady custom. I am in a fortunate situation and have not needed to receive lots of customers in order to keep it open. I have money set aside thanks to Ronald and Amanda.

Across the open space in front of me I can see rows and rows of white grapes, absorbing the sun, slowly ripening ready for harvesting. I am hoping to make my own wine next year. This year will merely be about testing and adjusting. I will have to teach myself how to make it. I have already read many books and watched many videos and lockdown was the perfect time to hone my skills. I am in no hurry. Perfection takes time.

I close my eyes as I feel the sun's rays warming my skin, which is deliciously tanned from living in the sun for just over a year. I like it. The area is peaceful, away from hordes of people. Only a few people enter my wine bar of an evening, which means I can easily handle the work so I do not have to hire any further hands. I still have a few odd jobs to do before I open the bar for this evening's bookings, but I am enjoying the sunshine. I often forget to sit and enjoy my surroundings. There was once a time that I thought enjoying a sunset and a glass of wine was pointless, but since being alive for real I do believe my mind has altered its perception on some things. I am required to speak to people as part of my job and I am learning to blend in with the local people and tourists. I interact with them when I need to, talking to them in a friendly manner. I have gotten a lot better at talking like she used to. A lot of my customers enjoy coming back to my bar again and again, so word of mouth is spreading. I even set up a website and a lady wrote a review saying that I was a lovely and welcoming host. I am not sure how it happened or why it works, but it does. I told you I had changed ... for the most part.

I must admit though ... I do miss her.

I have always put myself first. This body was always mine to begin with, but a small part of me misses my sister. When you have spent twenty-odd years inside someone's head you are bound to form an attachment. I often find myself thinking about her and wondering how she would react had she seen what I have accomplished with her body. She would probably laugh and find it hard to believe how much I have changed. I remember having to constantly try and convince her to look after herself and move away from her parents, but she never listened to me, yet she always complained about her life. I could never understand why. She always felt the need to be close to them. I guess that is the difference between a normal person and a psychopath. I do not feel the need to form an attachment to anyone. There have been men in my bar who have tried their best to flirt and persuade me to date them, but I have declined every single one. I do not need a man to make me happy. It is strange having silence in my head. For so many years I was in her head and she was in mine. I like to think she would approve of my new lifestyle and physical appearance, even though she would not have been brave enough to do it herself.

I breathe in deeply and then out slowly. Then it happens: the pain washes over me like a mountainous wave. It causes me to drop my glass, which smashes to the floor into thousands of tiny pieces. Oscar jumps to his feet and starts barking excitedly. He knows something is happening. I clutch my head with both hands and scream. Then I hear a voice that I had not been expecting to ever hear again. It is a familiar voice, a voice I have missed. It is her and she is back.

Hello, Alicia. Have you missed me?

The pain stops and I am left panting for breath as I slowly rise to my feet.

Hello, Josslyn. I did not expect to hear from you.

Surprise, Alicia!

My name is no longer Alicia.

What do I call you now?

I am Alexis Grey.

Did you like this book?

I really hope you enjoyed reading My Dark Self, the first novel in the "My ... Self" series.

If you liked this book please feel free to leave me a review.

Leave me a review on Amazon

Leave me a review on Goodreads

Connect With Jessica

Find and connect with Jessica online via the following platforms.

Sign up to email list via website to be notified of future books and her monthly author newsletter:
www.jessicahuntleyauthor.com

Follow her page on Facebook: Jessica Huntley - Author

Follow her on Instagram: @jessicah_reading_writing

Follow her on Twitter: @new_author_jess

Follow her on Goodreads: jessicahuntley88

Follow her on her Amazon Author Page - Jessica Huntley

Printed in Great Britain
by Amazon

71913582R00224